New York Times bestselling author **Maisey Yates** lives in rural Oregon with her three children and her husband, whose chiselled jaw and arresting features continue to make her swoon. She feels the epic trek she takes several times a day from her office to her coffee maker is a true example of her pioneer spirit.

Katherine Garbera is the *USA TODAY* bestselling author of more than ninety-five books. Her writing is known for its emotional punch and sizzling sensuality. She lives in the Midlands of the UK with the love of her life; her son, who recently graduated university; and a spoiled miniature dachshund. You can find her online at www.katherinegarbera.com

Also by Maisey Yates

Gold Valley Vineyards
Rancher's Wild Secret

Copper Ridge
Take Me, Cowboy
Hold Me, Cowboy
Seduce Me, Cowboy
Claim Me, Cowboy
Want Me, Cowboy
Need Me, Cowboy

Also by Katherine Garbera

Tycoon Cowboy's Baby Surprise
The Tycoon's Fiancée Deal
Craving His Best Friend's Ex
One Night with His Ex
One Night, Two Secrets
One Night to Risk It All
Her One Night Proposal

Discover more at millsandboon.co.uk

CLAIMING THE RANCHER'S HEIR

MAISEY YATES

IN BED WITH HIS RIVAL

KATHERINE GARBERA

MILLS & BOON

First Published in Great Britain 2020
by Mills & Boon, an imprint of HarperCollinsPublishers,
1 London Bridge Street, London, SE1 9GF

Claiming the Rancher's Heir © 2020 Maisey Yates
In Bed with His Rival © 2020 Harlequin Books S.A.

Special thanks and acknowledgement are given to Katherine Garbera for her contribution to the *Texas Cattleman's Club: Rags to Riches* series.

ISBN: 978-0-263-28007-4

1120

MIX
Paper from
responsible sources
FSC™ C007454

This book is produced from independently certified FSC™ paper to ensure responsible forest management.

For more information visit: www.harpercollins.co.uk/green

Printed and bound in Spain
by CPI, Barcelona

CLAIMING THE RANCHER'S HEIR

MAISEY YATES

One

Creed Cooper was a cowboy. A rich, successful cowboy from one of the most well-regarded families in Logan County. He also happened to be tall, muscular and in possession of the kind of good looks a lot of women liked.

As a result, nearly nothing—or no one—was off-limits to him.

No one except Wren Maxfield.

Maybe that was why every time he looked at her his hands itched.

To unwind that tight bun from her hair. To make that mouth, which was always flattened in disapproval—at least around him—get soft and sexy and get all over his body.

And he had that itch a lot, considering he and Wren were the representatives for their respective families' vineyards. Rivals, in fact.

And she hated him.

She hated him so much that when she saw him her eyes flared with a particular kind of fire.

Fair enough, since he couldn't really stand her either.

But somehow, years ago, a piece of that dislike inside him had twisted and caught hard in his gut and turned into an intensity of another kind entirely.

He was obsessed.

Obsessed with the idea he might be able to use that fire in her eyes to burn up the sheets between them.

Instead, he had to listen to her heels clicking on the floor as she paced around the showroom of Cowboy Wines, looking like a smug cat, making him wait to hear whatever plan it was she'd come to tell him about.

"Are you listening to me?" she asked suddenly, her green cat eyes getting sharp.

She was dressed in a tight-fitting red dress that fell to the top of her knees. It had a high, wide neck, and while it didn't show a lot of skin, it hugged her full breasts so tight it didn't leave a lot to the imagination.

Even if it had, his imagination was damn good. And it was willing to work for Wren. Overtime.

She had on those ridiculous spiked heels, too. Red, like the dress. He wanted to see her in only those heels.

He wasn't into prissy women. Not generally. He liked a more practical girl. A cowgirl who would be at home on his ranch.

Wren looked like she never left her family show-room, all glass walls and wrought iron furniture. Max-field Vineyards was the premier wine brand for people who were up their own asses.

And still, he wanted her.

That might be her greatest sin.

That she tested control he'd had firmly leashed for the last eighteen years and made him want to send it right to hell as he burned in her body.

Of all the reasons to hate Wren Maxfield, wanting her and not being able to do a damn thing to make himself stop was number one on the list.

He looked around the Cowboy Wines showroom, the barrels with glass tabletops on them, the heavy, distressed beams that ran the length of the room.

And then there was him: battered jeans and cowboy boots, a hat for good measure.

Everything a woman like Wren would hate.

A testament to just why there was no reason to carry a burning torch for her fine little body.

Too bad his own body was a dumbass.

"I wasn't listening at all," he said, making sure to drawl it. As slow as possible. He was rewarded with a subtle flare of heat in those eyes. "Make it more interesting next time, Wren. Maybe do a dance."

"The only dancing I'll ever do is on your grave, Creed."

The sparring sent a kick of lust through him. They did this every time they were in a room together. Every damn time. No matter that he knew he shouldn't indulge it.

But hell, he was afraid the alternative was stripping her naked and screwing her against the nearest wall, and that wasn't a real option.

So verbal sparring it was.

"What did I die of?" he asked. "Boredom?"

Those eyes shot sparks at him. "It was tragic. You were found with a high heel protruding out of your chest." Her magic lips curved upward and he felt it like she'd pressed them against his neck.

"Any suspects so far?"

"Your own smart mouth. Are you going to listen to me or not?"

"You're already here. So am I. Might as well."

He leaned back in his chair and, for effect, put his boots up on the table.

Her top lip curled up into a sneer, and that thrilled him just as much as if she'd crossed the room to straddle his lap. Okay, maybe not just as much, but he loved that he got to her.

"Fantastic. As you know, things at Maxfield Vineyards are changing. My father is no longer the owner. Instead, my sister Emerson, her husband, Holden, and our sister Cricket and I now have ownership.

"This plan is Emerson's idea. To be clear. As she is the person who oversees our broader brand." She waved a hand in the air as if to distance herself yet further from whatever she was about to say. "I had to defer to her on the subject. She doesn't think a rivalry is beneficial for any of us. She thinks we should join forces. A large-scale event where both of our wines are represented. As you know, wine tours and the whole wine trail in general have become increasingly popular."

"A rising tide lifts all boats and gets more people drunk?"

"Basically," she said.

"I'm not really sure I see the benefit to me," he said. "Seeing as everything is going well here."

"Everyone wants to expand," she said, looking at him as if he had grown a second head.

"Do they?"

"Yes," she responded. "Everyone."

"Well, the way I see it, our business is running well. We have just the right amount of staff, every family member has a position in the company, and it supports us very well. At a certain point, Wren, more is more. And that's it."

She looked at him, clearly dumbfounded. There were very definite and obvious differences between the Cooper and Maxfield families. The Coopers might be wealthy, but they liked their winery to reflect their roots. Down-home. A Western flare.

In the early days, his father had been told that there was no way he would ever be successful unless he did something to class up his image. He had refused. Digging in deeper to the cowboy theme was ultimately why they had become so successful. There was no point in competing with fancy-pants places like the Maxfields'. It wasn't the Coopers' way.

Joining up with the Maxfields made even less sense than trying to emulate them, in his opinion.

"Come on," she said. "You're ambitious, Creed, don't pretend otherwise."

And that was where she might have him. Because he didn't like to back down from a challenge. In fact, he quite liked a challenge in general. That she was issuing one now made him wonder if she was just baiting him. Taunting him.

He wasn't even sure he cared. All he knew was that he instantly wanted to take her up on it.

There was something incredibly sexy about her commitment to knowing her enemy.

"What exactly are you proposing?"

"I want to have a large event featuring all of the wineries in the area. A wine festival. For Christmas."

"That's ambitious. And it's too early to talk about Christmas."

"All the stores would disagree, Creed. Twinkle lights are out and about."

"Ask me if I care."

"I'd like to do a soft launch, a large party at Maxfield in the next month," she continued as if he hadn't spoken. "We'll invite our best clients. Can you imagine? The buzz we'll make joining forces?"

"Oh, you mean because everybody knows how profoundly our families dislike each other?" He paused for a moment. "How profoundly *we* dislike each other?"

It wasn't a secret. They were never civil to each other.

They never tried to be.

"Yes," she said. "That."

"And how exactly do you think we're going to get through this without killing each other?"

She looked all cheerful and innocent. "Look on the bright side. If I do kill you, you'll get that dance you wanted so badly."

"Well. A silver lining to every cloud, I guess."

"I like to think so. Are you in?"

The only thing worse than giving in to the attraction he had for her would be hurting a business opportunity for it. He didn't let other people control him. Not in any way.

Least of all Wren Maxfield.

And that meant he'd do it. No matter how much he'd rather roll in a pit of honey and lie down on an anthill.

"How is this going to work? Logistically. I'm not going to roll up to your event in a suit."

"I didn't think you would. I thought you might be able to bring your rather…rustic charm." The way she said *rustic* and *charm* implied that she felt the former did not go with the latter.

He smiled. "It goes with me wherever I go."

"Do you have to wear a hat?" She wrinkled her nose.

"That is nonnegotiable," he said, reaching up and flicking the cowboy hat's brim with his forefinger.

"I figured as much." She sniffed. "Well. I can accept that."

"You have no choice. We'll provide the food. Barbecue."

"You really don't have to do that."

"I am not standing at a fancy party with nothing but raw fish on a cracker to eat. And anyway, if you want my clients, you better have meat."

"With wine."

"Hey. We work hard to break the stereotype that cowboys only like beer. I myself enjoy a nice red with my burger."

"Unacceptable."

His gaze flickered over her curves. That body. *Damn* what he'd like to do to that body. "Too repressed to handle a little change, Wren?"

Color flooded her cheeks. Rage. "I am not. I just don't like terrible ideas."

"It's not a terrible idea. It's *on brand*." He said the last bit with no small amount of self-deprecation, and a smirk.

"Whatever. I don't care what you like with what. Really. I just want to know if I can count on you to help me put this together."

"You got it."

"I look forward to this new venture," she said. She smiled, which was strange, and then she extended her hand. He only looked at it for a moment. Then he reached his own out, clasped hers and shook it.

Her skin was soft, like he had known it would be. Wren was the kind of woman who had never done a day's worth of manual labor in her whole life. Not that she didn't work hard, she did. And he knew enough about the inner workings of a job like theirs to be well aware that it took a hell of a lot of mental energy. It was just that he also worked on his own ranch when he wasn't working on the wine part of things, and he knew that his own hands were rough as hell.

She was too soft. Too cosseted. Snobby. Uppity. Repressed—unless she was giving him a dressing-down with that evil tongue of hers.

And damn he liked it all, as much as he hated it.

The thing was, even if he'd been a different man, a man who had the heart it took to be with someone forever, to do the whole marriage-and-kids thing, if he'd been a man who hadn't been destroyed a long time ago, it wouldn't be her.

Couldn't be her.

A kick of lust shot through him, igniting at the point where their hands still touched. Wren dropped her hold on him quickly. "Well. Good. I guess we'll be seeing a lot more of each other, then."

"I guess we will. Looking forward to it."

"Dear reader," Wren muttered as she walked back into the family winery showroom. "She was not looking forward to seeing more of his arrogant, annoying, infuriating, ridiculous…"

"I'm sorry, what?"

Wren stopped muttering when her sister Emerson popped up from where she was sitting.

"I was muttering," Wren replied.

"I know. What exactly were you muttering about?"

"I was muttering," she restated. "Which means it wasn't exactly meant to be understood."

"Well. I'm nosy."

"I just had my meeting with Creed."

"Oh," Emerson said, looking her over. "Huh."

"What?"

"I'm checking you for burn marks."

"Why? Because he's *Satan*?"

"No. Because the two of you generate enough heat to leave scorched earth."

She narrowed her eyes at her sister. "You'd better be talking about anger."

Regrettably, anger was not the only thing that Creed Cooper made her feel.

Oh, Creed Cooper *enraged* her. She typically found herself wanting to punch him in the face within the first thirty seconds of his company.

He was an asshole. He was insufferable.

He was…without a doubt the sexiest man she had ever encountered in her entire life and when she woke up at night in a cold sweat with her pulse pounding between her thighs, it was always because she had been dreaming of him.

"Yeah," Emerson said. "Anger."

"What?" Wren snapped.

"It's just… I don't know. The two of you seem to be building up to some kind of hate-sex situation."

Wren shifted, hating that she felt so seen in the moment. "No."

"Why not?" Emerson asked.

"Several reasons. The first being that he disgusts me." Her cheeks turned pink when the bold-faced lie slipped out of her mouth.

"Is that what the kids are calling it these days?"

"You would know. You're...*on fleek* on the internet. Or whatever."

"That is an incredibly passé bit of pop culture there, Wren. And I think we both know disgust is not what he makes you feel."

She pulled a face. "Can we talk about business?"

"Sure, sure. So, what was your conclusion?"

"He's a dick."

"Yeah. I know. But what about the initiative?"

"Oh. He's on board. So I guess we'll be having a party. But he's insisting on barbecuing."

"Barbecuing?" Emerson asked, her sister's hand rising upward, bent at the wrist, her fingers curled.

"Yes." Wren lifted her nose. "Beef."

"I guess that's what we get for joining forces with cowboys."

"Says the woman who's married to one."

Emerson shrugged. "Sure. But I don't let him plan my parties. He has many uses, the primary one being that he allows me to do good work and save horses."

"Save horses?"

She batted her lashes. "Ride a cowboy?"

"For the love of God, Emerson."

"What? He's hot."

She was not here for her sister's smug married-frequent-sex glow. Emerson had very narrowly escaped an arranged marriage with a man their father had chosen for her. The whole thing with her husband, Holden, had been dramatic, had involved no small amount of blackmail and subterfuge, and had somehow ended in true love.

Wren still didn't quite understand it.

Wren also didn't understand why she felt so beset by her Creed fantasies. Or why she was so jealous of Emerson's glow.

Wren herself wasn't overly sexual.

It wasn't her thing. She'd had a few boyfriends, and she enjoyed the physical closeness that came with sex. That much was true. It had been a while since she'd dated anybody though, because she had been so consumed with her job at Maxfield Vineyards. She enjoyed what she did for work quite a lot more than she enjoyed sex, in point of fact.

Her dreams about illicit sex with Creed were better than any sex she'd ever had, and she found that completely disturbing.

Also, proof that her subconscious didn't know anything. Nothing at all.

"Great," Wren said. "Good for you and your libido. But I'm talking about wine, which is far more important than how hot your husband is."

"To you," Emerson said. "The hotness of my husband is an entirely consuming situation for me."

"Anyway," Wren said, her voice firm. "We get our joint party."

"But with beef."

"Yes," Emerson said. "And then hopefully in a few months we'll have the larger event, which we can presell tickets to. Hopefully we can bring a lot of people into town if we plan it right."

"I do like the way you're thinking," Wren said. "It's going to be great," she added, trying to affirm it for herself.

"It will be," Emerson agreed. "Have you talked to Cricket about it at all?"

Cricket was their youngest sister. She had been... She had been incredibly wounded about the entire scandal with their father.

The situation with their parents had gone from bad to worse. Or maybe it was just that they were all now aware of *how* bad it had always been.

The reason Holden had come to Maxfield Vineyards in the first place had been to get revenge on their father for seducing Holden's younger sister and leaving her emotionally broken after a miscarriage.

After that, Wren and her sisters found out their father had carried on multiple affairs over the years, all with young women who were vulnerable, with so much less power than he had. It was a despicable situation. Holden had blackmailed Emerson into marriage in order to gain a piece of Maxfield Vineyards, but he and Emerson had ultimately fallen in love. They'd ousted their father, who was currently living out of the country. Their mother remained at the estate. Technically, the two of them were still married.

Wren hoped that wouldn't be the case for much longer. Her poor mother had put up with so much. She deserved better.

They all did.

But while most of the changes that had occurred around the winery really were good things, their sister Cricket had taken the new situation hard. She had a different relationship with the place than the rest of them did. Cricket had been a late-in-life baby for their parents. An accident, Wren thought. And it had seemed like no one had the energy to deal with her. She'd been left to her own devices in a way that Emerson and Wren had not been.

As a result, Cricket was ever so slightly feral.

Wren found her mostly charming, but in the current situation, she didn't know how to talk to her. Didn't know what Cricket wanted or needed from them.

"She's been... You know," Emerson said. "Cricket. In that she's not really talking about anything substantial, and she's been quite scarce. She doesn't seem to be interested in any of the winery's new ventures."

"It's a lot of change."

"True," Emerson said. "But she's not a child. She's twenty-one."

"No," Wren said. "She's not a child. But can you imagine how much more difficult this would have been for you ten years ago?"

"I know," Emerson said softly. "It is different for us. It's different to have a little bit more perspective on the world and on yourself. I think she feels very betrayed."

"Hopefully she'll eventually embrace the winery. She can have a role here. I know she's smart. And I know she would do a good job, whatever Dad thought about her."

Emerson shook her head. "I don't think that Dad thought about her at all."

"Well, we will," Wren said.

The Maxfields had never been a close family in the way people might think of a close family. It wasn't like there had been intimate family dinners and game nights and things like that. But they had been in each other's pockets for their entire lives. Working together, deciding which direction to take their business. Their father was a difficult bastard, that was true. But he had entrusted his daughters with an extreme amount of responsibility when it came to the winery. It was weird now, to have the shape of things be so different. To have everything be up to them.

"Everything will be fine," Wren said. "It's already better, even if it is a little difficult."

Emerson nodded. "You're right. It's better. And things will only get even better from here."

"You agreed to do *what*?"

Creed looked at his older brother, Jackson, who had an expression on his face that suggested Creed might've said he planned to get out of the wine business and start raising corgis, rather than just coordinating an event with the Maxfield family.

"You heard me the first time," Creed said.

"What's the point of that? They're a bunch of ass-holes."

Normally, Creed would not have argued. Or even felt the inclination to argue. But for some reason, he thought back to Wren's determined face, and the way her body had looked in that dress, and he felt a bit defensive.

"You know the girls are running it now," he said. "James Maxfield absolutely was an asshole. I agree with you. But things are different now, and they're running things differently."

"Right. So you suddenly kissed and made up with Wren Maxfield?"

The idea of kissing Wren sent a lightning bolt of pleasure straight down to his cock. And the idea of… making up with her made his gut turn.

"Not a damn chance," Creed responded.

"So, the two of you are going to do this, while at each other's throats the entire time?"

"The logistics aren't exactly your concern. The logistics are my concern, as always. You just…be a silent partner." Creed narrowed his eyes. "You're awfully loud for a silent partner."

"I'm not technically a *full-on* silent partner," Jackson said. "It's just that I would rather invest money than make decisions."

"So then I'm letting you know what the plan is." Creed thought back to the moment he had told Wren that he was going to barbecue. Now he had to barbecue. "We have to bring some grills."

"I'm not even going to ask."

"Fine with me."

"I'm sorry, what are we planning?" Their younger sister, Honey, walked into the room. She was named by their mother, who had been so thrilled to have a daughter after having two sons that she had decided her daughter was sweet and needed a name that suggested so.

Honey had retaliated by growing into a snarky tomboy who had never seen the use for a dress and didn't know which end of a tube of lipstick to use. He had always been particularly fond of his sister.

"An event. With the Maxfields," Jackson said.

Her mouth dropped open. "Are you out of your mind?"

"I asked him that already," Jackson grunted.

"Well, ask again. Then check him for brain damage."

"No more brain damage than I had already," Creed said.

"Then why are we doing this?" Honey asked.

"Because," he said, taking a long moment to chew on the words that were about to come out next, because they hurt. "Wren had a point. She thinks we should join the wineries together. Make this area more of a tourist destination for wine. Wine trails, and things like that. There's no point in being competitive when we can advertise for each other. People like to try all different kinds of wines, and experience all different atmospheres when they're on vacation."

"You sound like a brochure," Jackson said.

He probably did. Mostly because Wren had sounded like one and he was basically repeating her. "Well. That's a good thing," Creed said. "Since we need some new brochures. And somebody has to write them. It isn't going to be either of you."

"True," Honey said cheerfully.

"You do have to help me barbecue. And you have to help set up this party. I need you two there. If for no other reason than to be witnesses."

"Witnesses to what?" Jackson asked.

"Just in case Wren decides to murder me."

"You could take her," Honey said.

Yeah. He could take her. That was for damn sure. But not in the way his sister meant. "You know I would never hurt a lady."

"That's far too gallant if the lady is willing to murder you," Honey said pragmatically.

"You could try to be less annoying," Jackson said.

"Look," Creed said. "She came to me. So, it's up to

her to behave herself. I didn't go to her, and I wouldn't have."

Though, truth be told, he would have to behave himself, too. The prospect of spending extra time with Wren Maxfield was definitely problematic. But he'd spent the last five years *not* touching her. A few weeks of working in close proximity shouldn't be an issue.

Hell. They *wouldn't* be.

Because when Creed Cooper decided something, he stuck to it. Control was what he was all about. He might be a rich cowboy who could have everything he wanted, but that didn't mean he *did* have everything he wanted. Not anymore. Not after he had experienced the disastrous consequences of that kind of behavior.

He had learned his lesson.

And he would never again make the mistakes he'd made as a kid.

That was for damn sure.

Two

Sometimes it still felt strange and disorienting to walk through the large Italian villa-style home, knowing their father would likely never return. That everything here had been previously certain but now…wasn't.

For as long as Wren could remember, her life had been on a steady course. Everything had been the same. From the time she was a child she had known she would work for Maxfield Vineyards. And the only real question had been in what capacity. Emerson's contribution had been based on her strengths. She was a social media wizard, but that was not something anyone could have anticipated, considering the medium hadn't existed in the same form when they were younger.

But Wren… Wren had always had a talent for hospitality. She had always been able to make people feel at ease. Even when everything had been going well in her parents' marriage, from the outside looking in, there had been an invisible band of tension in the house. The tension had only ever been worse when they were dealing with the Coopers. Whatever the reason, her father hated that family. And he had instilled a hefty dose of that dislike in her. Though, Creed had taken that dislike to a personal level.

Even so, Wren was an expert at managing tension. And making everything seem like it was okay. Delightful, even when it was decidedly less so.

Even when she and Creed wanted to dismember each other, they could both do their jobs. She imagined that was why he was in his position in his family company. The same as she was in hers.

Event planning and liaising with other companies in a personal way to create heightened brand recognition was something she excelled at. But, it had also been the only real surprise in her entire life. Apart from when James Maxfield had been utterly and completely disgraced.

Yes. That was really the first time her life had taken an unexpected turn.

She still wasn't sure how she felt about it. On the one hand, her father was clearly a monster. And, having never been…*emotionally* close with him—not in the way Emerson had been—it didn't devastate Wren. But it did leave her feeling adrift.

Now she was drifting into uncharted territory with this Cowboy Wines partnership, and she truly did not know how she felt about that either. But it was happening. So, there wasn't much to be done about it.

In fact, she was meeting with Creed this morning. The two of them were going to be talking logistics and deciding which wines to feature. They wanted to show-case the broad spectrum of what each wine label did best, while not stepping on each other's toes. Unusual, since generally they were deliberately going head-to-head.

But now they weren't. Another unusual thing in a slew of unusual things.

She got into her shiny little sports car and pulled out of the grand circular drive that led to the top of the mountain where the family home sat. She took the drive all the way down to the road, and as she put distance between herself and the villa, she was surprised to realize the pressure she hadn't noticed building in her chest began to get lighter and lighter.

And that shouldn't be what was happening. She should be feeling more and more stressed the closer she got to Creed. It didn't track with what she knew to be true about herself.

That she loved her family and her life and *hated* him.

She mused about that as she maneuvered her car down the winding two-lane road, through the pictur-esque main street of Gold Valley, Oregon.

Her family had been based here all her life, but she had always felt somewhat separate from it. She and her sisters had gone to boarding school on the East Coast, coming back to Oregon for summers.

All the men she'd dated had been from back east. Long-distance relationships that had become inconve-nient and annoying over time.

But those men had been like her. Educated in the same kinds of institutions, from families like her own. In fact, in those groups, often she was among the poor-est. Hilarious, all things considered. But that made her feel...somewhat out of place here. She didn't go out drinking at the Gold Valley Saloon, a favorite watering hole of most people who lived here.

She didn't have occasion to eat at any of the local restaurants, because they had a chef at home. They threw lavish parties at the villa, and ultimately... She just didn't often venture out of the estate. She had never considered herself sheltered. Not in the least. Instead, she had considered herself worldly by comparison with most of the people who lived in Gold Valley.

She had traveled extensively. Been to some of the most lavish resorts in the world. But suddenly it seemed obvious to her that she existed in a very particular kind of bubble—by choice—and there was something about having to face who her father really was that had...well, *disturbed* the bubble she lived in. It hadn't popped it altogether. She remained in it. But as she passed through town, the thoughts about her father passed through her mind, and she focused on getting her armor in place so she could deal with Creed.

Creed's family vineyard was beautiful. The winery facilities themselves were not her style at all, but they were pretty, and she could appreciate them. Rustic barns that had been fashioned into showrooms and event spaces, along with picnic tables that were set up down by the river, live bands often playing during the summer. She knew that food trucks came in during those events and added to the down-home atmosphere.

She could see why it appealed.

Now she really was worried that she had a headache. Wondering about the local bar and appreciating the aesthetic of this place. She snorted, pulling her car into the showroom lot and getting out, immediately scuffing her high heel on the gravel.

Oh, *there it was*.

All the ready irritation that she possessed for this place, and the man she was about to meet.

Her beautiful yellow leather pumps all scuffed…

And then, she nearly fell off her beautiful yellow leather pumps, because suddenly he was standing in the doorway, his arms crossed over his broad chest and his expression as unreadable as ever. He looked cool. His lips flattened into a grim line, his square jaw locked tight. His green eyes were assessing her. And that was the thing she hated the most. He was always doing that. Looking at her as if he could see straight through her dress. As if he could see through her chest. As if he could see things she wasn't sure she had ever examined inside herself.

She didn't like it.

Added to the *long* list of things she didn't like about him. That one went right below his being way too handsome for his—or her—own good.

"Howdy, ma'am."

"Sup, asshole." She crossed her arms, mirroring his own posture.

"I thought you were supposed to be a lady."

"That's the thing. I know how to behave like a lady in the right venue. I also know how to go toe to toe with anyone. A by-product of my private school education. Rich people are mean."

"Well. *You're* certainly mean."

She shifted uncomfortably. "Not always."

She didn't know why she felt compelled to strike at

him. Constantly. Why had they slipped into the space of open hostility with such ease?

You don't know?

Okay. Maybe she had a fair enough idea. But she didn't want to marinate on it. Not at all.

"Just to me?" he asked. "Aren't I special."

He moved away from the door and allowed her entry into the tasting room. There, he had several bottles of wine out on the table. They were already uncorked, glasses sitting next to them.

"Isn't this nice?" she asked.

"You didn't answer my question."

"You're certainly something," she responded. The answer seemed to settle between them, rather than striking immediate sparks. But that left an odd note lingering in the air. They just stared at each other for a long moment. And it was like everything in the air around them went elastic, stretched, then held tight.

"Nice to know."

She had hoped that his voice, his words, might banish that strange threat of tension. But it didn't. No. If anything, it felt worse. Because there was something about that voice that seemed to shiver over her skin, leaving goose bumps behind.

"Don't let it go to your...head." His eyes dipped down, to her lips, then lower.

"Let's drink wine," she said, far too bright and crisp and obviously trying to move them along from whatever was happening now.

"Did you bring some for me to try?"

"Yes. I have a crate in the car..."

"I've got it." He extended his hand.

"What?"

"Keys?"

"Oh." She dug in her purse for her key fob, and clicked it twice. "It's open."

He went outside and returned a moment later with a crate full of wine bottles slung up over his shoulder.

And it was... Well, it was impossible for her not to admire all that raw male beauty. His strength.

He had big hands. The muscles on his forearms shifted as he slung the crate down with ease onto the table, beginning to take the wine bottles out. They looked small in those hands. For some reason, she had an immediate image of those hands on her hips. All that strength, all that...largeness...

That was another thing.

She felt outside a lot of experiences here. And she had never... Well. Not with a man like him.

All of her past relationships had been based on having things in common. Liking each other. Being able to see a potential future, where she served as the appropriate ornament, and they served as the appropriate accessory.

The kinds of people who fit into each other's lives with ease, and because of that decided to make a go at fitting into bed with each other.

As a result, she hadn't had the most exciting sex life. It had been fine.

But she never had a wild...well, a wild anything.

She hadn't gone out to bars and hooked up.

Creed Cooper was a bar-hookup kind of guy. She just had that feeling.

That he was the kind of man women saw from across the room, all warm with whiskey and the promise of bad decisions, and thought... *He looks like a terrible choice.*

Before gleefully climbing on.

She had never done anything like that and there was something about him that made her think of those things. If she was honest, made her yearn for those things. A rough, bad decision like the kind she'd never made before.

"Let's get to pouring," he said.

And so they did. Portioning out samples for each other to try.

Infinitely safer and better than her standing there pondering the potential badness of climbing on top of Creed.

"Should we start here?" He picked up a glass of Max-field Chardonnay.

"It's as good as any as far as I'm concerned," she said. Though, now she was feeling fragile and like maybe she shouldn't be drinking around the man. Her thoughts were doing weird things. But she'd been in a weird space since she had driven away from the house today. Or maybe, since even before then.

She was familiar with this wine, and it was one of her favorites. Citrusy, with notes of white peach and apricot. It was a decent wine for her mood because of the tartness.

"Nice," he said. "Very nice."

"I thought it might pain you to admit that," she said.

"Not at all. Actually, I would be disappointed if I didn't like your wine. Because I would hate to be in competition with somebody who was terrible."

"I suppose that's a fair call," she said.

"Us next."

He offered her Cabernet Sauvignon, and the notes were completely different from the Chardonnay. Smoky oak and rich espresso. It reminded her of him. Full-bodied and rich. Tempting, but a very bad idea to over-indulge in.

"Nice," she said.

"A compliment from you," he said dryly. "What an achievement."

"Not one I would think you'd care about."

"I didn't say I *cared*. I was just remarking."

"You're irritating," she said, taking another sip of the wine. They moved through the wines, and she felt a looseness in her limbs. Relaxation pouring through her. She knew how to taste wine without getting drunk. So she had to assume the feeling had something to do with him. Which was honestly more disturbing than thinking she might have overindulged.

"Why shouldn't I be irritating? You're no better."

The smug male arrogance in those words rankled. He tipped his too handsome face backward and took another sip of wine. "You know, this event might also need a bouncy castle."

"No," she said.

He wasn't serious. She knew that. That was ridiculous. This was not going to be some family Sunday picnic. He knew her well enough to know that, whether he agreed or not.

"A dunk tank."

"Absolutely not," she responded. "It's happening in October."

"This is your problem, Wren. You can't think outside the box. You want to bring two labels together that historically have never had anything to do with each other. You want to bring together two very different types of people."

"The kinds of people that are at my winery do not want bouncy castles. Or children running around anywhere."

"Oh, they want perfect little Stepford children just like all of you were?"

Irritation twisted in her stomach. "You don't know me. You don't know us."

"Don't I? You're proving that I do. You're all worried about appearances here, like you always have been, when this whole thing with your daddy should have taught you appearances don't mean much of anything."

"How dare you?" She was trembling now, irritation turning to total outrage. "How dare you bring my father into this?"

"It was too easy."

"I've been through enough. We've been through enough. I don't need you flinging things at me about my family that I can't control. You want to talk about living in a box… You've never even left here, have you?"

"We both know that's not true. A fair amount of travel is required to do this job."

"Did you even go to college?" she asked.

"No," he responded. "I was too busy working to build the family label. I guess you think attending college makes you smarter than me, but all it means is you were from a different sort of family. You see, we are not from money. Not like you. You think that makes you better, but it doesn't. Because you know what else? My dad never sexually harassed a woman either. Unlike yours."

Raged poured through her and she fought to keep from showing just how mad he'd made her. He was doing it on purpose. He didn't deserve the satisfaction of knowing he'd succeeded in getting to her.

"Where is your damn wine cellar?" she asked. "I want to go look at what else you have."

"You don't want to keep having this conversation?"

"I never wanted to start having it," she said, each word coming out in a monotone. Because if she allowed her voice to amp up, she was going to say something she would regret.

Not that there was much she could say in anger that she would regret having spat out at Creed. It wasn't the anger that scared her. It was everything that hummed underneath it. That it could still hum underneath when she was so infuriated with him. When he was being such a...such an unrepentant asshole.

"Wine cellar's this way," he said.

He led the way to the back of the barn, where there was a staircase that led straight down.

She was reluctantly charmed by it. By the uneven rock walls that gave it the vague feel of a French country home. The thick, uneven slabs of wood that made up the staircase, making it feel old-world and resonant.

She was irritated she didn't hate it. She was irritated that he had homed in on the exact thing about herself that was bothering her at the moment.

That he had managed to poke at her exact point of insecurity. All the things she had been thinking of when she had driven into town. About how there was this whole other life here—a whole other life in general— that she had never even considered living because she was a... *Stepford child*. It was exactly what she had been.

Going where her father had chosen for her to go, growing into exactly what he had wanted her to grow into. Taking the job he had given her. And she was still doing it all. All of the exact same things she had done before her father had gone away. Before he had stepped down from the company in disgrace.

And it did make her wonder... What creature had she been fashioned into?

And for whom?

She didn't think there was an alternative reality where she would be in favor of a bouncy castle at her event, but she truly didn't know. She could only speculate.

Everyone is a product of their circumstances. Don't be so hard on yourself.

She nearly nodded at the affirmation she gave herself. The problem was, she couldn't agree. Because she wasn't actually ever all that hard on herself.

She never made any mistakes. Not in the way that she thought of mistakes. Because she had always, without fail, done exactly what she had been charged with.

By your father.

And still, her father had never been effusive about his pride in her. But she had lived for that praise. Because who didn't? Who didn't want to make their father happy? And her father was... He was a monster.

All these thoughts had her feeling absolutely and completely off-kilter. And that was only serving to make her even angrier at Creed. How could she handle all of this stuff *and* him? And how dare he cut her so close to the bone?

He didn't know her. He didn't have the right to say the things he'd said. To say things that made her feel more seen than anything anyone in her family had ever said. That was for sure.

"So, the Cooper family is just all rainbows and butterflies?" she asked as they made their way through the aisles of wine.

"And horseshit," he said. "Which wine were you thinking?"

"I don't know. Pick something good."

"The array of wine upstairs is good," he said. "That's why I picked them."

"Something different." She felt difficult and she didn't care.

"Rainbows and butterflies," he reiterated. "And my dad's not a criminal."

"And all of you work here at the family winery because you just love each other so much."

"Is that difficult for you to believe?"

It wasn't. Not really. There was a reason she was choosing to stay at the Maxfield winery, after all.

A reason that went beyond just being afraid to start over, or not knowing what else she would do.

Emerson was her rock, and Cricket needed her.

"I'm close with my sisters," Wren said. "I love them."

"And I love *my* family. You ought to love your family."

"I'm just saying. I'm not in a box. I just know who I am." Those words had never felt less true. Not that she loved her family. She did love her family. It was just that right now she felt like she was wearing a Wren suit and somewhere inside was a different creature. She felt like she was inhabiting the wrong body. The wrong space.

"Honestly, Wren, if you believed that, you wouldn't be so bound and determined to try to convince me."

"You don't know me," she said. "You're not my friend."

"Something we can agree on."

"You don't get to say what I know or don't know. You just don't."

"Too late. I did."

"You're such a… You're ridiculous."

"Just take a bottle of wine so we can get on with this. I will feel a lot better dealing with you if I'm drunker."

"This isn't exactly a picnic for me either," she said. "You are without a doubt the most insufferable man I've ever known."

"You don't like me, Wren?" he asked, taking a step toward her. "However will I survive?"

"The same as you always do, I imagine," she said. "High on an unearned sense of self-confidence and a little testosterone poisoning."

He huffed. "You like it," he said.

"I'm sorry, what?"

"You like it. My testosterone. You'd like to be poisoned by it, admit it."

"There's that sense of unearned self-confidence," she said, her heart hammering steadily against her chest. "Right on time."

"It's not unearned. I watch you. When we fight. Your face gets all flushed."

"That's called anger."

"Why? What is it about me that makes you so damned angry?"

"You… You are just…a useless, base ape."

"Base?" He asked the question with a dangerous sort of softness to his voice, and it made her tremble. "That's what you think? That I'm like an animal who can't control himself?"

"Yes," she spat. "I know all about you and your reputation. You get drunk at the bar, you pick up women every night of the week."

"I don't get drunk," he said. "That's not me."

"Maybe that's how you see yourself, but it's not what I hear. I hear that you're just a big, dumb, blunt instrument. You might go on and on about how you pulled yourself up by your bootstraps, but your daddy made all this happen. You might wear a cowboy hat, but there's a silver spoon in your mouth the same as mine. So don't you dare go acting like you're better than me just because you can't be bothered to put on an ounce of refinement. Because you don't have the manners to leave my dad out of a conversation. Just because you can't be bothered to try to be a…a civilized human being."

"You think I'm an animal, Wren?" he asked again, his voice low and rough. "You think I don't control my baser instincts? I have, Princess. You don't even know. Maybe it's time you saw what it looks like when I don't."

And that was how she found herself being backed up against one of the stone walls in the wine cellar, six-foot-plus of angry man staring down at her, his green eyes blazing. "You want an animal?" He put his hand on her hip, and she nearly combusted. "I've half a mind to give you one."

Her heart was thundering so hard she felt like it might rattle the buttons clean off the front of her blouse. And if it did, it would leave her top open. And then he would be able to…

She was throbbing between her thighs, her throat utterly and completely dry. This couldn't be happening. This had to be some kind of fever dream. The kind of dream she had every other night when she had to deal with Creed.

When anger turned into something much hotter, and much more *naked*.

But it couldn't be real. Anger couldn't really turn into this seething, hot well of need, could it? This couldn't really be what was beneath all of their fighting. That was... That was her being confused.

Her having some kind of fantasy that allowed her to take control of him.

That was just what she told herself whenever she had sex dreams about him.

That sure, he might be hot, but she didn't actually want to *have sex with him*. It was just that the idea of manipulating him with her body appealed to her subconscious, because it was always such a sparring contest in real life.

And the idea that maybe her breasts could reduce him slightly was tempting.

But that wasn't real. People didn't really do this.

She didn't really do this.

You're just trapped in a box...

And suddenly, she wondered what it might be like if she did really do this. If she dared. If she returned his volley right now.

If she let herself be the animal she'd accused him of being.

She'd gotten to him. Really and truly. Something about her accusing him of lacking civility and control clearly irritated him. And she wanted to keep on doing it. She wanted to push him.

She arched her hips forward, and her pelvis came into contact with the evidence of just what he was feeling, there in the front of his jeans. He was hard. He might be mad, but he was hard. For her.

"Oh, I see," she said. "So that's your real problem. Pulling my pigtails on the playground because you like me?" She rolled her hips forward, and she nearly gasped at the sensation. She might be taunting him, but she was on the verge of overheating. Spontaneously combusting. "If you want me to lift up my skirt so you can see my panties, you should've just asked."

"You're infuriating," he bit out.

"No more so than you."

"You know what, I'm tired of that smart mouth of yours. Maybe it's time you found something else to occupy it with."

And before she could say anything else, those lips had crashed down on hers. He was kissing her, hard and deep. And he was so… Hot and strong and male. So far and beyond any man she had ever touched before. She was used to civilized men. And he might be angry that she'd called him uncivilized, but the fact remained that he was. Dangerously so.

She was panting, writhing against him as he cupped the back of her head so he could take the kiss deeper. His tongue was hot and slick against hers, and the friction made a well of need open up between her thighs. She felt hollow, she felt… Like she might die if she didn't have him. Thrusting hard and deep inside her.

"You talk big," she said against his mouth. "I hope you've got the equipment to back that up."

"I've never had any complaints, Princess."

"I'm sure I could find a few."

"No, baby. You're not going to have any. Not after this."

"Are you just going to talk? Or are you going to fuck me?"

She had never spoken to a man like that in her life. Had never even dreamed of saying something so raw and carnal. Because she'd never been this desperate before. And it didn't matter. Because it was Creed Cooper, and he didn't even like her. So it didn't matter what he thought of her. Didn't matter if he thought she was dirty or bad or wrong for talking to him that way. For demanding that he take her up against a wall. For fighting with him with one breath, and demanding he do something about the heat between them with the next.

There were no boxes here. That was the beautiful thing. There was nothing but this.

"My pleasure."

Then her shirt was torn open. Buttons scattered all over the floor, and she didn't care. He pulled her bra down, exposing her breasts, and then those big, rough hands were cupping her tender flesh, his thumbs skimming over her nipples.

She gasped, arching toward him, reveling in the way she filled his palms. She had never been like this.

And suddenly, as he stripped layers of clothes off her skin, she felt like that suit had been removed along with it. That layer that had felt so foreign. So wrong. And even though she had never in all her life behaved like this, the situation suddenly felt more real. Suddenly felt more like who she was. Like the Wren beneath all that she had been created to be.

It was her turn next. She pushed his shirt, shrugged it over his shoulders, and revealed a body that put her wildest fantasies to shame.

She hadn't known. Not really.

She hadn't even begun to guess how beautiful the man was. How much all those muscles would appeal to her. His chest hair, the scar on his side. Everything that made him a rough, uncultured-looking man, the likes of which she had never had before.

And everything after that became a blur.

A fumble born out of desperation.

She worked at his jeans while he pushed her skirt up over her hips, hooking his finger around the elastic on her underwear and shoving it to the side while she freed his cock. It was big and thick, gorgeous. And she had never particularly thought that part of the male anatomy was *gorgeous* before, but that was the only word for it. A thing of actual beauty. She was far too happy for herself to be annoyed with him that his outrageous ego was not in fact misplaced. He had earned the right to be full of himself.

And all she wanted was to be full of him, too.

"Please," she whispered against his mouth.

"That's the first time you've ever asked me nicely for anything," he growled, pressing the head of his arousal to the entrance of her body, teasing her, teasing them both.

She'd never been so wet so fast in her life. So ready. She had never craved penetration like this before. She had never craved another person like this before.

She had never thought much about her sex drive, because it had never really felt like a drive. She had thought of it as something like a sweet tooth. Something people had to varying degrees, and sure, sometimes a piece of cake would be nice. But she just wasn't one of those people who obsessively craved sugar, or sex.

This felt like a drive. An urge. Something that came from deep inside her that she couldn't control or minimize. This was something like insanity.

"Did you still want that fuck, sweetheart?" His voice was a growl, feral and compelling.

"Yes," she said. "Please yes."

And then he was inside her.

He was so big that it stretched at first. Hurt a little bit. But in the best way.

Every time he drew away and then thrust back into her body, he did so with a growl. And she clung to him, the hard drive of him deep inside her everything she had fantasized about and more. She had not truly known that it could be like this. She had thought that people made up stories. She had thought for sure that...

Well, when her sister had lost her mind over Holden, Wren had judged her.

But she hadn't known it could be like this.

Raw and terrifying. Wonderful. Electric.

There had been no more denying this than there was denying herself air.

It seemed to make perfect sense now. This thing that had mystified her only a moment before. This anger turned need that rocked everything she was.

Of course, this was right next to the anger that was always threatening to combust between them. Of course, this was the other side of all that need. Of course.

How had she ever thought it was anything else?

He whispered things in her ear. Dirty things. Shocking things. But he called her beautiful. And he kissed the side of her neck, and it made her feel like she might break apart. She didn't know why.

And then suddenly, everything came to a head, and she couldn't breathe. All she could do was cling to him, to keep herself from collapsing onto the ground, to keep herself from flying into a million pieces. She dug her fingernails into his shoulder and cried out as pleasure took over. He wasn't far behind. On a growl, he found his own release, his body pulsing inside her. And when it was over, they both collapsed there against the wall, sweaty and breathing hard.

"This wine," he said, reaching around her. "This will do." He grabbed the bottle, then bent and picked his shirt up from off the floor. He righted his clothes disturbingly fast, and then left her standing there.

She tucked her blouse as firmly into her skirt as she could, crossing the bottom ends and getting the thing to more or less cover her breasts. And then she just stood there for a moment, shell-shocked.

She'd just had sex with Creed Cooper against the wall.

And he had walked away like they hadn't missed a beat between talking about wine and screwing each other senseless.

She pushed the skirt down over her hips. If it wasn't for the intense throbbing between her legs… If it wasn't for that, she would have thought she had hallucinated it all. Because how… How had that just happened?

She grabbed another bottle of wine, not even reading the label, and walked back upstairs. He was in position, his face like absolute granite.

"Want to finish tasting?"

"Are you… Did you hit your head down there?" she asked.

"Where?"

"Why are you acting like we didn't just have sex?"

"It's done," he said.

There was something bleak in his green eyes, and it disturbed her. She was a woman. Wasn't she the one who was supposed to freak out about this kind of thing? She wasn't particularly worried about how many partners she'd had, but it was one of those things other women often seemed to worry about. But he was the one who looked...well, vaguely ashamed.

"It's just that..."

Those green eyes were hard as emeralds now. "I don't really want to talk about it."

"Why not?"

"It's not going to happen again."

Well, on that they could agree. Because there was no way—absolutely no way—that she would ever do anything like that with him again. It had been stupid to do it the first time.

Even though it had felt amazing. She wanted to tell him that. She wanted to cling to him, for just a little while longer. To make him hold her up, because her knees still felt weak. To tell him it was the best sex she'd ever had, and she didn't know what to do with the knowledge that the man who could make her body do things she hadn't known it could do was the one man she had decided she hated more than any other.

She wanted to ask him why that was, because he had taken pleasure with her, too, so maybe he could understand it. He'd certainly had more partners than she had. Had more experience overall. So surely he should be able to...

And she realized she was being a ridiculous stereotype. A woman who was putting emotions into something that had been purely physical.

She had been caught up in that moment. In being outside herself. Well, she had done something out of character. And that was that. There was no going back. But there was also no need to continue on with it now.

He was still Creed. She was still Wren.

She didn't like him any more now that she'd seen him naked than she had before.

Well. That wasn't true.

The man had given her the most insane orgasm of her life. It would be impossible not to like him slightly more now than she had before.

"I trust you to make your selections," she said. She felt numb and shaky. And maybe he had a point that the two of them should act like nothing had happened, but she couldn't do it while in the same room as him.

"I'll just leave you to it."

"You're leaving?"

"Yes," she said. "We'll be in touch."

It wasn't until she got back in her car, and was safely back on the road, that she started shaking. She had lived out some kind of fantasy she hadn't even fully realized she'd had. She'd had sex with her enemy up against the wall. She didn't intend to have a relationship with him. They couldn't. They couldn't even be in the same room without biting each other's head off.

She didn't like him. He didn't like her.

It had been just... Just to feel good.

And then, in spite of the shaking, in spite of the nerves riding through her body, she felt a smile curve her lips. Maybe what she'd done had been out of character. But it had been her choice. And she had liked it. She had liked it a lot. And what was wrong with that? What was wrong with doing something wild? She hadn't hurt anybody, not like her dad. And she hadn't done it for anyone else. She had done it for her. She had done it because she hadn't been able to make any other choice. Because she had wanted it so damn much.

That was a Wren choice. The real Wren. The Wren who lived somewhere deep inside her. Who didn't just do things for approval, or because it was easy. Because it was the next step on the path.

She couldn't help but be proud of herself for that.

And she couldn't be ashamed of it either.

For the first time in her life, Wren Maxfield had done something truly spontaneous. And she was just going to enjoy it.

Three

Eighteen years of flawless self-control had been completely destroyed in under an hour. He could throw a whole parade fueled by his guilt and regret. The trouble with guilt and regret, for him, was that it was such a tiresome old standby that his body immediately converted it to anger.

He was currently outside on his ranch trying to burn off the rage that was firing through his veins. She had done this to him. She had made him into something he didn't recognize. Or worse, something he did recognize. Someone he knew from a long time ago. Someone who had made mistakes others had to pay for.

Damn Wren Maxfield.

And damn his libido.

He was thirty-four years old. He was better than that. Better than a quick screw against a wall. Better than ignoring her and what had happened right after.

Dammit. He had not handled that well.

He picked up a large boulder, hefted it upward, then walked about five feet before dropping it down in the spot where he was building a retaining wall near his house.

The ground was soft and slick here, made of clay, and when it rained, it had a bad habit of turning into a flood, and quickly. So he was building a wall to make sure that the water funneled where he wanted it to funnel. He'd already dug a trench, which had helped with a little of his frustration. Lifting boulders would hopefully be the antidote for the rest of it.

"I thought I might find you here."

He turned and saw his brother, Jackson, standing there, leaning against the stone post at the bottom of the driveway.

"What are you doing here?"

"Thought I might ask you the same thing. Since you didn't show up to the winery this morning."

"I had work to do here." He gestured to the stones.

"Looks like it. Except… Normally you let us know when you're not coming in."

"Since when are you so up in all the winery stuff?"

"I always have been. It's just that I don't usually have to come looking for you. So maybe you don't notice."

"Did Dad send you?"

"No. But he did ask after you."

"Well, Dad needs to keep himself busy."

In the two years since their mother had died, their dad had become something of a hermit. The work at the winery had shifted more to Creed, Jackson and Honey. It was difficult for Law Cooper to deal with the loss of his wife. In fact, it could be argued that he hadn't dealt with it at all. He'd simply buried his head in the sand, doing things on the ranch that didn't require him to interact much with people.

"You know, I'm not sure I believe Dad asked after me."

"He did," Jackson said, a strange blankness in his expression. "He worries about you. He worries about all of us. Hell, I think he worries about everything these days."

"Maybe he should start doing winery work again. It might take his mind off things."

"Might."

"Anyway. Now you know where I am. You could have called like a normal person."

"You wouldn't have answered. Because you're avoiding me."

"What makes you think I'm avoiding you? I don't come into work one morning and you immediately think it's about you? Nice ego on you, Jackson."

"All right, not me specifically," Jackson said. "But something."

"It's just this whole thing planning the party." Creed figured he would get close enough to the truth without actually giving his brother all of it, and that would probably be more believable. "That woman is giving me hell."

"Scared of a girl?" Jackson took a swing at him, verbally. He was his older brother, and Creed knew he lived for that.

Creed wasn't in the mood.

He shot his brother a dead-eyed look. "I live for the day a woman gives you hell."

"Not going to happen," Jackson said. "I'm not going

to let myself get tangled up in knots over a woman. Especially not a Maxfield."

"The only other Maxfield is Cricket. And she'd kick your ass if you came near her."

Jackson snorted. "I'd kick my own ass ten ways till Sunday if I ever did anything that stupid. She's... young." He grimaced. "Wren, on the other hand, is perfectly age appropriate. If you want her, just have sex with her and get it over with."

Creed gritted his teeth. "That's not always the answer, Jackson."

"Look," he said. "I know you had a bad experience. But it's not like you're a monk."

"No," Creed responded. "I'm not. It isn't that I quit having sex, but I don't let my body tell me what to do."

Too bad he had. Too bad he had one hundred percent followed his libido and nothing else.

And he knew that he should talk to Wren about the fact that they hadn't used protection. But she was a grown woman. She was probably on birth control, and if she wasn't, she would handle anything she needed to on her own.

"The problem is that you banged her already," Jackson said, his expression suddenly going sly. "And you're pissed about it."

Creed about ground his teeth into powder. "Go away."

"You did. Well, what the hell are you going to do about it now? Is there any point beating yourself up over it?"

His brother's question gave him pause. "I mean, I think there's always a point in beating yourself up about something."

"Yeah, but you're a martyr. So, let that go for a second. You're a grown person, she's a grown person. You don't like her, who cares? You've been with plenty of women you don't even know."

"Sure. But then the *possibility* for liking them exists."

"What does it matter? You're not going to be in a relationship with her."

"No, but it seems…like the wrong thing to do."

"Sometimes the wrong thing to do feels pretty damn good. Maybe you should try it."

"You forget. I did."

"You're not sixteen anymore. Neither is she. You're not going to have your life gutted by some girl and her family intent on keeping her to the straight-and-narrow path they put her on."

And that was the bottom line of it all. Creed had to keep control, because he knew what happened when he didn't. And more to the point, he knew the way that other people could then take control of your life.

"I know that."

"Yeah, but you act like you don't sometimes."

"If I didn't learn from a mistake like that what kind of fool would I be?" Creed asked.

"The normal kind."

"Well, whatever is going on with that now, you don't know what it's like to disappoint him quite in the way that I did."

Jackson only chuckled. "You don't know everything about my life, little brother. And I don't claim to know everything about yours. But quit moping. We have things to do."

"Since when do you care about any of it?"

"I don't. But honestly, talking about this joint venture with the Maxfields is about the only thing that's gotten a reaction out of Dad in way too long. He was interested in it. And… I care about that."

Well, so did Creed. Anything to get their dad out of his depression. They'd already lost their mother. They didn't need to watch him slowly slip away, too, because of his sadness.

"Then it'll get done. Don't worry about it."

And maybe Jackson even had a point about himself and Wren. They were adults. And as long as everything proceeded with a bit more planning and caution than they had yesterday, what was the harm?

Maybe it was possible for Creed to drink his wine and have his beef, too. Or something like that.

"I'll be down at the winery in a couple of hours," he said. "I really do need to finish this wall."

"All right. See you back at the ranch." His brother tipped his hat, and turned and walked back toward his truck. And he took with him Creed's excuses.

Creed supposed he should write his brother a thank-you note for that. He was right. Creed was good at self-flagellation when it came to losing control. But sex with Wren had been incredible.

What was the harm in going back for more?

That was, if she wasn't too angry at him.

A slow smile spread across his face. Of course… Anger, with them, didn't seem to prevent the sex from happening.

Quite the opposite.

He might never have experienced anything like this before, but he was eager to experience it again.

* * *

Wren had managed to keep her interactions with Creed confined to text messages for the last couple of weeks. His responses had all been short and on-topic, and that weirded her out more than anything else. There was no teasing. No goading. Of course, she hadn't teased or goaded him either.

It was weird and unsettling. To not be engaged in some kind of sparring match with him. She would have said that she wanted this distant professionalism that didn't leave her feeling hot, bothered or angry. Anyway, it got all of the planning done for the event. And today it was all ready to go. An open house, of sorts, set out on the front lawn of Maxfield Vineyards.

Thankfully the late October weather was playing nicely, and it was sunny and warm. Oregon Octobers were a gamble. They could be infused with all the warmth of spring, with deeper golds infusing the air. Or they could be gray, damp and snarling, with a harsh bite in the wind.

Today was golden, and so was the event.

There was no dunk tank. Neither was there a bouncy castle. But there were barbecues and smokers, coupled with lovely covered seating areas, and some places that had quilts set out like an old-fashioned picnic. She had to admit, the barbecue was a nice touch. It did make everything seem welcoming.

And people from Gold Valley, along with folks from the neighboring town of Copper Ridge, seemed to be pouring in to engage in the event.

It was a success. And she was… Well, she was thrilled.

But she felt like she should be something more.

Maybe that was the problem. She was mentally pleased. But she wasn't as happy as she might have been. Because she knew that Creed was going to be here soon. If he wasn't already.

She had spent a few hours early this morning making sure everything was ready to go, so she could go off and get herself dressed and also maybe so she could avoid him.

Anyway, they had a very good team hired to take care of all the logistics, so it wasn't as if she needed to micromanage anything.

Her stomach twisted, butterflies jittering there. She told herself it was because the event was about to begin, and that always made her feel a little bit nervous.

But she could no longer pretend that was the case when it felt like the crowd parted and the sun shined down upon those who had just arrived. Law Cooper, Jackson Cooper, the family's friend and surrogate son, Jericho Smith, and petite, feisty Honey Cooper.

But it was Creed Wren couldn't look away from.

Creed, with a black cowboy hat on his head, a black suit jacket, white shirt opened at the collar, showing a wedge of chest that she now knew full well was as spectacular as advertised.

He had not shown up in jeans and a T-shirt.

Often, even at formal events, he did wear them, as if he was very intentionally flouting convention. He somehow never looked unprofessional. And she knew that had to do with the fact that his choices were just so damned intentional. He wasn't rolling into places that way on accident. No, he was wearing his country roots like a second skin, and it was provocative in their sorts of circles.

But for this, he had dressed up. For this, he had worn a suit. She wanted to…

Well, there was no use marinating on what she wanted to do.

The things she had wanted to do every day since the last time he had touched her.

She had tried to simply appreciate the triumph of a good rebellion. But it wasn't that easy. Because her body was so greedy and desperate for more of what he had given her. For more sex as it existed for others, more of this realm that had been completely unknown to her prior to Creed's touch.

She was *so* messed up.

She probably did need to see a therapist. What had happened with her dad was no small thing, and now she was climbing on top of men who were mean to her. That had to say something about her mental state.

But her physical state had enjoyed it quite a lot, and it was difficult for her to accept it as a one-off. Especially when she kept having sweaty dreams about it.

"Well," she said, looking him up and down. "Don't you clean up nice."

"You, too," he said.

She was very aware that the eyes of every member of his family were on her.

In fact, she was so certain, it took her a while to absorb it since the fact was vaguely embarrassing. But when she did catch his father's eyes, she did not see the speculation she had expected. Instead, he had a strange, wistful look on his face.

"Wren," he said. "Right?"

"Yes," she said.

"You look very much like your mother."

She blinked, feeling a strange sensation at the comment. Her mother was beautiful. But Wren didn't have a lot in common with her. At least, she'd never felt like she had.

Over the years her mother had become more and more quiet. More withdrawn.

And Wren could understand why now. Because clearly not all had been well in her parents' marriage. Her mother must've had a sense that her husband was unfaithful at the very least. A predator at worst.

"Do you know my mother?" she asked.

"A long time ago," he said.

"Let's go find you a place to sit," Honey said, grabbing hold of her father's arm. "Nice to see you."

The youngest Cooper clearly didn't think it was all that nice to see Wren. Jericho and Jackson, on the other hand, were perfectly pleasant. They were both stunningly handsome men, Jackson as tall as his brother, and a bit broader, his eyes the same green. Jericho was even taller, with darker skin and brown eyes, and wide shoulders that looked capable of carrying any number of burdens upon them.

She found them both aesthetically pleasing. But her reaction wasn't the same as what Creed made her feel.

Which was a shame, really, because Jericho and Jackson were so much more pleasant.

"Good to officially meet you," Jericho said, extending his hand. She shook it, then Jackson's.

"It's a great event," Jackson said. "A great idea."

"Well, it's my sister Emerson's doing. Actually, a whole lot of this new direction is."

"I hear her marriage started the tidal wave."

Wren laughed. "The blackmail did."

"Was the blackmail related to the marriage?" Jericho asked.

"Oh, yes," Wren said. "Well, not now. I mean, in the sense that Emerson and Holden are totally fine and no one is being blackmailed to stay in the marriage. It's complicated."

At least, it had been. But now Holden and Emerson just loved each other.

Jackson and Jericho left, which put Wren and Creed far too close to each other.

"Nice to see you. In fact, I was beginning to think you had vaporized."

"No," he said. "Just getting my head on straight. Figured it would be best to focus on the planning of all of this."

"I suppose so," she said.

"Looks amazing."

"You were right about the barbecue. People love it."

"Now, I'm surprised you didn't burst into flame."

"You know, I might have, but recent events left me somewhat inoculated."

"Good to know. I thought they might have left you…"

"Oh, now you're concerned? You certainly didn't show any concern when you decided to pretend nothing happened."

"Is that what you want to fight about now?"

"I don't know. I haven't decided yet. There's such a huge array of things we could fight about. Considering we haven't seen each other in a couple of weeks and a whole lot has happened. Though, I do think the obvious thing to fight about would be the sex that we had, which you're still trying to pretend didn't happen."

She had not intended to open with that. She hadn't

intended to be talking about this with him with guests all around them, and members of their family in close proximity. But it just kind of poured out of her. Maybe it was him. But maybe it was her, too. Maybe it was everything that she was.

Everything that she had become in the last couple of months.

This creature she was trying to remake herself into, in her own image, and not that of her father.

And really… What was the point of watching what she said around Creed? Everything was already as horrifying as it could ever be. Everything was already ruined. There was no dignity left to be had.

She had climbed him like a tree and had an earth-shattering orgasm seconds after he had thrust into her. She was sure she'd left him bleeding from digging her nails into his back. She'd probably caused hearing damage with how loud she'd screamed when she'd come.

There was pretty much no coming back from that.

Her dignity was toast.

He knew how much she wanted him. But the flipside was she knew how much he wanted her. And she suspected the fact that he had pretended that nothing had transpired between them was only evidence of just how much he wanted her.

Something about wanting her bothered him.

But then, he had come to this event all dressed up.

She couldn't figure the man out.

And as much as it pained her to admit it, she sort of liked that about him. That he wasn't easy. That she didn't intimidate him. That he didn't want her money or her influence. Everything about him that was so annoying was simultaneously also compelling, and that was just the whole thing.

"Come here," he said, his voice suddenly hard. "I want to show you something."

There was a big white tent that was still closed, reserved for an evening hors d'oeuvre session for people who had bought premium tickets, and he compelled her inside. It was already set up with tables and tablecloths, everything elegant and dainty, and exceedingly Maxfield. Though there were bottles of Cowboy Wines on each table, along with bottles of Maxfield select.

But they were not apparently here to look at the wine, or indeed anything else that was set up. Which she discovered when he cupped her chin with firm fingers and looked directly into her eyes.

"I've done nothing but think about you for two weeks. I want you. Not just something hot and quick against a wall. I need you in a bed, Wren. We need some time to explore this. To explore each other."

She blinked. She had not expected that.

He'd been avoiding her and she'd been so sure it was because he didn't want this.

But he was here in a suit.

And he had a look of intent gleaming in those green eyes.

She realized then she'd gotten it all wrong.

"I… I agree."

She also hadn't expected to agree.

But her heart was about to fly out of her chest, and she was achy and wet between her legs already. She sort of wanted to ask him if they could try it up against the wall of the tent. But she had a feeling that would only culminate in the two of them falling through the filmy fabric and embarrassing themselves.

She just didn't have the willpower to resist him.

"I want you now," she whispered, and before she could stop herself, she was up on her tiptoes and kissing that infuriating mouth.

She wanted to sigh with relief. She had been so angry at him. So angry at the way he had ignored this. Because how dare he? He had never ignored the anger between them. No. He had taken every opportunity to goad and prod her in anger. So why, *why* had he ignored this?

But he hadn't.

They were devouring each other, and neither of them cared that there were people outside. His large hands palmed her ass, pulling her up against his body so she could feel just how hard he was for her. She arched against him, gasping when the center of her need came into contact with his rampant masculinity.

She didn't understand the feelings she had for this man. Where everything about him that she found so disturbing was also the very thing that drove her into his arms.

Too big. Too rough. Crass. Untamable. He was everything she detested, everything she desired.

All that, and he was distracting her from an event that she had planned. Which was a cardinal sin in her book. And she didn't even care.

He set her away from him suddenly, breaking their kiss. "Not now," he said, his voice rough. "Tonight. All night. You. In my bed."

"But can't we just…"

"We are in a tent."

"I don't really care," she said, amazed.

"You don't?"

"Maybe I'm having a nervous breakdown," she said. "It's entirely possible. It has been a very weird few months. And I just… I don't know. I don't know who I am anymore. I'm not sure I want to know who I am. You're right. I've been in a box. And I didn't want to admit it. I just wanted to be mad at you. I just wanted to yell at you. But then we kissed, and then we did other things, and I've spent the last two weeks being incredibly confused about it. But you know what confuses me most? That I'm not ashamed. But I'm not sorry. I think it was good. Because even if it was the biggest mistake of my life, at least it was my mistake. I've done everything that's ever been asked of me. I've dated only men that were expected. I've never had sex outside of a relationship."

"It's fun," he commented.

"Apparently. I know that now. And…it was just for me."

"I don't know about that. I got something out of it, too."

"Well, good for you." She sighed heavily. "Okay. I'm not baring my soul to you or anything like that. But… Look, it's been weird. The whole thing with my dad. I swear to you, I didn't know how awful he was."

"I'm sorry that I brought your dad up the other day."

"No. It's okay. I mean… It's not. It was painful. But I'm working through things. And, I think I'm getting there. Better. This is part of it."

The left side of his mouth lifted. "Sexual healing?"

"Why not?" she asked. "Nothing else has worked." She took a breath, and then everything just poured out. "I worry about Cricket. Because she's not really talking to anyone. My mom is just kind of… Well, she's doing what she does. She's hiding. Emerson has Holden, and she seems to be coming out of it just fine. I feel like I'm in a weird space. I can't exactly live in denial. I'm too involved in this business. I feel the loss of my father too much. But I don't really feel okay about any of it. Or over it. I'm not sure that I feel okay about me. I need to figure out what I want."

"You're not thinking about leaving the industry, are you?"

"No," she said. "I think I feel like *this*—" she gestured to the interior of the very Maxfield tent "—is mine. But… What I'm saying is a little rebellion is what I need right now."

"Happy to be a part of it."

"Yeah, well." It was unexpected just how easy it was to tell him all of this. Somehow, she couldn't really be embarrassed around this man.

She had yelled all kinds of unflattering things at him over the years. She was not the best version of herself when he was around. It was like he tapped into some unfettered part of her that she didn't normally have access to. And when he was in the room, she just let fly.

It now extended to sex, apparently, and again, she wasn't even embarrassed about it. She had a total and complete lack of inhibition with him.

And right now, that felt like a gift.

Because she'd had nearly thirty years of being inhibited. Of following a very specific path. And Creed represented something wild and free that she'd never thought she could be.

Maybe that was the real reason he made her so angry.

That he had been free in about a thousand ways she was sure she never would be.

"Then let's go do our jobs," he said. "The sooner we get finished with all of this…"

The last part was left unspoken, but the promise in his tone was clear. And her whole body responded to that. Effortlessly. Deeply.

And she knew she had made the right choice. To continue down this path with him.

It might end badly… But there was something in her that didn't fear the consequences. Not really.

She had gone down the expected path before. She had done it all of her life. And look how that ended. With her father…

There were no guarantees.

There were no guarantees. And she would rather live free.

Four

His body was on fire.

He was burning for her, and he'd decided to jump into the flames. That was control. He'd made a choice and he was resolved in it.

Or he'd just decided to take his hands off the wheel and let the car steer itself. One or the other.

He had to admit that the event was going well. His father even looked like he was enjoying himself. Though, his entire countenance had taken on an odd tone after he had met Wren.

Creed didn't really understand it.

He knew that there was…weird blood between the Maxfield and Cooper families, but he didn't fully know why. He had always assumed it was because they were business rivals, but effectively… They weren't anymore. Maybe it was just old habits dying hard. Except there had been no animosity in his father's bearing. None at all. He'd shown a strange kind of wistfulness. A sadness. But then, everything his father did these days was wistful and sad.

The old man missed his wife, and there wasn't much anyone could do to fix that.

They all missed their mother. It didn't matter that it was the natural order of things to lose a parent. You knew that you would. If everything went according to plan... You did.

But you were never ready for it. It was never time.

It would always feel too soon.

But it *really* had been too soon.

And they'd been suffering the aftereffects of grief, as a family incomplete, ever since.

Incomplete and different. Jackson had been distant. But Jackson had always been closest to their mother. Still, it was just another thing.

Creed hadn't had a drink or a bite to eat all day, mostly because he felt like he was being fueled by desire for Wren, but he was about ready to go and get himself some brisket when everything inside him went still.

He'd experienced this a couple of times in his life. But not for a long while. And it was never for a *good* reason. It was only ever for one reason. He closed his eyes, steeling himself.

Why the hell would she come to this?

He turned slowly, and that was when he saw her.

Louisa Johnson. Her accomplished doctor husband, Calvin Johnson. And as far as all the world was concerned, their four children. Including their oldest son, who was taller and broader than his father.

As a matter of fact, the boy looked a hell of a lot like Creed.

His stomach went acid.

He hadn't seen the kid in... Maybe going on four years.

The boy was eighteen now. Creed knew his birthday. Every year marked itself on his heart. A deep groove. A line in a particular chart that spoke of the hours, weeks, months, years that he'd been father to a son he could never acknowledge.

It was a small town. He couldn't always avoid Louisa. But her actually coming to one of his events was a study in sadism. Even he didn't think she could be quite that evil.

Just self-centered and hell-bent on creating the life she wanted. Never willing to admit she had given her virginity up to somebody other than her longtime boyfriend. And that when she'd gotten pregnant at sixteen it had not been with Cal Johnson's baby. But she'd gone and fixed that uncomfortable fact really quickly, slept with Cal right away and claimed the kid was his.

Creed knew the truth.

Creed had thought they were in love.

A virgin himself, he'd believed that having sex with her meant something. That her climbing into the bed of his truck with him had mattered. And he'd been so overwhelmed by desire that he hadn't stopped to think about anything.

He was sure... He had been so sure that it meant she was going to break up with that college-bound boy for him. Even though he wasn't from a fancy family, wasn't a future doctor. He'd been sure she'd fallen for him all the same.

But no.

And even when she had found out she was pregnant...

He wondered, to this day, if Calvin knew who fathered the kid. Wondered if he didn't especially care, not given the life they had built on the back of that lie.

Creed realized he had been standing there frozen for a full minute, and Louisa hadn't even looked his way.

The kid was harassing a younger sibling, laughing.

And then Calvin reached over and playfully punched his oldest son in the arm, gently telling him to knock it off.

They were a family. Built by years and birthday parties, Christmases and good-night kisses. By fights and celebrations and soccer games and barbecues in the backyard. In the face of all that, genetics didn't matter.

Except they mattered to Creed.

Because he'd had eighteen years of never getting to know that kid, and all the regret that went with it.

But what was he supposed to do? She hadn't put his name on the birth certificate, refused to admit they'd ever had sex. Creed's father had tried, he had damn well tried to get a court-ordered paternity test, but the judge refused to do it. To subject an underage girl to scrutiny, to call her a liar when she said staunchly that the only boy she'd ever slept with was her longtime boyfriend.

There had been nothing Creed could do, and everyone had said that he was just mounting a smear campaign against a girl who had rejected him. A girl who'd already found herself in a *delicate situation*.

They were happy. Clearly. She had Calvin. Their four kids.

What was he?

He didn't even know.

Suddenly, he felt a soft hand on his shoulder. "Is everything all right?"

He turned and saw Wren. Louisa wasn't looking at him, not even with the full force of his anger turned in her direction. But Wren had seen him.

"Fine," he responded.

"You look like you're about to start a fight."

"No," he said, turning away. "I'm not."

"Good."

Suddenly, the feeling inside him went from hungry to ravenous. And he needed this damn thing to be over so he could lose himself in Wren's body.

He lived with the mistakes of his past every day. But having to stare them down was a particular kind of torture he was never quite prepared for.

And he needed something, anything, to find a little oblivion. If it wasn't Wren, it would be the liquor on the table, but he would rather have her.

It was strange, the exchange they'd had back in the tent, and this one. Because it wasn't as sharp and hard-edged as most of their interactions.

But it was still tinged with that same kind of raw grit. Which he recognized now as just desire. Only not desire like he'd ever known it before.

The closest thing that came to it was that sixteen-year-old lust haze he'd found himself in with Louisa. But that had been born out of inexperience. Out of desperation to know what it felt like to be inside a woman.

Well, he knew what it felt like now. That wasn't why Wren created this wildness in him.

It wasn't about knowing what it was like to be inside a woman, but what it was like to be inside *Wren*.

He knew the answer to that now, but a simple answer wasn't enough. He wanted more. He wanted her.

And that want began to eclipse the pain in his chest.

He was desperate for it. Because the promise of it— of her—was so big, so intense, with the capacity to take away this hurt. And he wanted that. He damn well did.

Needed it. Especially now.

He bent down slightly, careful to make it look like they were just having a business exchange, and not like they had shared any kind of intimacy.

If you could call sex against a wall *intimacy*.

"I can't wait until you're naked beneath me," he said.

She arched a brow. "Who says I'll be beneath you? I was kind of thinking I might like to be on top."

"There's time for that," he said. "There's time for a whole hell of a lot."

"So many promises."

"I promise you one thing—you're going to be screaming my name all night."

She looked up at him, her eyes glittering a challenge. "You'll be screaming mine."

"I plan on it."

They parted then, the tension between them so intense it would combust if they didn't release their hold.

So they did, because they both knew they were in a public setting, and a professional one. And whatever the hell he thought of Wren, whatever she thought of him, they were both damn good at their jobs.

He turned away then. From the direction that Wren walked. From the place where Louisa stood with her family.

A piece of his family. A piece of his heart.

He would focus on getting through all of this. And then he would focus on getting Wren into bed.

That was his life.

Work. Sex.

What the hell else did he need?

Everything was done, everything was cleaned up, and Wren was sitting in the driveway of Creed Cooper's house. She had made her excuses to her family about being tired, having a headache and a few other things she couldn't readily remember, and scampered off almost immediately after the last guest left.

She knew Emerson thought she was acting strange, but Wren didn't much care.

Wren was obsessed with Creed.

And if she were honest with herself, she could admit she had been obsessed with him for quite some time.

She might have couched that obsession in irritation, but the fact of the matter was, it had been deeper than that.

He hadn't annoyed her at all today.

No. Quite the opposite. He had been wonderful at his role during the event, and more than that, she had seen humanity in him that she didn't particularly want to see.

She had no idea what had been going through his mind when he had been standing there staring into the crowded party right before she had come up to him. But she had seen that it was something. The intensity that had come off him in waves had been palpable, at least to her.

She wasn't entirely sure whom he had been looking at, but she thought it might have been Louisa Johnson, a woman Wren knew because she and her husband frequented the winery and often had birthday parties and events there. It was common for wealthy families to come to Maxfield for special events. It was a status symbol. And Louisa had always seemed like the kind of woman who enjoyed her status.

Wren quite liked her. Louisa was nice, and she was funny, and a generous tipper to the waitstaff.

If it was Louisa that Creed was staring at, though, Wren had the feeling that he *hated* her.

And there was really only one reason for people to hate each other like that.

Love gone wrong.

Wren screwed up her face.

Well, there were actually a lot of reasons for people to hate each other. She and Creed hated each other, for no real reason.

Except, as she got out of her car and walked toward his front door, she couldn't find any of the hatred that she normally felt. She only felt giddy. Excited to have his hands on her, to have him make good on all those promises he had issued earlier at the event today.

She liked it when their verbal sparring had a bit of an edge, even if it wasn't a fight.

There was something electric and exciting about their exchanges.

She liked the danger that came with talking to him.

She just did.

She walked up to the door, prepared to knock, when it opened, and she found herself being dragged inside and pressed against that door, six-foot-plus of muscular man pinning her there as he kissed her. Kissed her with all the pent-up longing she knew had been building in both of them for the entire day.

She kissed him like he might hold all the answers she was so desperately seeking.

"Please let's make it to a bed," she whispered against

his mouth. "I like the desperate stuff, but I really just want to see you naked."

"I can oblige," he growled.

He picked her up off the ground and carried her straight to a staircase, taking them two at a time. There was an edge of darkness to all of this that was so different from how it had been before. That first time had been charged by anger, the kind of anger they commonly felt toward each other, reasonable or not.

But this was different.

He seemed fractured, broken in some way, and like he thought perhaps this might put him back together. She was used to him looking at her and being irritated. And that one day down in the wine cellar he had found pleasure. But today, he seemed to be after something altogether deeper, and she wasn't entirely sure she could help him find it.

But she wanted to.

And that was perhaps even more surprising than his looking to her for something deeper in the first place.

He pushed open the door, revealing a large bed made of heavy wooden beams. The bed was the largest thing in the room, a clear indicator of exactly where his priorities were.

His house was Spartan. Everything about it was serviceable, practical. And she knew full well he didn't need that much mattress for sleeping.

No, he was a man who clearly used his bed for more athletic pursuits. And she knew already he was a man who did those pursuits well.

"You said you wanted to see me naked." He set her down lightly on her feet. Then he moved away from her, unbuttoning the crisp white shirt she'd been looking at all day. Exposing that gorgeous chest, those impressive abs. He shrugged the shirt and jacket off, his body a thing of outright beauty the likes of which she had never seen before she'd seen him.

"Trading," he said, gesturing to her.

She reached behind her back and grabbed hold of the zipper tab on her dress, pulling it down slowly, letting her dress pool at her feet. She was wearing only heels and a matching red lace bra and panties.

She wasn't insecure about her body. Men, in her experience, were quite simple about things like that.

But the hunger in his eyes surpassed anything she had ever experienced before from other men. This passion, which seemed to simmer so intensely it was bound to bubble over, was something foreign to her. Something entirely different from all her previous experiences. Sure, she had found sex pleasurable before. But she had not found it to be fire and hunger. She hadn't found it to be the air she needed to breathe. She had never felt like the urge to be touched was so intense it was a physical agony.

And she could see all that she was feeling mirrored in his face as he looked at her.

She hadn't known. Hadn't known that having him, this man—this man who didn't even like her—look at her like she was… Like she was a wonder. Like she was perhaps the most beautiful thing he had ever seen…

Like she was seen.

Her.

Wren Maxfield.

This new version of herself that she was finding, inventing and creating as she went along…

He was captivated by her.

He wanted her.

It was a revelation.

Because she wasn't insecure about her body, but she felt new and fragile in her skin. In all that she was, in all that she was going to be.

Didn't even know what that might be in the end.

But when Creed looked at her, she thought she might be closer to finding it.

And it didn't make sense, how it was somehow more affirming to have it be him who made her feel that way, but it was.

Maybe because her sister Emerson would be supportive of her no matter what. Her mother would say that she loved Wren regardless of what she did.

Creed wouldn't. Creed found her intolerable.

He would never tell her anything just for the hell of it. He wouldn't pretend that he wanted to touch her, kiss her, be inside her. He would only do what he wanted to do.

It was freeing.

And with all the freedom it gave her, she reached behind her back and undid her bra, throwing it to the ground, glorying in the look of absolute need on his face.

She wiggled out of her panties, leaving herself standing there in nothing but her high heels. And then, she leaned backward on the bed, arching her breasts upward, letting her thighs fall slightly apart. She knew she looked like a wanton. And she had never been one, not particularly.

But she wanted to be.

Here. Now. For him.

She wanted to take this thing between them and test

it to the breaking point. Wanted to test *herself* to the breaking point.

And whatever dark emotion was rolling beneath the surface of his skin... She wanted to unleash it.

Because she wanted to go as far as she could. She wanted to take them both to the edge.

This felt safe, with him, because it wouldn't be forever.

Because they didn't have a relationship, and they wouldn't. Because it was only this. Only her trying to figure out who she was, and only him trying to contend with whatever demons were clawing at him right now.

She could take it. For now.

And he could take her. Imperfect and new and unsteady.

They could both please themselves.

It was a miracle.

And she badly needed a miracle.

Creed didn't disappoint.

Because then he dropped to his knees, a position of submission she had never expected from him. He was beautiful from this angle, too. The planes of muscle on his shoulders and chest intoxicating. His strength, bowed before her...

Oh, she shivered with it.

Of course, immediately following that submissive posture he revealed that it was not submissive at all. Because he grabbed hold of her ass and pulled her forward, burying his face between her legs and licking her until she screamed.

Until she couldn't breathe.

He had all the control. There was no restraint. No quarter given.

He tortured her with pleasure, and if that wasn't the most Creed Cooper thing on the planet, she didn't know what was.

That he sank to his knees and yet managed to still have all the control.

And she didn't want to fight it. Didn't want to stop it. No. She surrendered to it. To just taking. Everything that he wanted to give. To the slow glide of his fingers inside her, and the wicked friction of his tongue against her. She surrendered to all of it. To the absolute glory of knowing this man needed to taste her.

Because that's what this was.

He *needed* to taste her.

He had no control. His movements didn't have finesse. It was a devouring. He had fallen upon her like a beast, like a man possessed.

Because of her.

Tension coiled inside her, and she just let go. When her orgasm broke over her like a wave, she cried out with her pleasure, completely unembarrassed by the sound that came from her body.

She felt remade, and she wanted him to feel the same. She scooted herself back farther on the bed, her thighs open even wider, an invitation.

"Take what you need," she said.

A shudder wracked his big frame, and he undid his belt buckle, sliding it slowly through the loops and letting the belt fall to the floor. He undid the closure on his pants, and took his shoes, socks, pants and underwear down to the ground. And then she could see him. Fully naked, fully erect.

Hands down the biggest guy she'd ever seen.

He was stunning.

She'd thought so the first time, too. But now she had a moment to really look. And…

Truly, he was beautiful. She couldn't wait to feel him inside her again.

He reached over to the nightstand and grabbed a condom. And something, a small alarm bell, went off in the back of her mind. She dismissed it. Pushed it to the side.

He tore it open, rolling it onto his length before positioning himself at the entrance of her body. Those green eyes, her adversary's eyes, meeting her as he slid inside her, inch by agonizing inch. She felt full, of him, of desire. Of need. She had been so ready for him that she let her head fall back, a deep sigh of pleasure on her lips.

And then he began to move, slow and languid at first, letting her feel each delicious inch of him on his slow glide out, and back in.

And then it all became harder, more frantic, a desperate race to completion. She wrapped her legs around his hips, letting him thrust deeper, harder. And she arched against him each time, meeting his every thrust, chasing a second climax, which before, for her, had been unheard of.

But it was Creed.

It was Creed making her feel these things.

And when their eyes met again, and she saw the hollow bleakness there, she felt him all the way down in her soul.

She kissed him.

She kissed him deep and long and hard, and she tried to…to give him some of the wonder and pleasure inside her. Because if he could feel her pain, then maybe he could feel her pleasure, too.

She didn't want him to be hurt. And he was. She could see it.

And even if it was over another woman... Well, Wren wasn't his woman. Not really. This was just sex. And she would make it the best ever. She would make sure she took away some of his loneliness. Some of his bleakness.

She got a perverse kind of pleasure out of that. That she, a woman he didn't even like, might give him something that the woman he had once loved denied him.

Wren was making assumptions. But she was pretty sure she was assuming right.

He thrust into her, hitting the spot deep inside that sent sparks shooting off behind her eyes, made her come so hard she could scarcely breathe. And then he followed right along with her, shaking and shuddering his pleasure as he came deep inside her.

And she just held him for a while. Pressed his head against her breasts as they both lay there breathing heavily.

She didn't want it to be over.

"We're just getting started," he mumbled, and she wondered if she had said the words out loud.

She was afraid she might have.

"You wanted to be on top, remember?" he mumbled.

"Yes, but I think you killed me. I'm too weak."

"I have food," he said. "I have cake."

She lifted her head. "How do you have cake?"

"My sister. She makes excellent cakes."

"Well, I could have some cake."

"If you eat my cake, I'm going to expect you to put out."

"I will put out for cake."

"Will you ride me?"

"Only if you promise that later you'll tie me to that headboard."

She was shocked by the words as they came out of her mouth. Because she'd never wanted anything quite like that before. And at first it had just been to dare him, but now she found she really wanted it.

"I think that's a deal I can stick to."

And some of the bleakness from his eyes did seem to be gone, so she supposed she had accomplished her goal.

She wouldn't think about what would happen after tonight.

She didn't want to.

Tonight, she just wanted to be the Wren she was becoming with him. Tonight, she wanted to be new.

Tonight, she wanted to be with Creed.

Five

It had been two weeks since he'd last had Wren Maxfield in his bed. Two weeks, and she was all he could think about.

It was starting to impact…well, everything. His work, his sleep, his ability to be a halfway decent person and not be an absolute dick anytime someone in his family wanted to talk to him.

He wanted her again, but he didn't know how to justify it. Sure, they were going to be working together on that big cross-winery event, but it wouldn't just be the two of them working on it.

He didn't know if that night after the party had been transformative because he'd been in a really dark place, or if… He just didn't know. All he knew was that he wanted more. And Wren didn't seem to be coming back for it. Which was a damn shame.

And then, as if his thoughts had conjured her up, he looked through the windows of the tasting room and saw her standing outside. She was staring at the door, not moving.

He watched her, without changing his position, until she turned and her eye caught his. There was something bleak and strange in her expression, and he didn't know how to read it. So they just stared at each other through the window.

If she was waiting for him to make the first move, she was out of luck. She was the one who had come here to knock on his door. She was the one who was going to have to close the gap.

Finally, she did.

Finally, she walked through the door, but then she stood there in the entry, her hands clasped in front of her. "We need to talk."

"We do?"

"Yes. We do."

"I've been waiting to see you," he said, "and I have to tell you, it's not talking I want to do."

"Well, it's talking we need to do. Creed…" She closed her eyes and swallowed hard. "Creed, I'm pregnant."

Suddenly, he felt like he was falling into a chasm. A chasm that led to some moment eighteen years ago. A moment he didn't want to relive.

But you knew this might happen. You did. He pushed the thought to the side. *You tried not to think about the fact that you screwed her without a condom, but you know you did.*

No. Wren was the same age as he was. It didn't seem possible that the woman wasn't on birth control. Or that she wouldn't have said something about the condom if she wasn't taking something.

You didn't say anything about it either.

"I didn't even think," she said. "After the time in the wine cellar. I didn't think. It didn't occur to me until we were at your house and you took a condom out of your bedside drawer that I realized...that we didn't."

"You're not on...the Pill or anything?"

"I haven't been in a relationship in like a year and a half. And I... I didn't really like the way I felt on it. It made me gain weight, so I quit taking it after I broke up with my last boyfriend." She grimaced. "I'm not really somebody who hooks up."

"Well," he said, his voice rough, "I am. I am, so I sure as hell should've thought of a condom. Because I use them all the damn time. I... I'm sorry. I should have thought of it. I should've done better."

"No," she said. "That's stupid. I should have, too. I... Creed, I want to keep the baby."

Cold fear infused itself into his veins. "You want to keep the baby?"

"Yes. I understand that it might surprise you. But I... I'm thirty-two years old. I would like to have a baby. And I'm at a point in my life where I don't really know what's coming next, what I want to do. And this pregnancy feels like... Well, it feels like a pretty clear sign of something that I could do to change my life. Because it's happening. And I... I want it. When I found out a couple of days ago, I cried. I spent the entire day crying. I've been avoiding my family. Because I knew that I needed to tell you first. But I also knew... I knew immediately that I wanted the baby. I... I just *do*. And I don't need anything from you. I'm completely fine and taken care of. I have a house, I have a business, and I don't need you to be involved at all."

"I will be fucking involved," he said, his voice hard.

"I didn't mean you *couldn't* be," she said. "I just didn't want you to think I was making demands of you, or your money…"

"This baby is mine," he said.

"Of course it is," she said.

"No," he said. "You misunderstand me. That wasn't a question. It was a statement. This baby is mine, and that means I will be involved. I am this baby's father."

Echoes of everything that he had lost were shouting inside him. Because he knew how easy it was for a woman to take a child from a man.

A *girl* to take a baby from a *boy*.

That was the thing. They'd been kids. And everything about it had been messed up. All of it.

But he was not a child anymore, and he would be damned if anybody took anything from him.

His child.

For his son, it was too late. He couldn't have his son. Not now.

He had just seen that boy with his…with the man he thought was his father, with his siblings. They were a family. Creed never could be. He was just a man who had donated the material that had created the boy.

That wasn't being a *father*. He could never have that back. That boy was grown.

Even if he found out about Creed someday… He could never be the boy's dad.

No, he had lost that chance. But he would never lose that again. Never again.

"You're going to marry me," he said.

"I… I most certainly am not," she said. "That is… It is not a good reason for people to get married."

"It is the only damn reason for people to get married. It's legal protection, Wren. For both parties involved."

"That's not how the world works anymore."

"It is damn well how the world works. What's to keep you from taking my name off the birth certificate?"

"I won't."

"What's to keep you from preventing me from seeing my baby?"

"I won't," she repeated. "I won't do that. We were both involved in this and…"

"You say that, but you don't know. You don't know how it will go. You're marrying me. You're marrying me, and we're going to live in the same house. I am not missing a moment of my child's life."

"Creed, I didn't say that you would. But we are not in a relationship. We don't even like each other, let alone love each other."

"That doesn't have anything to do with this. This isn't about us."

"Be reasonable. I didn't even think you would want this baby."

"Because you don't know me," he said. "Not at all. We were naked together, that's it. But you don't know me well enough to think that you know whether or not I want this child. I do."

He did. With every breath in his body.

And the resoluteness he felt over what needed to be done was as intense as it was real.

"I am not letting you take this baby from me."

"Creed, I won't. But I don't have to marry you to…"

"We are getting married."

"Or what?"

Everything in him turned to ice. If she wanted an ultimatum, he would give it to her.

"Or I'll do what I have to do to make sure that most of the custody is with me."

"What?"

"Do you think it's fair? For one parent to only be with the child on weekends? Do you think it's fair for one of us to miss that much of the child's life? Because I don't. But if you think it's fair, then you won't mind if it gets flipped on you. Do you think it'll be fair to miss a week of the baby's life?"

"I'm the mother," she said.

"And I am the father," he said, the conviction in his voice shocking even him. "I'm the father," he repeated. "I'm not missing this."

"Creed..."

"You listen to me," he said, speaking with all the firmness he could when his life had just been turned completely upside down. "You listen to me, Wren Maxfield. Either you become my wife, or I'm going to have to make this difficult."

"You listen to me," she said. "You might be used to issuing edicts, but you don't get to tell me what to do. Because I've lived my entire life walking on another path that was set out for me by someone else. By a man. I will not be dictated to. If you want to fight, I will give you a fight, Creed. You can bet on it."

And then, she turned on her heel, walking out of the room.

And he could see that she was certain that she could get her way.

All he could see was another woman walking off with his child.

It wouldn't happen. It wouldn't.

It wasn't for another hour that the shock wore off.

And that was when he clutched his chest like he might be having a heart attack and leaned against the wall of the tasting room.

He was going to be a father again.

And Wren Maxfield was the mother.

And he had no idea how in hell they were going to survive this.

Six

She was a coward. She had run away from him, and she could see that whatever was driving him to be unreasonable, and make actual threats, came from a place she didn't understand.

She could see that, and still, she had run away from him rather than sticking out the conversation to see where it might go. And wasn't that basically what he was saying? That he assumed she would be a coward when push came to shove? That she would keep their child from him because it was easier or less challenging, because she didn't want to deal with him?

And maybe... Just maybe it had been easier for her to assume he wouldn't want anything to do with the baby. Maybe that's why she'd been able to come here and tell him about the pregnancy.

Before that, she had spent two days in agony.

She hadn't been lying to him when she'd said she

cried. She cried enough to make a flood. It just wasn't good timing. At least, that was what she told herself in the beginning.

Wrong time.

Wrong man.

And then she thought… Maybe he was the right man. Because he wouldn't want anything from her. Because he was not a paternal type, and there was no way he was secretly yearning for a wife and family.

She had never considered herself particularly maternal, either, but when she looked at the situation objectively, she could see that, well, this was an opportunity.

Because she had everything she needed to raise a child, including the assumed support of her family. She had job security. Money. A place to live. A great many things that people took for granted. From that standpoint, she was in a spectacularly great place to raise a child. And the more she thought about it, the more she had wanted to grab hold of this major life change and see where it took her. The more she thought about it, the more she had felt…a sense of excitement, rather than one of despair.

But her revelation had been selfish. Utterly and completely.

It had never included him.

She didn't know how to include him in that.

And then he demanded that she did.

Honestly, he'd demanded it in the most extreme way she could have imagined. Even if she had let herself truly think about a scenario in which he wanted the baby, wanted to be in the baby's life, she had not imagined that he would…demand marriage and issue threats.

But that's what he'd done. And it became clear that

she really didn't know all that much about him, and that lack of knowledge actually mattered.

Having sex didn't mean they knew each other.

Oh, they knew things *about* each other. Creed knew things about her that no one else did. She had done things with him she hadn't done with any other man.

Including that moment of absolute loss of control. The lack of protection.

But that didn't mean they knew each other.

And so she was now looking for the person she should have gone to in the first place.

Emerson was at the house she shared with Holden, working from home today, which was something Wren could never have imagined Emerson doing before. Given that Emerson had been wholly and completely tied to the family home.

But not only had she moved away from the estate, she seemed to prize the separate life she and Holden had built.

Wren would be fascinated by it if she didn't find it so annoying.

She parked her car and got out, walking to the door. It took a couple of minutes, but her sister opened it, wearing a large, elaborate-looking robe, her hair piled on her head, her fingernails manicured to perfection, a giant wedding ring that she'd gotten from Holden glittering on her finger.

"Well," Wren said. "Good afternoon to you, too."

"I was taking pictures," she said.

She swung the door open wider, and Wren saw that the couch and coffee table were set just so, a glass of rosé in her sister's glass, and a book sitting next to it.

"Are you reading?"

"I was taking pictures," Emerson said dryly. "It's a great afternoon to indulge in a little Maxfield luxury and *hashtag self-care*, don't you think?"

"I think that I'm glad you run the internet properties and not me. Since I don't understand any of this."

"Luckily, you don't have to. Because I'm a savant."

"An influencer savant." But Wren smiled, because she really did find her sister to be a wondrous magical creature.

Emerson should be annoying. She wasn't.

"Where's Holden today?"

"He's gone to visit his sister. She's getting settled in her new house after getting out of the rehab facility. We are hopeful that she's going to keep doing better and better."

"I'm glad to hear it."

Holden loved his sister, and Wren and Emerson's father had caused her immense distress. Wren was rooting for her.

"So what brings you by? Because you look like an absolute disaster."

Wren stepped into her sister's house and craned her neck so she could see her reflection in the mirror on the wall. Emerson wasn't kidding. Her makeup was smeared, in spite of the fact that she hadn't been crying. She assumed that maybe she had wiped her fingers firmly across her eyes to try to keep the tears back. But she hadn't even been conscious of doing it.

Her hair was in disarray, and there was just something…shocked looking about her expression. Her skin was pale, and her cheeks seemed especially hollow.

"Well, I feel terrible," she said. "So that's fair." She sighed heavily. "I have to tell you something."

Emerson looked bemused. "Am I hiding a body? Should I get a shovel? Because you know I will."

"I do know you will." Wren sighed heavily again. "I don't think I'll need your help with that. Though, I guess we'll see how all this goes. I'm pregnant."

Her sister's schooled expression became very serene. Wren could tell that Emerson was covering shock, because there was no way she was that serene about such an announcement.

"Congratulations," she said. "I didn't expect that."

"Well. Just wait until you hear the next part. Creed Cooper is the father."

A bubble of sound escaped Emerson that was almost a laugh, but not quite. "That doesn't surprise me at all. I actually figured you were here to tell me that you slept with him. But obviously that ship sailed a while ago."

"Multiple times," she muttered.

"I mean, I can't exactly lecture you."

"Why not?"

"Well, I jumped into bed with our father's enemy while I was still engaged to somebody else. So, when it comes to making good sex choices... I mean look, luckily, I married him. It all worked out in the end. But, I get how men can make you really stupid. And I didn't get that before Holden."

"Well, Creed doesn't make any sense to me. I don't like him," Wren said helplessly. "I don't like him and yet... I want him. I want him so much. And the sex is so good. It's the best sex I've ever had. I mean, that's weak. It seems like just the thing you say. But sex with him is like a whole other thing."

"I get it," Emerson said. "I mean, I profoundly get it."

"I guess you managed to use condoms, though."

"Yeah," Emerson said. "That we did."

"We forgot. And…"

"What are you going to do?"

"Well, I was all resolute. I'm not a kid. I'm in a great place to raise a child, and everything has been so out of whack I just… I kind of *want* to. I mean, I really want to. I was shocked by the realization, but it's true. I want to have a baby. I want to have *his* baby. It'll be… so cute. But I didn't think he would want me to have a baby. And I didn't think he would care. I thought this would be just my decision, but he told me today that I have to marry him."

That successfully shook Emerson's composure. *"He what?"*

"He demanded that I marry him. Like, demanded. *With threats.*"

"I mean…" Emerson blinked. "Okay, that's shocking."

"I know."

Emerson's expression turned thoughtful. "Well, obviously something happened to him."

"You think?"

"If I know one thing about hardheaded, alpha cowboys, it's that usually demands like that spring from an emotional wound."

"With all the experience you have with them?"

"I may not have experience across a vast section of them, but the one I married was basically a giant walking open wound."

"Gross."

"I know. But everything he did, seducing me, forcing me into marriage, tearing my dress off…tying me to the bed… What was the point I was making?"

Wren narrowed her eyes. "This isn't helping me, Emerson."

"Right. My point. *My point* is everything he did that was awful came from a place of being so angry on behalf of his sister. And a lot of things got twisted up inside him, but he couldn't quite deal with all that anger. It took time for him to sort it out. But ultimately he did. Ultimately, *we* did. But he wasn't being an asshole just to be an asshole. My experience is they're all just lions with big thorns in their paws."

Wren's mouth flattened into a line. "And you want me to... What?"

"I mean, find the thorn. Identify it. Pull it out."

"I'm not going to end up like you," Wren said. "I... I can't say that I hate him anymore, but I also don't really want to marry him."

She imagined the bleakness that had been on his face that last time they were together. She had cared about that. About the pain he was experiencing.

"He *is* hurting," Wren said. "I just don't really know why."

"That's what you have to find out."

"I don't know how to talk to him. Every time we do talk, it... Well, it's exactly what just happened—we fight. Or we have sex. Fighting or sex. Those are the two options."

"Would either one be so bad in this situation?"

"I probably shouldn't have sex with him again."

"Honey, the horse has bolted from the barn, and is in the pasture with the stallion, and is already knocked up."

"I meant emotionally, for *emotional reasons*."

"Right, right," Emerson said, waving her hand.

"You still think I should have sex with him?"

"You seem to want to. And it sure makes men act nicer," Emerson said. "Anyway. As established, I make bad decisions on that score." An impish grin crossed her face. "But I don't regret them."

"I don't know if I regret this. I don't know what I regret."

Wren wanted the baby. She was sure of that. It was all the other things she couldn't quite figure out, including how she felt about Creed. *That* she couldn't quite navigate.

But if Emerson was right, if there was a thorn in Creed's paw, so to speak, then Wren was going to have to approach him differently.

She might not know all she needed to know about him, but she knew him well enough to know she was going to have to come in with a plan. A counteroffer. He wasn't simply going to accept her *no*. She was going to have to come up with an arrangement that would make him happy.

And in order to do that, she was going to have to identify that thorn.

And she couldn't identify the thorn without talking to him.

That was the problem.

She didn't especially know how to talk to Creed.

She knew how to fight with him. She knew how to fuck him.

She wasn't sure she knew how to do anything else.

But they were going to have to figure it out.

For the sake of the baby, if for nothing else.

She realized that for the first time in a very long time, her thoughts weren't consumed with the winery.

The winery was something she loved, but not something she had built with her own hands.

She found herself suddenly much more concerned with her life, her future.

And even in the midst of all the turmoil, that was an interesting development indeed.

Seven

Creed knew he had basically lost his mind earlier, but he didn't regret it.

In fact, he was making plans to call his lawyer. He was going to do whatever he had to do to get his way. That was when Wren showed up on his doorstep.

She looked strange. Because she was wearing jeans and a T-shirt, and she looked smaller somehow, and yet resolute.

It was the resoluteness that concerned him.

"I'm sorry I left things the way they were earlier," she said, breezing into his house without an invitation.

She wandered into his living room, sat on his couch.

When she had come before, she had been in his bedroom, his bathroom and his kitchen for a cup of coffee before she had run out in the early hours of the morning.

Not his living room. But there she was, sitting on

the couch like a satisfied, domesticated feline. Except he had the feeling that nothing about Wren was particularly domestic.

"What exactly are you here for?"

"Not to agree to your demands. Sorry. But it's ridiculous to think that we have to get married just because we're having a baby."

"Is it?"

"It is to me. I'm pretty much one hundred percent *not here for it.*"

"That's a shame. Because I'm one hundred percent…" He frowned. "Here for it? What the hell does that even mean?"

"Why?"

She was glaring at him with jewel-bright eyes, and it was the determination there that worried him.

"What do you mean 'why'? I told you earlier. It's because I'm not going to take a back seat to raising my child."

"Why? I mean, you don't even know the kid."

"Neither do you, and you're sure that you want it."

"Sure. But I'm…you know, carrying it. I sense the miracle of life and whatever," she said, some of the wind taken out of her sails.

"No, if you can be certain then *I* can be certain."

"You have to be honest with me," she said. "Because when I left here earlier what I realized was that I don't actually know anything about you. We have worked in proximity to each other for the last five years. And we fight. We… We create some kind of insane electrical surge when we are together, and I can't explain it. And somehow in all of that, I convinced myself that I knew you. But that night that we were here together after the party, there was something wrong. I knew it, even though I didn't know what it was. And when I told you I was pregnant... Look, I didn't expect you to be thrilled about it. But I didn't expect you to demand that I marry you. And I think the problem is, we just don't know each other."

"We know each other well enough. I'd be good to you. I wouldn't cheat."

She didn't look convinced. Not by his offer, not at all. And she should be. What the hell more could she possibly want? Love, he supposed. But here they both were in their thirties, not anywhere near close to settling down, and they were having a kid. Neither of them was young enough or starry-eyed enough to think there was some mystical connection out there waiting for them.

He'd lost his belief in that a long time ago.

Maybe Wren hadn't.

But he didn't see Wren as a romantic. Particularly not after the way things had worked out in her parents' marriage.

"What?" he asked.

"There are other reasons to get married. I just... You would really be faithful to me?"

"Wren, I can't even think about other women when I'm with you. I can't imagine taking vows to be true to you and then betraying them."

"That's nice," she said. "But a lot of men can. You know, my father, for one."

"So that would matter to you," he said.

"Yes," she said. "If I was going to do it... I don't share."

"So now you're considering it."

"I need to know *why*."

"It's not important."

"I have a feeling that it is."

Why not tell her? After all, his family knew. Well, Jackson did. And so did his father. Creed had never talked to Honey about it, but she had been a baby. A kid.

But anyway, it wasn't like no one knew. And he had never agreed to keep it quiet.

Wren looked at him directly. "Does it have something to do with Louisa Johnson?"

The name hit him square in the chest. "How do you..."

"I saw you looking at her. At the barbecue. And afterward..."

"It's not what you think," he said.

"Look. If you needed to be with me to deal with seeing an ex, it's fine. I knew what was happening."

"I wasn't thinking of her. I wasn't using you. Not in the way you mean." He was surprised how much it mattered to him for her to know that.

She looked at him, bemused. "Then what is it?"

"Do you know her at all?"

"They do birthday parties and things at the winery sometimes. That's it. I know her in a vaguely professional capacity."

"So you know her husband, then, and her kids."

"I've seen them. Yes."

He shook his head. "Her oldest son is mine."

For the second time in a couple of days, Wren felt like the ground had tilted beneath her feet.

Her thoughts were coming in too fast for her to grab hold of them.

He had a son.

Creed had a son.

"He… He…"

"You may not remember this, seeing as you didn't go to school here. But Louisa got pregnant in high school."

"I always got the impression that…"

"Yes. By design. That Cal is the father of all her children. She and Cal were dating at the time. She and I started… We were in a study group together, and I developed some pretty strong feelings for her. I knew she was with Cal, but you know how it is when you're young. And you think things will work out just because you want them to. That your feelings have to be good and true and right. Well, I thought mine were. I was a virgin, and what we got up to in the back of my truck sure felt like love to me. I thought it was the same for her. We made a mistake. So, now that you're pregnant… This isn't the first damn time I've made this mistake, Wren. I swore that I never would again. Twice is just… It's damn careless. Especially when you've got eighteen years between who you were and who you are now. I ought to know better."

"I mean… Yeah, I can't really argue with you there. I'd like to reassure you, but that does seem…"

"She didn't put my name on the birth certificate. She wouldn't even look at me at school. She acted like she didn't know me. And when I confronted her about it, she said we never slept together. She told everybody that the baby was Cal's. She was a virgin when we slept together. I knew the baby was mine. But she must have gone and slept with him right after to make sure he believed her. I doubted myself sometimes over the years. I thought maybe… Maybe I was the crazy one. Maybe she hadn't been a virgin. Maybe the timing was all off."

"He looks like you, though, doesn't he?" She felt sick to her stomach. "I don't know him that well, but I remember seeing them all together, and I wouldn't have looked at him and thought he was your doppelgänger or anything, but now that I know…"

"I don't doubt it either," he said. "I haven't ever spoken a word to him. Never been close to him. And the fact of the matter is, he's not really my son now, is he? I didn't raise him. I'm not the one who taught him what he knows. I'm not the one who's been there for everything and paid for his upbringing and… I'm just a guy who had sex with a girl once a long time ago, and got left with a scar that's never going to heal. I can't do that again, Wren. I lost a child already. And I was never going to… I was never going to try to become a father again. I couldn't see any reason to. After all, I never had my first kid. But now it's happening. And I can't go through a loss like that. Not ever again."

"And you think I would do that to you?"

"I thought I was in love once, and I thought the woman loved me back. *We* don't even like each other."

Her heart felt bruised, sore.

He'd been so young to go through something like that. And she could see that it still affected him profoundly. How could it not? But she couldn't go paying for the sins of another person. It wasn't fair.

"We are going to have to get to know each other," she said, resolutely.

"No," he said. "I'm sorry. I'm not budging on it. You're going to marry me. One year. I want us to get married, I want legal acknowledgment of the kid, and I want us to try for one year. And then if you want to divorce, God bless you, but we're going to have to work out a real custody arrangement."

"Creed, it doesn't make any sense," she said. "We can't just get married."

"I won't accept anything less," he said. "I won't accept anything less than marriage."

She looked at him, and she could see that he was absolutely serious. More than that, she could see that what her sister had said was absolutely right. His demand was coming from a place of pain. Unimaginable pain. And it wasn't about simply pulling out a thorn. He wasn't even going to let her get close enough to touch it, never mind remove it.

It was going to require trust. A hell of a lot of trust, and she could see that he was fresh out.

This was his vulnerability. His weakness. The situation they were in, it was the man's worst nightmare. And she couldn't make it work with him if she was continually trying to hold her position, fighting him just for the sake of it.

She wanted her freedom. Her life. The chance to make a future for herself the way that she wanted it made. But not at the expense of their child having the best life he or she possibly could.

Creed might irritate her, but he was a good man. She knew it.

He could be the kind of father her own had never been.

Right now, they had the freedom to make whatever future they wanted. Whatever future they thought was best. She wasn't under the tyranny of her father, and she didn't have to pass any of her pain, any of her issues, on to her children.

Something her own parents hadn't managed.

But it all needed to start here. It had to start with this.

She took a breath, and then she sat down at one of the tables. "Okay. Get a notebook."

"What?"

"Get a notebook. We're going to write out what we both need. What we both expect. Creed, we are not going to make it through this if we don't trust each other. I can understand that you want marriage in a legal sense. If you need that, I can give it to you. But, during the pregnancy, that doesn't have to mean anything. It's not like we need to live with each other or be in any kind of relationship until the baby is born."

"You think that, huh?"

"I do," she said. "I think we need to focus on putting our child first. And we need to build some trust between each other. I would not take your baby from you, Creed. But I understand why you don't just take my words at face value. And, I'm not going to suffer for it either. I just found my life. I just found my purpose. Everything in my world got turned upside down when my dad… I've had to rethink everything. Everything I believe in. Everything I am. I'm not giving everything up to you. Sorry."

He looked hollow. Almost helpless, and that made her stomach drop into her feet.

"I can't bend on this," he said.

She looked at him. And she knew he was telling the truth. His face was drawn and haggard, his tone was tortured.

"I know you can't. I'm going to bend as much as I can right now so we can find someplace where we can meet."

He stood, left the room for a moment, then returned with a pen and a notebook. He thrust it into her hand. "All right. Start listing your demands."

"First of all, if you want to be involved, you need to be involved. It's really important to me that you're either hands-on or hands-off with our child. All in, or all out." She looked at him, her jaw set, her posture determined.

"Why is that?"

"Because I won't have any of this lukewarm BS. That's how my dad was. He was there just enough to make us...try to perform for him. To make us try to do the very best we could to please him. But he never gave us anything back. Not really. I'm not going to put my kid through that. I want more for them."

"I want *everything*," he said, his voice rough. "I lost eighteen years with my son. I'm not losing any more time. I'm not losing that ever again."

"I won't ask you to. I promise. And that's why...my next thing. No more sex."

"Are you out of your damn mind?"

"No. I'm absolutely *in* my mind. We need to be able to deal with each other, and with this. I need to be able to have you at my house. You need to be able to be around for whatever you want, whenever you feel you need to have time with our child. If we have our own feelings in the way, our own situation, then this isn't going to work. We have to be able to be in the same room and not fight. And not... Well, you know that other *F* word that we seem to be so fond of."

He snorted. "If we had that kind of control, we wouldn't be in this situation."

"But you know as well as I do that getting out of control isn't going to work. It just wouldn't. It couldn't.

We have to make this list and stick to it so we can give each other what we need. And I don't think we can do that if we get…all that emotion involved."

"Is that what you think?"

"Well, don't you? Don't you think it's too big a risk?"

His face went hard. Neutral. And then finally, "You're right. And really, it's all just a little control. Which, I had plenty of until you."

"Well, that's flattering. But, I don't doubt you can find it again."

"Sure. What else?"

"Holidays?" she asked.

"Together. Obviously. At my family place," he said.

Always with his family. Was he kidding? But the child was currently a zygote so as pressing matters went, that wasn't a huge one. "Okay, I think we can actually wait on that."

"Marriage," he said. "For the first year."

"Until the baby is born," she said. "I'll give you that. Marriage until the baby is born so you can be sure you have your legal protection. And then we can work out whatever custody agreement you want. We can cohabitate, whatever. But, if the primary concern is custody, and you making sure that you have all your parental rights… I'll go that far."

"I can deal with that. For now. Let's go get a marriage license, then," Creed said, fully and completely matter-of-factly, as if they'd worked out everything.

"What, *right now*?"

"Do you have a better time frame?"

"I don't… I wasn't exactly thinking of a time frame. But… I'm like six weeks pregnant, Creed. We can chill out."

"Nope," he said. "It may have escaped your notice, Wren, but I don't have any chill."

"It didn't escape my notice at all. Nothing about you suggests that you have chill."

But he was already gathering his things, and he was ushering them both out the door and toward his truck.

"I can't... We're just going to go get a marriage license?"

"This isn't Vegas. We can't get married the same day. We need to figure out all the specifics."

She made an exasperated sound and got into the truck behind him. As they drove to town, she was completely and utterly overwhelmed by an out-of-body sensation.

Because *surely* this wasn't actually happening to *her*. She wasn't really going down to the courthouse to get a marriage license with the man who irritated her more than...

"You don't even like me," she said.

"I'm not pretending to *like* you."

That shut her up, because it was true.

He wasn't pretending to like her. He wasn't pretending that there was anything to this other than a legal practicality.

And that was how she found herself standing in front of a clerk's desk in the old brick courthouse, filling out forms.

They could get married three days after the license was purchased.

"Then we'll get married in three days," Creed said.

She didn't reply, or say anything while they finished signing off on all the papers. But when they were back outside the courthouse, and walking on the sidewalk down Main Street, heading back to where they had parked the truck, she gave him the evil eye.

"You have to be joking," she said. "Three days?"

He lifted a shoulder. "Do you want a hamburger?"

"Do I look like I want a hamburger?" Her stomach growled. She frowned furiously at it. She did in fact want a hamburger.

"I think you do," he said. "Let's go to Mustard Seed."

"You don't know what I want more than I do, Creed Cooper," she groused, trailing along after him as he abruptly reversed course and headed to the small, unassuming diner that was just off the main drag.

"I believe I'm pretty good at anticipating what it is you want, Wren Maxfield."

"In bed," she muttered as he pushed open the door, holding it for her.

She stepped inside and looked around. She couldn't remember the last time she had been here. Maybe once. When she was a kid, and she had tried to hang out with some of the local teenagers during the summer. The floor was made of pennies, all glossed over with epoxy, making a coppery, shimmering surface. There was quirky local art everywhere. Little creatures made out of spoons and forks.

The tables were small, and there was a bucket of dry-erase markers on each one, everyone encouraged to create their own removable art on the surfaces.

"Do you come here often?" she asked him.

"Yes," he answered. "My favorite burger place."

"Oh."

A waitress who looked like she was probably the same age Wren had been the last time she had come into this place approached the table. "Chocolate milkshake," Creed said. "Cheeseburger, extra onions, French fries."

"I'll have a Diet Coke. And a cheeseburger. And sweet potato fries."

Then they sat staring at each other across the small table.

He was her fiancé.

A hysterical bubble of laughter welled up in her throat.

"What?" he asked.

"Well, of all the ways that I imagined getting engaged, it wasn't being dragged down to a courthouse to sign papers, then being taken out to a diner for a burger."

"Oh, right. I imagine you figured it would come with something fancy."

"And a diamond."

"Do you *want* a diamond?"

She had a sudden image of him getting down on one knee. Sliding a ring on her finger. And that felt...

That felt too close to real.

And the feeling in her chest was far too tender.

"No," she said. "A diamond won't be necessary."

"So what is it you think this is going to be?"

"In name only," she responded. "You want legal protection, and while I'm sure we could manage that without a marriage, I can appreciate the fact that this is maybe the simplest route. And... It's fine with me. We're having a baby together. I'm not going to act like this is somehow...going to bond us together in a way that it isn't." She sighed heavily. "It's weird, though. Because I certainly never expected to be starting a family without being *really* married. I never expected I'd do it with you."

"My brother seems to think it was inevitable."

"The baby?"

"No. The events leading up to the baby."

"My sister seemed to think that, as well."

"What do they know?" he asked, smiling ruefully.

A few moments later their food appeared, and Wren realized how hungry she was. The food was amazing, and she mentally castigated herself for any snobbery that had kept her away from a burger of this caliber.

"Okay, good suggestion," she said.

She tucked into the burger, and between bites, he looked at her. Hard. "So, you think this is going to be an in-name-only marriage. Does that mean you've changed your mind? You think it's all right if we sleep with other people?"

"Well, we can't sleep with each other," she pointed out.

"Right. Because you seem to think that's unreasonable."

"I do. It will only cause problems. I don't know what kind of marriage your parents had. My parents' marriage is a disaster, and it's only gotten worse as time has gone on. You know, for obvious reasons. I just… You and I don't have a great relationship. It's a weird relationship, but all the fighting… It's not personal. I think we can be okay. I think we can make something out of this and be good parents. And I have a lot more confidence in our ability to do that if we keep it simple."

"So, again, you now think it's all right for us to sleep with other people during this yearlong marriage?"

Discomfort rolled through her, and something like

sadness. "Well, I'm not going to be sleeping with anyone."

"Why not?"

She stared at him. "I'm pregnant. Not exactly going to go out and find a new lover while I'm gestating a human being. I can't imagine anything less sexy."

He lifted a shoulder. "A lot of men like that sort of thing. I think you could find someone if you had a mind to."

"Do you *want* me to go find someone else to sleep with?"

"Just checking."

"For your information, I was celibate for eighteen months before we had sex." She dipped her French fry into the pink sauce so hard it bent. "I'll be fine for the next nine."

He leaned back in his chair and fixed her with a bold stare. "I don't do celibacy."

She was surprised at the zip of emotion that shot through her. Possession. Anger. She didn't like that. She didn't like the idea of him sleeping with other women. She stared at him. And she had to wonder if that reaction was what he was pushing for. If he was pushing to see if she was actually okay with all of this.

"Maybe I *will* find someone, then," she said. "How about this, I'm probably not going to be actively looking for a lover, but if one presents himself... Who am I to say no?"

"Hey, you have needs, I'm sure."

Now he was just making fun of her.

"Do you have to be such a pain in the ass? What is it you want? Why can't you just say it?"

His gaze went sharp, intense. And everything inside her…shivered.

She wished she hadn't asked for honesty, because she was sure she was about to get it. Now she wasn't entirely certain she wanted it.

"Here's what I want," he said. "I want for no man but me to ever touch you again. How about that? But that's not reasonable, is it? Because this is just a temporary marriage and you want it to be in name only. And we need to have a *relationship* for the sake of our child, not based on *F* words that involve nudity—your words, not mine."

"Oh," she said.

She was equally surprised by how satisfying this was, that he was showing he was possessive. It went right along with the possession she had felt a moment before.

This was all very weird.

"That's it?" he asked.

"Well, what do you want me to say?" she asked. "You're right, it is unreasonable."

"And you're totally fine with other women touching me while we live together? While we have a marriage license?"

"No." She bit into her French fry fiercely and chewed it with much more force than was necessary. "I hate the idea about as much as I hate you. Which is *a lot*."

"What are we going to do about that? Because it seems to me that it's going to be pretty difficult for the two of us to find neutral ground. We're never neutral. You want to prevent hard feelings by us not sleeping together, but we've got hard feelings already. If there's another lover in play neither of us are going to be nice, and you know it."

"We can't make it worse," she said, feeling desperate and a little bleak. "And we would. We could. It seems obvious to me. I mean, look at us now, after just a couple of... I don't know. Just after a few times. It's already an issue. We can't... We can't do that to our child."

"We could," he said, his tone horrendously pragmatic. She wanted to punch him. "Plenty of people do."

"I..."

"I know," he said. Something in his gaze shifted. "This is my only chance to do it right. I didn't intend to ever have the opportunity to do it again."

"I can't imagine," she said, her heart squeezing. "I can't really explain how it felt to find out I was pregnant. Because I was terrified. And it wasn't like I had completely positive emotions. I didn't. But I feel conviction. I know having this baby is what I want."

He shook his head. "I didn't know. When she told me she was pregnant I was terrified, too. I was sixteen. I wasn't ready to be a father. But I knew what I would do. I knew I'd be there for her. That I'd be there for the baby. Even if it felt scary. And then suddenly... The whole story changed. She acted like she didn't know me. She acted like we never slept together. It was losing the opportunity to be a father that made me realize how much I wanted it. But even then, I didn't really know. I was a kid. There was part of me that was relieved. Relieved that I didn't have to change my life at all. And damn, there's a lot of guilt that goes with that."

She nodded slowly. "I can imagine there is."

"But I've seen him, over the years. So there's never been an opportunity to really forget what I'm missing, what I don't have." His voice went rough. "I can't get over feeling like a piece of myself got stolen. It's just out there in the world, walking around. And sometimes I ask myself if it can't just be enough that he's happy. Because all the rest of it is selfish, I guess. He's got a dad. He's got a family. He's not missing anything because I'm not in his life."

"That's not true," Wren said. "He doesn't have you."

She was treated to a rueful, lopsided smile. "That's weird that you think not having me is a deficit, Wren."

"Well, what I mean is… Creed, if I didn't think that you would be a good father I wouldn't have bothered to try to include you in our baby's life."

"Maybe that's the thing," he said. "Maybe she just didn't think I would be a good father."

"She was sixteen. I imagine it's more that she didn't think. At least, not about anything much deeper than herself."

"Well, that probably is true."

"We'll do this right," Wren said.

He nodded. "So what do we do about the two of us?"

"We have nine months to figure it out. To figure out how we navigate sharing…a life. Because that's what we're doing. It's going to be complicated, and we don't need added complications. I'll tell you what… No relationships for either of us. For nine months."

He grimaced. "All right."

"Sorry. Get used to cozying up with your right hand."

He snorted. "In more ways than one, it's like being sixteen again."

"The fact of the matter is, we have got to find a better way to deal with each other than we have been. And

I mean, we really do. So, we certainly don't have room for anyone else in this whole… situation."

"Fair enough."

"All right," she said. She extended her hand.

He looked at it. "I'm not shaking your hand."

"Why not?"

"Because it's not business, Wren. And it isn't going to be. You and me can't ever be business, sweetheart."

She lowered her hand, her heart fluttering. "I approach everything that way. Because of my dad."

"It's okay," he said. "We just… We are who we are. Can't do much about it."

"I want to do something about it, I guess. This whole figuring-myself-out thing is going to weave together with figuring out how we can be a family."

She would never have thought she would become family with Creed Cooper. But here she was.

"I guess so."

"Well." She looked down at her cleared plate. "I guess that's it. For now."

"For now. The wedding will be in three days."

"Are you going to invite your family?"

"Hell no," he said. "Just you and me."

"Don't we have to have a witness?"

"Bring your sister."

"Okay."

Then she stood up, and the two of them walked to the counter. Creed paid the bill.

"You didn't have to do that," she said.

"You're feeding my baby."

She looked around, feeling a little embarrassed. It wasn't like they would be able to hide it in the upcoming months. "I guess it can't really be a secret, can it?"

"Why does it have to be?"

"It doesn't," she said.

He had been treated like a secret before. And Wren wasn't about to do to him what Louisa had done.

Wren couldn't hate Louisa for it, though. She'd been sixteen. Who hadn't done a host of stupid things when they were sixteen? It was just that when Wren had done stupid things, they hadn't affected someone else for the rest of their life.

"It really doesn't," she affirmed.

Then the two of them walked out of the restaurant together, engaged.

It was so strange, because just a few weeks ago Wren had the sense of being on a different path from the one she had been on before. But she hadn't imagined that the path would lead here.

But this was one of those moments where she had to change.

It was actually a good thing. Because she needed a change anyway.

The only way to handle all of this change was to keep on going.

So that was what she would do.

The fact that she had to keep going with Creed... Well, they would figure it out.

They had no other choice.

Eight

It was his wedding day.

He hadn't ever imagined a wedding day. Hadn't figured he would ever get hitched. But then, what he'd said to Wren at the diner had been true. He had never planned to be in a situation where he got a do-over on the biggest regret of his life.

A slug of something hard hit him in the gut. It wasn't really a do-over. Because it wouldn't give him time back with his son. His son whose name he couldn't even think.

Because it wasn't a name he would've given to his kid. And it served as a reminder of the ways in which Creed wasn't part of his son's life.

But that didn't matter.

Today Creed was going to make sure he never missed out again. And the more he'd thought about it over the last few days, the firmer a conclusion he'd come to.

Sure. He could understand where Wren was coming from—she had the idea that they might be able to exist in a middle ground. And that the middle ground would be better than trying and failing at having a marriage.

But what she didn't understand about him was that he didn't do middle ground. He was all in. Or not in at all.

If he decided to make a marriage, then he was going to make it. And there would be no living separately. No other relationships.

No amicable divorce when the year was up.

He wanted to be in his child's life. He didn't want to have regrets. A real marriage was the simplest way to that path he could think of.

He would talk to her later.

After their wedding night.

As it was, he'd gone and dressed up for the occasion. Because she had liked it so much when he had dressed up for their winery event, so he was sure she would like it for this.

She'd said she would meet him at the courthouse. He assumed she was driving there with her sister.

And when he arrived, Wren was standing in front of the red brick building, wearing a simple white dress that fell just past her knees. On either side of her were her sisters. And her mother was there too, looking pale and drawn.

"Well, I didn't realize the whole family would be joining us," he said.

Wren grinned at him, then took hold of his arm, leading them ahead of her sisters and mother. "I had to bring them all," she said. "And they don't know the whole situation."

"Meaning?"

"They don't know that it's temporary."

He nearly said right then that she didn't seem to realize that temporary was off the table. But he decided to save that for after the vows. Instead, he bent down and brushed a kiss across her cheek. The action sent a slug of lust straight down to his gut.

She turned to face him, her eyes wide.

"You look beautiful," he said.

He heard a rustle of whispers behind him. And he gave her a knowing look.

"Thank you. So do you."

He knew she wasn't lying. She *did* think he looked good.

The heat between them was real.

It was all way too real.

Her mother looked between them. "I do wish we could've had a real wedding."

"You know why we have to do it quickly," Wren said.

"Nobody cares anymore if a woman is pregnant at her wedding, or if they have a baby in attendance," her mother replied.

"I care," Wren said.

"I was impatient," he said. "I just couldn't wait."

"Indeed," her older sister, Emerson, said, looking him in the eye with coolness.

"You don't approve of me?" he asked.

"I'm deeply suspicious of you. But then, I would be deeply suspicious of anyone marrying my sister."

"I hear tell that your husband is a pretty suspicious character, too."

"And Wren did her sworn sisterly duty by being skeptical of him."

Well, that was fair enough.

It was the youngest sister, Cricket, who gave him the kind of open, assessing look that made him feel actual guilt.

"You had better be good to her. Our father was terrible, and Wren deserves to be happy."

"I'll be good to her," he said.

He would be. Her happiness mattered. He told himself it mattered only because of their baby.

But somehow, he suspected it was more.

"Good," Cricket said. "Because if you aren't, I'll hunt you down and I'll kill you."

She said it cheerfully enough that he suspected she wasn't being hyperbolic.

They all filed into the courtroom, and he and Wren took their position up near the judge's bench. They exchanged brief pleasantries with the woman before getting down to business.

It was surprisingly quick. Pledging his life to another person. When the ceremony was stripped away, a wedding was just a business deal where you held hands.

Wren's voice trembled on the part about staying together until death separated them.

His own didn't. But maybe that was because he didn't feel like he was lying. He felt as committed as he could be to this. To her.

Maybe it was that simple for him because he didn't have other dreams of love, marriage or anything of the kind. He imagined that Wren, on some level, dreamed of romance. Most women did, he assumed.

He wondered what his sister would say if he leveled this theory at her. She would probably bite him. Honey didn't like to be what anyone expected.

And she would also be annoyed at him for having a

wedding and not inviting her. Probably, she would be irritated at him for not telling her that he was going to be a father.

But Honey was a problem that would have to wait.

"You may kiss the bride," the judge said.

And this... Well, this was the part Creed had been waiting for.

He wrapped his arms around Wren and pulled her against him. The look in her eyes was one of shock, as if she hadn't realized they would be expected to do this. As if she hadn't realized that whether a wedding was permanent or not, in a courthouse or not, if you were trying to pass it off as something real to your family, you were going to have to kiss.

And so they did.

It was everything he remembered. Her mouth so soft and sweet. She was a revelation, Wren Maxfield.

And he tried to remember what it had been like when he wanted to punish her with his passion.

That wasn't what he wanted now. No.

Now what he wanted was something else altogether.

A strange need had twisted and turned inside him, upside down and inside out, until he couldn't recognize it or himself. He might not know exactly what was happening in him, but he knew desire. And desire flared between them whenever they touched. No question about it.

When they parted, her family was staring at them, openmouthed.

He shrugged. "There's a reason we had to get married so quickly."

That earned him a slug on the shoulder. Wren looked disheveled, and furious. And he wondered if he had set a record for husband who got punched soonest after the vows were spoken.

When it was over, they went to his truck, and sat there. Silence ballooned between them.

"I thought you weren't going to involve your family?" he asked.

"I… I didn't know what to tell them. I didn't want to tell them I was getting married to you just because of a legal thing. It felt stupid. And then it snowballed."

"Wren…"

"So, can I come to your house? Just for a while?"

She was making his whole seduction plan a hell of a lot easier than he had expected it to be. He had thought he would have to contrive a way to get her to spend their wedding night together, but it turned out she had walked herself into a situation where she was going to have to do it anyway.

"Gee, I think I can think of something for us to do."

"Creed…"

"You can't deny that it's real between us, Wren. Whatever else—the desire between us is real."

Wren stared at her new husband.

She had to wonder if all this time she had simply been lying to herself. By increments, stages and degrees. Lying to herself that they could be together and *not* be together, that they could somehow have a platonic relationship that wouldn't be affected if the other one ended up with a different partner. That they could be friends, and keep everything easy for their child.

But she realized now that perhaps the real issue in her parents' marriage had been honesty. And maybe it wasn't even honesty with each other, but honesty with themselves.

Wren didn't really know how to be honest with herself, that was the thing.

The realization shocked her about as much as anything else had since she'd started this thing with Creed. About as much as their kiss at the altar, and as much as how real the vows had felt.

It was just so different from how she had imagined. He was different from how she had imagined.

They were different together.

"Take me home," she said softly.

And he did.

The truck moved quickly around the curves as he maneuvered it expertly along the rural road.

"Did you ever want to do anything but work at the family winery?" she asked.

His eyes were glued to the road as he drove. "I have my ranch. Not a huge operation, because, of course, I'm tied up a lot of the time with Cowboy Wines. But I've found a way to do what I want, and what I feel like my responsibility is."

"So it feels like a responsibility to you?"

"Yes. It does. And more so in the years since my mother died."

Her heart went tight. "I'm so sorry. About your mother."

"I'm sorry about your dad," he said. "I know I wasn't very nice about it before. I'm not proud of what I said, Wren. But sometimes I get my head buried in the sand. I turned your family into an enemy, because you were competition, and because I was pouring myself into making our winery better. Since my mother died, I felt like I was on some crusade to make my dad interested in life. I lost sight of some things. But I'm good at that. I'm good at losing sight of things. Sometimes intentionally."

"Does that have to do with…"

"My son?"

"Yes."

"Trying to ignore that pain certainly didn't improve my disposition, let's put it that way. And it's a wound that hurts worse the older I get. The more I realize what I missed. What I can't get back. Kids always make you aware of how time passes, as I understand it. Mine comes with accompanying grief and regret."

She could see that. How that would work. At sixteen, everyone was short on perspective and long on time. But at their age… That's when a person realized how precious it all was, and that feeling only increased with the years. The desire to hang on to what was important.

Of course, she wasn't sure it was age that had given her that perspective.

"You know, losing my relationship with my father the way I did is what forced me to look at my life more critically," Wren said. "It's what forced me to ask myself why I was doing anything. And I think it's what made me feel ready for the baby. But even with those changes, there are so many things I still don't know how to navigate. So many things I'm not sure about. Because all these revelations are so very new and I…" She looked at him. "People like to be comfortable, don't we? We don't want to change. And usually, life doesn't ask us if we want to go through the things that most define us. We just have to go through them."

"I'm sure losing your dad the way you did is a lot like losing my mom."

She shook her head. "No. You can't see your mom anymore. I don't want to see my dad. It's a loss, Creed, but I wouldn't compare the two. My dad was never who I thought he was."

His truck pulled up to the long gravel driveway that led to the ranch. His house was so different from any she would have imagined herself living in before. Her place at Maxfield Vineyards was styled after the vineyard house itself, which was her parents' taste. Or maybe just her father's taste. Maybe what her mother wanted didn't come into it at all. Wren didn't know.

It bothered her, going from a house that had been decided on by her parents, straight to a man's house.

He stopped the car and looked at her. "What's wrong?"

"I've never had my own place. Not really. I don't know what I like. I don't know…who I am. I try to think of what kind of house I would choose and it's just a blank in my head."

"What *do* you know, Wren?" he asked.

"I know that I want you," she said, meeting his gaze.

Because that was one choice she had made in the middle of all of this, the one choice that had been down to her—kissing Creed Cooper in the first place.

They'd made a deal. A deal to not do this. But she didn't think she could stick to the deal. Didn't think she could be near him, with him like this, and not have him.

So maybe just once?

Maybe just for their wedding night.

Whether it made sense or not, it was what she'd chosen.

That desire for him hadn't come from anywhere but

inside herself. And there was something empowering about that.

Maybe the wedding had been his idea, but wanting him… She knew that was all her. Nothing anyone would have asked her to do. Nothing her family was even all that supportive of. Some might have argued it was a bad thing to have given in to, on some level, but it had been her own choice. And right now, sitting in a truck that wasn't hers, in front of the house that wasn't hers, having taken vows that weren't her idea, the desire between them at least seemed honest.

And wasn't honest what she really needed?

Yes, she was trying to be smart, whatever that meant in this situation. Yes, she was trying to do the right thing for her child, but if she didn't know what the right thing was for herself… How could she be a good mother?

She thought about her own mother. Soft but distant, somebody Wren had never connected with.

Because she didn't *know* her. She didn't know her mother, and Wren had to wonder if the other woman knew herself.

"Yes," she repeated now. "I want you. I want you, because I know that's real."

He threw the truck into Park and shut off the engine. Then he got out, rounded to her side and opened the door. He pulled her out and into his arms, carrying her up the front steps and through the door. Then he carried her up the stairs, set her down in his bed.

And when they kissed, she felt like she might know something.

Something deep and real inside herself.

She didn't have a name for it. But it didn't matter.

Because all she wanted to do was feel.

This was different from the other times they had been together. It wasn't fast or frantic. And when it was over, she drifted off to sleep. She had the oddest sensation that in his bed, without her clothes, without any of the trappings that normally made her feel like her... She was the closest to real that she had ever been.

Nine

Wren began stirring in the late evening. They had skipped straight to the wedding night before the sun had gone down, and Creed was certain he would never get enough of her.

Then she had fallen asleep, all soft and warm and satisfied against him, and he would've thought that he'd find it…irritating. That he still wanted sex and the woman had fallen asleep.

But he didn't. Instead, he just enjoyed holding her.

It was amazing how much less of a termagant she was when she was asleep.

As soon as she began making sleepy little noises, he hauled himself down to the kitchen and put together a plate of cheese and crackers, and grabbed a bottle of sparkling cider, which he had bought a couple of days earlier.

How funny for Wren not to be able to drink wine. Wine was their business. It was what they were. But, of course, it wouldn't be part of her life for the next few months.

That meant it wouldn't be part of his either. No wine, but she got him as a consolation prize.

He imagined it was all a very strange turn of events for her.

He brought the food upstairs just as Wren was sitting up, scrubbing her eyes with the backs of her hands, the covers fallen down around her waist, exposing her perfect, gorgeous breasts.

"Happy wedding night," he said, holding up his offerings as he made his way toward the bed.

Her eyes took a leisurely tour of his body, and he could tell she enjoyed the view.

That she had ever thought the two of them could keep their hands off each other was almost funny.

Almost.

The problem was, he didn't find much funny about the way he wanted her. It flew in the face of everything that he was. Everything he knew about himself.

Everything he knew about keeping himself separate.

All the decisions that he'd made about his life eighteen years ago seemed... They didn't seem quite so clear when he was staring at Wren. The woman carrying his child.

The woman who was now his wife.

"Well, this is nice," she said.

"I can be nice."

She chuckled, and pushed herself up so she was sitting a little taller. The covers fell down even farther, and he set the food and drink down on the nightstand next to her, then yanked them off the rest of the way.

"Hey," she said.

But he was too busy admiring her thighs, and that sweet spot between them, to care.

"It's my payment," he said.

"I retract what I said about you being nice."

"If you keep showing me all this glory, I might go ahead and drop dead. And then you can do a little dance on my grave. I really would like to see you dance."

She smirked, then shook her hips slightly as she got up onto her knees, leaning over and taking a piece of cheese off the tray.

"Honestly, I would have married you a lot sooner if I'd known you came with room service."

"Room service and multiple orgasms," he said.

"You know, if you have to be the one to say it…"

"You know you're sleeping with a woman who has more pride than sense?"

"Nothing wrong with that," she said. "A little bit of pride never hurt anybody."

"Neither did a little bit of submission."

"That's where you're wrong," she said. "It hurts unless you want to give it."

"You say that as an expert?"

She shook her head. "Definitely not. Being totally honest, I've had a few *very* underwhelming boyfriends. And none of them have enticed me to do the kinds of things that you entice me to do. So there you have it."

"I haven't had girlfriends. None." He got into bed with her and stretched out alongside her, running his knuckles along the line of her waist. "I hook up. It's never about any one woman in particular so much as about my desire to get laid. That's actually vastly unsatisfying."

"Tell me more." She narrowed her eyes. "And this better end in a way that compliments me and makes me feel singular, magical and like a sex goddess."

"I can't keep my hands off you," he growled. "More to the point, I can't keep my mind off you. When I'm not with you, I want to be with you. And when you said you didn't want our relationship to be physical… I didn't know what I was going to do with that. I think about you, and I burn, Wren. Even if we weren't having the baby, even if we weren't together tonight because it was our wedding night, I think we would still be in my bed."

The frown on her face made his chest feel strange.

"We don't like each other," she said.

"I think we're both going to have to let go of that idea. Because obviously it's more complicated than that."

"We don't mesh," she said.

"We seem to mesh pretty well."

She poured herself a glass of the sparkling cider and took another slice of cheese, leaning back against the headboard, sighing heavily. "My parents' marriage has always mystified me. They don't really talk. It was very civil, but very distant, and I think I always imagined that's what marriage was. I tried to find a similar thing with the men I dated. This kind of external compatibility. We never fought. And anytime I ever broke up with someone… It just sort of fizzled out. Like I would notice it had been a while since we'd seen each other and I didn't really care. Or we were still going to events together, but not even bothering to have sex after. Or worse, we did have sex and I basically spent the whole time thinking about which canapés I liked best at the party, and not about what we were doing. I knew I didn't want that in a long-term relationship. Boredom before we got to forever, you know?"

"Sure."

"But there was never *this*. There was never any fighting, there was never any passion. I just thought passion was for other people."

"Why did you think that?"

She sighed. "It's stupid."

"Look, Wren, you know all about the worst thing that's ever happened to me. You tell me why you can't have passion."

"I never think about it. It's one of those things usually buried in my memory. You know when you're a kid you think you're going to be all kinds of different things. From a unicorn on down the list. For a while, I even fantasized about being a police officer. Chasing bad guys, solving mysteries. And then I realized that I don't like to run, and I never want to be shot at, so that kind of takes being a cop off the table."

He snorted. "Yeah, I can see how that would be an issue."

"But when I was a little bit older, I thought… I got really good grades in math. I really liked it. I also really liked art, and a teacher at school, at the boarding school I went to, told me that combination was sort of rare. She said it made me special, that I could think creatively and wield numbers the way that I did. She talked to me about the kinds of things I could do with a talent like that. One of the things we spoke about was architectural engineering. I was really fascinated by it.

By the way you could put different materials together. Marrying form and function. Art with practicality. My father said it just wasn't what he saw me doing. He said my brain would be useful for the brand, and that I needed to remember the school that I went to, the clothes that I wore, everything that I was, came from the winery. Which meant I needed to invest back into the winery. I understood that. I really did. And I just didn't think about architectural engineering anymore after that. I got my degree in hospitality and marketing. And I've found that I really love my job. But I've just been asking myself a lot of questions lately. About who I might've been if my whole life hadn't felt so rigidly *decided*."

"Do you want to go back to school?"

"I have to take care of the winery. Cricket doesn't have any interest in it. Emerson is awesome, but she does a very particular thing, this kind of global brand ambassador stuff that requires lots of computer savvy. She's brilliant. It's actually a very similar kind of skill set as the one I have. She's so good with algorithms, but she's also great at finessing public branding. Doing posts that are visually appealing and that have a result. I mean, I get to use my gifts in my job. It's just every so often I wonder if I had known who my father was back then, would I have worked so hard to make him happy?"

"I don't think you can know that. The same way I can't actually know what kind of father I would've been. The honest truth is, Wren, I can get myself really angry about what was taken from me, and when I do that… Well, in my head I'm the best damn teenage father ever. I give up everything for my kid. Women and drinking and partying and being carefree." He paused, working hard to speak around the weight that settled over his heart. "But I didn't do any of that, I didn't have to. Louisa did. So did Cal. *They* are the ones who ended up sacrificing. They're the ones who gave my son a family. They're the ones who gave him his life. Yeah, in hindsight I can make myself a hero. But I don't know that I would've been. We can't actually know what we would have done. We can just do something different now."

As soon as he said those words, he realized how true they were. And they made his chest feel bruised.

He looked at Wren, and he felt a sense of deep certainty. "From this day on, Wren Maxfield, you can be whoever you want. You've chosen to be the mother of my child, and I appreciate that. Whatever else you want to be, I would never hold you back from it. I'd support you. If you wanted to quit working and just take care of the baby, I'd be fine with that. If you wanted to go back to school, I'd be fine with that, too. Whatever it is you need, I will help make that a reality."

"Why?" she asked.

"Because I've had more what-ifs in my life than I care to. And this... This gives me the chance to answer a lot of my greatest ones. Getting to be the father that I've wondered if I could be... I want to be a father. Everything else... Everything else doesn't matter as much."

"You don't expect to hear that from men," she said.

"Maybe not. But most men didn't lose out on the chance of fatherhood the way that I did. So for me... If you're going to get a second chance, you gotta be willing to pour everything into it. And that includes caring about your happiness, Wren. I want you to stay my wife."

"Creed…"

"Like I said, be whatever you want along with that. I'll support you. I swear it."

He had assumed so many things about her. He had looked at her and seen the glitter and polish, had associated her with her father and the kinds of things her father had done, and Creed had imagined her to be avaricious and shallow, because it was so much easier to reduce people to stereotypes. Because it was easier to do that than to see her as a person.

Because now that he saw her as a person, he had to contend with the complicated feelings she created inside him. And he knew he had been avoiding that. Avoiding it because something in him had recognized a connection to Wren the moment they first met.

He had no doubt about that.

And he had been running from complicated since the first time emotional entanglements had bit him in the ass when he was sixteen.

But he hadn't known anything then. And he hadn't known anything for a lot of years after because he had simply clung to his anger at Louisa and used it as a shield.

But age forced him to see everything with a hell of a lot more nuance, and being in this situation again demanded the same thing.

He was having to contend with the fact that Louisa didn't seem like such a villain anymore. And that the fact didn't make the past hurt any less for him.

Having to contend with the fact that there was a lot

of mileage between just sex and whatever this was between him and Wren.

And whatever their feelings were, whatever they could be, they were having a baby. And he wanted this child to have the benefit of everything his son had.

If there was one good thing about Creed never busting into his son's life, it was that he'd given him a family. He'd honored and respected that.

But now, Creed wanted the same kind of family for this child.

So he would give Wren anything. Absolutely anything.

"I don't know what I want yet," she said, looking almost helpless. "I'm not sure that I can make that decision while I'm still in the middle of this big…change."

"It's okay," he said. "I understand. Maybe it's not the best time, but my offer stands no matter when you take it."

"Thank you." She looked at him again. "For now, can we just focus on cheese and sex? Because those are decisions I feel like I can make. I would like both."

"And I can accommodate."

And that was when he pulled her into his arms again, and they quit talking about the future, about anything serious.

Because there was a whole lot of uncertainty out there, and in the future. But there was no uncertainty of any kind between them when it came to their mutual desire. It was certain, and it was real. And it made everything else seem manageable. Like it might be the easiest thing in the world for them to find some way to make this marriage and parenthood work.

Creed was determined in that.

If sheer stubbornness could will something into being possible, then he knew he and Wren would succeed.

Because they were two of the most stubborn people on the planet.

He just had to hope they could do it without deciding they wanted different things. Because in the end, that would end up tearing both of them apart.

She and Creed had been living together for two months.

She'd wanted a wedding night… She was getting a full-on honeymoon.

She'd wanted to do all this with a clear head. Had wanted to make plans for the baby, for how they would conduct themselves…

She'd wanted to do it all in a lab-like environment. As if they were talking heads who could divorce feeling and desire from everything else.

But they couldn't do that.

He'd set something free inside her and she didn't want to deny it. Didn't want to put it back. He'd asked for permanent and she didn't feel like she could answer him.

Was afraid to.

But she'd be lying if she said she wasn't fantasizing about it.

They had been sleeping together, talking to each other, eating cheese in bed. They'd talked about Christmas, and not just in the context of the event they were planning.

Their memories of it. The way they liked to decorate. She liked it sparkly. He liked it homespun.

She liked a full turkey dinner. His mom had always made spaghetti, lasagna and bread.

They opened a present on Christmas Eve. He was scandalized by the idea. Christmas morning only.

She liked fake trees because they were perfect and didn't shed.

If he'd had pearls, he'd have clutched them. He'd been subjected to the virtues and tradition inherent in going to the woods and getting your own tree.

Another discussion they'd tabled for later, in terms of how they'd raise their child.

It was so difficult for her to reconcile the man that she was involved with now with the one she had first kissed all that time ago.

She could hardly remember hating him. She didn't hate him now. Not even close. She *couldn't* hate him. Her feelings were starting to get jumbled up, and it was frightening, to be honest.

But no more frightening than when she came home and saw that a real estate sign had been put up at his ranch.

"What is this?" she asked.

"I'm selling this place. Because I want us to pick out our own place."

"What?"

"You heard me. Wren, you told me you didn't know who you were. And that you were going from a house designed to your father's taste to one better suited to mine. I don't want you to feel that way. I don't want that for you. I don't want that for us."

"So you put your house up for sale without talking to me about it?"

"I didn't go out and buy a house without talking to you. That would have defeated the purpose."

She looked at him, and boggled. Because as much as she was coming to feel affection for him, he was still a big, stubborn, hardheaded fool.

And she cared about him an awful lot.

"I can't believe you would do this for me. This is your place. Your ranch."

"That's the only requirement I have," he said. "I do need to have property, or I need to be close enough to property I can lease."

"Don't be silly. That would be inconvenient."

"I don't care about the house," he said. "It can be whatever you want it to be. We could build too if you want, but that would take a lot of time."

"We need a place sooner than that."

They didn't waste any time. They started to house hunt after that. They went overboard looking at places, and Wren felt giddy with the independence of it.

That she was choosing a place. A place to call her own. One that would be shaped around this life she was sharing with Creed and...

She wondered when she had accepted it. That they were going to make a try at this together.

That she wasn't going to leave him after a year. Or when the baby was born, or whatever she had told him all those weeks ago.

Because she knew now that she wasn't going to do that. That there was no way. Because she knew now there would be no separating the two of them. They were forming a unit, as strange as it was.

And somehow, Wren found that their unit didn't

compromise her desire for independence. Rather, it supported it.

He supported it.

There was a strange sort of freedom, having this giant brick wall on her team. She couldn't fully explain it. But there it was. True as anything.

The house that stole her heart surprised her.

It was a white farmhouse with red shutters, new, but styled in a classic way. She could see how their Christmas styles might even meet here. A little glitter, a little rustic.

The kitchen had gorgeous granite countertops and white cabinets. Light and airy, but not too modern. Perfect for Christmas Eve lasagna, and Christmas turkey.

She loved the layout of it, the great big living room that she could imagine being filled with baby toys, and a big old Christmas tree.

Fake or real, it suddenly didn't matter.

The way the bedrooms were configured, with one just down the hall from the master bedroom that she knew would make the ideal nursery, was perfect. More than she had ever dreamed. For a life she hadn't been able to imagine before, but could now, so vividly that it hurt.

"What do you think?" he asked.

"This is it," she said.

A life that was theirs. A life that didn't belong to anyone else.

"Yes," she said. "I think this is going to work."

Let it never be said that Creed Cooper was a coward, but he had been avoiding having meaningful conversation with his family for far too long. They were all dancing around the issue of his marriage, and his impending fatherhood. And it was obvious that whatever leash had been holding Honey back had just broken.

He was in his office, finalizing details for the upcoming joint winery event, when Jackson, Jericho, Honey and their father walked in. Or rather, Honey burst in, and the others came in behind her.

"Are we just not talking about this? About the fact that you got married?"

"I mean, there's not much to say."

"You married a Maxfield."

"I did," Creed said.

"She's pregnant."

"Honey, do I have to walk you through how that happens, or did you get sex ed in school?"

"I'm good," Honey said, her tone dry. "Thanks, though. My point is, what exactly is going on?"

"I got her pregnant. I married her. That's what a gentleman does."

Honey rolled her eyes. "I was under the impression a gentleman waited until he was married." She looked like she was deciding something. Then, decision made, her lips turned up into a smirk. "Or at the very least used a damn condom."

"Can you not say the word *condom*?" Creed asked.

"Why? I would assume you'd prefer to think that I was using them rather than not."

"I would prefer not to think about it at all."

"You've given *me* no such luxury. Since you clearly had *unprotected sex*. Like a…horny goat."

"Are you just here to lecture me on protocol or…?"

"Do you love her?"

"What does love have to do with anything?" And

the words sat uncomfortably in his gut. Because he felt something for Wren, sure as hell. He was selling his ranch for her, moving into another house.

As if she could read his mind, Honey's gaze sharpened. "Is she *making* you leave your ranch?"

"No," he said. "I suggested we get a place that's more about the two of us."

"You...*did*?"

"It was the least I could do. Considering I basically forced her to marry me."

"You didn't," Honey said.

"I did," he responded.

His sister stared at him, and he could feel his older brother mounting a protective posture. At him? That was ridiculous.

"Honey," Jackson said. "Maybe just leave it alone. Like we told you to when you were ranting a few minutes ago."

"You guys are terrible bouncers," Creed said, addressing his brother and Jericho. "You let her come right through the front door."

"I just don't get it," she said. "Why you would marry somebody you're not in love with."

"There's a lot of reasons to get married, sweetheart," he said. "And they often don't have anything to do with love."

"Then what?"

"Well, lust comes to mind."

"You don't marry somebody just because you lust after them. That's silly."

"Fine. The pregnancy."

"I still don't understand how you could be so stupid. You're not a kid."

"Honey, I pray that you always keep your head when it comes to situations of physical desire."

She tossed her pale brown hair over her shoulder. "I would never get that stupid over a man."

The three of them laughed at her. Well, chuckles, really, but Honey looked infuriated.

"Spoken like a woman who's never wanted anyone," Jericho said.

Honey's face went up in flames. "You don't know *anything*," she said, planting her hand on his chest and shoving him slightly.

"I know plenty enough," he responded.

"Did you guys just come to my office to bicker? To yell at me about something I can't change?"

"They're our rivals," Honey said. "That's what I don't get. Now you're married, and did you do anything to protect the winery when you made that deal?"

No. They hadn't signed a prenup of any kind. And in hindsight that probably wasn't the best decision. But all he'd been thinking of was making sure he was protecting his rights as a father.

He hadn't thought to protect his monetary assets at all.

"Everything will be fine," he said.

"How could you be so shortsighted?"

"I was only thinking about one thing," he said, his patience snapping. "I'm really glad that you can sit there on your high horse. But virgins don't get to talk about what it's like to be carried away by desire. I've made this mistake before." That made his sister look shamefaced, shocked. "And the woman took the kid from me, okay? I missed out on eighteen years of raising my son because I didn't make sure my rights were protected, and I wasn't going to do it again. I did what I had to do. My kid was more important than the winery."

Finally, his father spoke. "You compromised the winery for this marriage?"

"There are things that are more important than a winery, Dad. I would think you would know that."

He couldn't read the expression on his old man's face. "I protected the winery all this time," he said. "It was my...new dream after it became clear I wasn't going to get the first thing I wanted. And I never compromised for it."

"No," Creed agreed. "You didn't. Down to not wanting to make too big of an incident out of me getting a girl pregnant when I was sixteen. Yeah, Dad, you protected the winery. But I protected my son. Can you say you did the same?"

Suddenly, Creed was done. Done with all of it. Done with all of them.

It was easy for them to pass judgment, but they didn't know what they were talking about.

His father had gotten everything he wanted in his life. He'd had a wife, had his children.

And then the old man had withdrawn into himself when his wife had died and let his children take over the running of the winery.

Yeah, he'd used them to protect the winery. At the expense of everything else. His father had asked endless sacrifices of Creed.

Creed was out of damn patience for his family.

"All of you spare me your lectures," he said. "A virgin and an old man who don't know what the hell they're talking about." He shook his head and walked out of the building, breathing in the sharp early-morning air.

He wasn't going to justify his decision to marry Wren. His course was set.

And whatever Honey thought, love did come into it. The love for his child. Nothing else mattered.

Ten

The big cross-vineyard event was tonight, and Wren could hardly keep the nerves from overtaking her.

She got tired much more quickly than usual these days, and her midsection was beginning to get a bit thicker, which made the dresses she normally wore to things like this slightly tighter. She had spent countless hours trying on gowns in hers and Creed's bedroom, until he had grabbed hold of her and said very firmly that he loved her body like it was, and that absolutely everything looked good on her, or off her.

That had ended in him nearly destroying her makeup with his kisses, and she had scolded him roundly about the fact that they didn't have any time to get busy.

She had been filled with regret about that decision, however. And the fact that making love to him seemed a whole lot more interesting than readying herself for something she was supposed to be excited about irritated her.

As she slipped into the formfitting green dress she'd decided on, she tried to tell herself she was irritated simply because having a baby was such a big deal.

It was harder and harder to care about other things right now. She was consumed with the fact that in six and a half months she and Creed were going to be parents.

And for some reason, it kept sticking in her mind even more that they were still going to be husband and wife, for six more months and longer.

The baby was supposed to be what mattered.

And first, this event.

Her family was acclimating to the fact that she and Creed weren't rivals anymore. That they had to be friendly, to an extent, with Cowboy Wines. But it wasn't smooth sailing.

Not entirely. For some reason, Cricket was being difficult about playing nice. And while Wren had a lot of patience for what they were all going through under the circumstances, her sympathy still didn't make it easy to accept Cricket's behavior.

All dressed and ready, Wren kissed Creed goodbye and told him she needed to get to Maxfield Vineyards early.

He grumbled about being reluctant to let her go, but she pointed out that she hadn't been back home since they'd moved. Not to the house, anyway. She'd gone to the winery itself, to the public areas, the tasting rooms. There had been weddings and dinners and other things since she and Creed had gotten married. But she hadn't actually been in the house.

For some reason, she felt like she needed to do that today. And she felt like she needed to do it alone.

Nerves overtook her when she realized part of the reason she felt an urgency to visit was that she hadn't actually been alone with her mother, Cricket and Emerson altogether since the wedding.

When Wren arrived at the house, her mother looked impeccable, but stone-faced, and Emerson looked as radiant as ever. Cricket was wearing jeans and a T-shirt.

"What are you doing, Cricket?" Wren asked.

"Oh, I'm not going," Cricket said.

"Why aren't you going?"

"Because I don't want to," she said defiantly.

"But it's a family event."

"No, it isn't," Cricket said. "It's an event for the winery, and I don't have to be there. There's absolutely no reason for me to get dressed up and parade myself around. I'm not really part of anything that happens with the winery. It's never been me."

Wren was shocked, but she had to wonder if she would feel the same way had she been Cricket's age when their family had fallen apart.

"I'm divorcing your father," her mother said.

"What?" Wren asked.

"I'm divorcing him," she said. "I haven't seen him in months. What's the point of staying married? What was the point of any of it?" Her mother, who was often so quiet, sad even, seemed…not herself.

"More and more I question the point of any of this. I have this beautiful house, but your father never loved me. I have you girls. The only good to have come out of my life in the last thirty years. Everything else is shallow. Pointless. I thought this winery mattered. This house. The money. It doesn't."

"And if it doesn't matter to her," Cricket said, "why should I pretend that it matters to me?"

"I'm all for bids of independence," Wren said. "And I'm not going to say I haven't been on a soul-searching mission myself these last few months. But save your breakdowns so they're not right before my big event?"

"Sorry it's not convenient for you," Cricket said. "You getting married and abandoning me wasn't great timing either."

Wren had a feeling that was directed at both her and Emerson.

"Cricket," Emerson said. "You don't have to go if you don't want. But if you're upset, maybe we should talk."

"We should talk now," Cricket said. "Because this family is a mess, and Wren is just making the same mistakes Mom did. Marrying Creed because she's having a baby, when they don't even love each other. You can pretend all you want but I don't believe you magically fell in love with him. It's going to end like this. Big house, lots of money. Maybe a winery conglomerate. Sad adult children and divorce."

"That's enough," her mother said. "I judge myself for the decisions I made for money. For comfort. For… for turning away from somebody who did love me for somebody who never could." Wren stared at her mother for a moment, not fully understanding what she was talking about. "But the one thing that I'm at peace with is anything I did for the sake of you girls. Wren made a decision for the sake of her child's future. And Creed Cooper isn't your father."

"No," Wren said, her tone firm. "Creed is a good man. He loves this baby. So much. You have no idea."

"Well, I don't have to participate in any of this."

Cricket turned and walked out of the room. Emerson put her hand on Wren's shoulder. "Don't worry about her. She doesn't know what she's talking about. She doesn't know what it's like."

There was something in Emerson's gaze that scared Wren, and she couldn't pinpoint why.

Didn't know what *what* was like? Relationships?

That she would believe. Her sister had led a cloistered life on the vineyard, and hadn't gone away to school the way Wren and Emerson had. In many ways, it had felt like their parents had given up by the time they'd gotten to Cricket. For all that the expectations of their father had been hard on Emerson and Wren, Wren suspected there had been no expectations at all of Cricket.

And that the low bar hadn't done her any favors.

But Wren didn't think that's what Emerson was talking about. And the alternative possibility made her stomach feel tight.

"Mom," Wren said, turning to her mother, deciding to reject any thoughts she was having about herself and deal with her mother instead. "What did you mean about 'someone who could love you'?"

"The Coopers are good men," her mother said. "If Creed is anything like his father, he has a lot more honor than James Maxfield ever did."

Wren's whole world felt shaky, and she decided not to press the issue, because she didn't think she could take on any more right then.

Instead, Wren and Emerson went down to the grand event hall, which was decorated and lit up, overlooking the valley below. It was all pristine glass, floor-to-ceiling windows and honey-colored wood beams. A huge fake Christmas tree was at the center, lit up, merry and bright.

It looked elegant and perfect, and stations for each winery were beginning to come together. Lindy Dodge, from another local winery, was there, setting out samples and arranging small plates of food, her big, cowboy husband, Wyatt, helping with everything. The sight of those two people, so very different from each other—Lindy, petite and polished, and Wyatt, big, rough and ready—did something strange to Wren's insides. Made her long for something she didn't think was even possible.

She turned away from the couple, and made a show of looking at some of the displays put up by the other wineries before busying herself with the fine details of their own.

And when Creed arrived, her world spun to a halt. Just looking at him made her mouth run dry. Made everything in her go still, and her sister's words echoed inside her.

She doesn't know what it's like.

Not a relationship. No, nothing quite that simple. Not attraction either. Because that was not deep enough.

No, what Cricket didn't understand was what happened when a man entered a woman's life, who was wrong in every way, but fit so beautifully.

Who seemed to take all the jagged pieces and press them together, turning something ordinary into something new. Making each fractured line seem a beautiful detail rather than a fatal flaw.

What Cricket didn't understand was the miracle involved in loving someone she shouldn't.

Loving someone who made no sense. And the way that it rearranged one's life into something unrecognizable.

What Cricket didn't understand was that love was a storm.

Wren had always imagined that loving somebody was civil. That it was something she could pick out, like selecting the perfect wine in a refined cellar.

But no. That wasn't how it was with Creed.

He was a brilliant and glorious streak of lightning, shooting across the sky, a low, resonating boom of thunder that echoed in her heart. He was nothing she would have ever looked for, and everything she was beginning to suspect she needed.

And that need wasn't comfortable.

Because just like a storm, she couldn't control it, didn't know how much damage it might cause, didn't know what the landscape would look like after it was finished raging.

Feelings like this, they could uproot trees. Reorder the slopes of mountains.

Damage her heart irrevocably.

She didn't know what to do, because she couldn't unthink all these things. Couldn't unknow the feeling that made her heart squeeze tight when she looked at the man. That made her want to mess up her hair and makeup and make love to him on the floor before an important event.

That made her want to test all his rough against her soft. That made her feel enamored of their differences, rather than disdainful of them.

The reason she had fought with him from the beginning was because she had been desperate to keep him at bay. She could see that now, with stunning clarity.

It was the wrong time to be realizing all of this. Any of this. Because she had to focus on this event. It mattered. It was the reason they were together in the first place, these initiatives.

Is it?

Or had she been unable to see a way forward without Creed because she had been desperate to spend more time with him?

Desperate to make him a part of her life and part of her business.

Honesty.

Hadn't she dedicated herself to finding honesty in who she was and what she wanted?

Her heart felt tender as she gazed at the tall, striking figure of her husband across the room, at a different winery station from her.

She didn't even know how that was going to work. They were separate. Though they were married.

And it wasn't just because they worked at different places. But because there was a very deliberate barrier between them when it came to emotion.

Creed had made it plain he wanted the marriage to last, but she knew that he was motivated by a deep, feral need to keep his child close to him.

It had nothing to do with her, and he'd never pretended it did.

It does, a little bit. He doesn't want anyone else to have you.

It was true. But was that the same as wanting her? Really wanting her?

She didn't know.

And she didn't even know why it mattered.

Why it suddenly felt imperative that there be love between them.

Because other than your sisters, have you ever felt like anyone really loved you?

The question bit into her, and she tried hard to keep on doing her job while it gnawed at all she was.

Eventually, she was unable to keep herself away from Creed any longer.

"This is looking good," she said.

"It is," he responded. "It's good."

She wanted him to say that he was proud of her.

But wanting his praise made her feel small and sad.

Because was she ever really going to be different? How could she ever be new? When she was still just simpering after the approval, the love, of a man who wasn't going to give it back?

Maybe he will. Maybe you just need to ask him.

She looked at his square jaw, at his striking features that seemed as if they were carved from stone.

He had been hurt. Badly. But did that mean he couldn't feel anything for anyone anymore? She knew that he loved their unborn baby. That he was intensely motivated by that love in everything he did.

Although, he had never said those words exactly. He didn't talk about love. He talked about opportunities, responsibility. He talked about not wanting to miss anything. But he had never said the word *love*. That didn't mean he didn't feel it, but it did give her questions about just how much he knew his own emotions.

Considering her own were a big giant news flash to

her, she didn't think it was outrageous to suspect that he might not be fully in touch with his own.

He held himself at a distance. She looked down at his left hand, at the ring he wore there.

He was her husband. And it wasn't a secret. She closed the distance between them, kissing him on the cheek. "I'm glad that we did this."

The look in his eyes was unreadable.

"Me, too."

She didn't know if she had meant the event. The pregnancy. The marriage.

How could she feel something so deep for this man? This man she had thought she felt only antagonistic things for a few months ago. Well, she felt chemistry with him, but she hadn't known him. Hadn't known that deep wound that he carried around. The intensity with which he cared about things.

And whether or not he knew it was love, she did.

He had been ready to set everything aside at sixteen and become a father.

He bled responsibility. He was everything her father wasn't.

And then he had let her choose their house, had sold a place that meant something to him. His own house, so they could build a life together. He'd asked her about her dreams, and he'd said that what she wanted was important.

No one had ever said those things to her. No one had ever offered the things to her that Creed had.

All that, and it came with the kind of intense passion she hadn't even known existed.

How could she not fall in love with him? How could she have ever not loved him?

She swallowed hard and leaned against him, pressing her face against his suit jacket and inhaling his scent. "Thank you for dressing up for me again."

"It was appropriate," he responded, his voice hard.

She could feel him pulling away, not physically, but emotionally. And perversely it only made her want to cling to him even more tightly.

She couldn't help herself.

She was supposed to be focusing on the triumph of the evening. A few months ago, she would have been. It would have been all-important to her. Because she would have gotten approval out of it. Approval from her father.

It was such a different thing to be doing something for herself. She still cared about the winery. It was just that she already knew she approved of the job she'd done. She wasn't waiting for recognition. She was good at what she did, and she didn't question whether or not she could execute something like this.

It freed up her mind to worry about other things. It made all of this less all-consuming. Less important. Because it wasn't an essential part of her happiness. Wasn't an essential part of who she was.

She did this job for the winery. But she was also a sister. A daughter. A wife. Soon to be a mother.

She was interested in other things, and Creed had reminded her of that.

This event, and what happened at the winery, was no longer the highest-stakes thing happening in her world.

She wondered what kind of mother she would be. And she was worried about being a good wife.

About her husband's feelings for her.

This was satisfying. And it mattered.

But it didn't feel half so important or potentially fatal as it would have only a few short months ago.

And suddenly she thought maybe the transformation she'd been going through wasn't so much about becoming a different version of herself, but expanding what it meant to be Wren Maxfield.

Wren *Cooper*.

A woman who could want more than one thing, care about more than just her father's good opinion and this winery.

A woman whose definition of love could expand to accommodate a storm.

A woman who could be proud of what she had done all by herself.

It was a relief.

Because she had been worried. Worried that she might have to break all that she was into pieces and scatter them over the sea, bury them there, so she could become something completely and entirely new and foreign to herself.

But she didn't have to do that. She didn't.

She could just be.

She didn't have to worry about whether or not Cricket approved, or if it made any sense to anyone else that she had married her business rival.

That she loved him.

Her life belonged to her now. And she imagined it would change shape a great many more times before it was over.

But they would be shapes formed by her hands, her heart.

And the people she loved.

No, she couldn't anticipate the landscape and how it would look in the end.

But whatever it was, she knew she would find a way to navigate it, and if necessary, find ways to change it again.

Because she wasn't easily broken.

She was strong.

And she was trying to find a way to make her bravery match that strength. Her instinct was to continue to protect herself, but she didn't think the answers lay there. After all, it had been the strangest choices, the bravest choices, that had brought her here to begin with.

From deciding to join forces with her enemy, to kissing him. Deciding to raise her baby. Agreeing to marry him.

There was that honesty again.

Honesty took so much bravery.

Not fearlessness, but bravery indeed.

The party was packed full of people, and everything went wonderfully. She could feel the bonds she was building between her family business and these other wonderful family-run operations here in Gold Valley. She felt connected. In the same way she had felt disconnected that day she'd driven to town and realized all the things she had missed here, she could feel herself growing roots in the place that she had been planted from the beginning.

A place she had always felt might not be for her.

She had anticipated this cross-promotion being a boon for her business, but she had never expected all of this could matter so much to her personally.

Emerson was standing at the station for Maxfield,

with her extremely handsome husband, Holden, at her side. Lindy was still standing with her husband.

And Wren made a decision, then and there.

Rather than going over to the station for Maxfield Vineyards, she went to the one that had been designated for Cowboy Wines. And she took her spot next to Creed.

She had no loyalty to a label.

She had a loyalty to this man. To all that he was, and more than that, all that they were together.

Yes, Maxfield would always be her family winery.

But Creed was her family now.

Creed was her heart.

Such an easy decision to make. Because now, she knew exactly who she was.

Eleven

Creed didn't know what the hell had gotten into Wren tonight, but it was as unsettling as it was arousing. She had been glued to his side the entire evening, tormenting him in that emerald dress that clung to her expanding curves. He loved the way her body was changing. The way her waist was getting thicker, the slight roundness low on her stomach speaking to the life growing inside her.

And, of course, he was enjoying the fullness in other parts of her curves.

She was beautiful in every way, but he was especially enjoying her current beauty because he was responsible for the changes. There was something intensely sexy and satisfying about that. But there was also a look in her eye that he was afraid he couldn't answer, and he didn't know what to make of it.

She had driven over to the winery on her own, but she left with him.

There was a determined sort of gleam in her eye, and it made his heart thunder, low and heavy.

Echoing like thunder inside him.

Like a storm.

She gave him a little half smile as they got into the house. And then she took his hand and led him over to the couch. He sat down, his legs relaxed, his palms rested on his knees.

Her eyes met his, and she reached behind her, unzipping that dress that had been torturing him so, and letting it fall from her curves.

His heart stopped. Stilled.

Everything in him went quiet. He couldn't breathe.

They'd made love countless times. Hadn't been able to keep their hands off each other these last few months. It was a storm of sensation and desire that had been building between them for years, and now that they lived together, now that they shared a bed every night, neither of them ever bothered to resist. But there was something different about tonight. There was an intent to her expression, a dare glimmering in her eyes.

Wren was never shy about sex. She was bold, and she was adventurous, but this was something else altogether. Still wearing her high heels, she unclipped her bra, removed it from her shoulders and let it fall to the floor. She did the same with her panties, standing there looking like a heavenly, dirty pinup that, thank God, was within arm's reach.

He didn't have to confine himself to just looking. He could touch.

He didn't know why he held himself back. Except that it was her show, and part of him was desperate to see exactly what she was going to make of it.

She pressed her hands to her stomach, slid them up her midsection and cupped her own breasts, teasing her nipples with her thumbs. Her eyes never left his.

"You know," she whispered, "you were my most forbidden fantasy. I tried to pretend that I didn't dream about you. About your hands on my body. But sometimes I would wake up from dreaming about you, wetter than I ever was from being with one of my other lovers."

"You have no idea," he ground out. "The dirty dreams I used to have about you."

"Is that why sometimes you were so mad at me when you would come and see me at work? Because you'd been dreaming about me naked, on my knees in front of you?"

And then she did just that.

Dropped to her knees in front of him, her dark hair cascading over her shoulders, the look of a predator etched into her beautiful face.

She pressed her hand over his clothed arousal, stroking him before opening up the closure on his pants. And then she leaned in, licking him, slowly, from base to tip, before making a supremely feline sound of satisfaction.

"I want you to know, I've never fantasized about doing this. But with you... I used to think about getting on my knees and sucking you to make you shut up. I could get off thinking about putting you in my mouth. That's not normal. Not for me."

And then she licked him again, and his world went dark. There was nothing but streaks of white-hot pleasure behind his eyes. Nothing but need. Nothing but desire.

She was a wicked tease, her mouth hot and slick and necessary.

How had she become *this*? He had thought her spoiled. Silly. Insubstantial.

You never really believed any of those things.

He closed his eyes and let his head fall back as she continued to pleasure him with that clever mouth that he had loved all the times it was cutting him to shreds, and now as it sent him to heaven.

No, he'd told himself those things. Because it was easy to disdain her, but much, much harder to have the guts to give in to a connection like this. A need like this.

Because this had nothing to do with the right thing, the good thing. With a pregnancy, or being a good father. It had everything to do with Wren. With his deep desire to wrap her in his arms and never let her go. With the intense possessiveness he felt every time he looked at her. And now, every time he looked at her and thought *wife*.

His wife.

His woman.

He hadn't asked for this. Hadn't wanted it. Had worked as hard as he could to avoid it, but all that work had been for nothing. Because here he was, and the inevitability of Wren, and his desire for her, suddenly seemed too big to ignore, too great to combat. And he was struck by his own cowardice. He had told himself so many stories about this woman that he had now seen weren't true, so many different things about the way he felt for her, that he could have easily examined and found to be lies.

He could tell himself he hadn't wanted this.

Because intensity had led to ruin all those years ago, and because he had failed.

Had failed as a father. Had failed as a man.

All because of desire. All because of wanting. The wrong woman. The wrong time.

But this was the *right* woman. The *right* time.

He gritted his teeth, rebelling against that thought as Wren's hand wrapped tight around the base of his arousal, squeezing him, sending his thoughts up to the stars and making it impossible for him to concentrate on anything else.

Impossible to do anything but feel.

She was a study in contradictions, so delicate and feminine as she destroyed his resistance with a kind of filthy poise he'd never imagined might exist.

He'd had sexual partners in the past. But he hadn't had a lover. Not really. Wren had become his lover. She'd learned his body, learned where to touch him and how, though he wondered if all these paths had been blazed by her hands, by what she wanted, by what she liked, because she seemed to conjure up sexual necessity out of thin air, make it so he couldn't breathe.

Couldn't think.

Wren had a spell cast on him that was unlike anything he'd ever experienced.

He had been smart to avoid it. Smart to try to turn away from it.

But he couldn't anymore. Not now.

Because she was here, and she was his wife. And everything she did was dark velvet perfection that took his control and ground it into stardust, glittering over the blank, night sky of his mind until she was all there was.

And without her, there would be only darkness.

And then what would he be?

Pleasure built low inside him, and he could feel his control fraying to an end.

"I need to be inside you," he ground out, lifting her up and away from his body, pulling her into his lap. Her knees rested on either side of his thighs, that slick, hot heart of her brushing his arousal. He brought her down onto him, over him, the welcome of his body into hers like a baptism.

Like something that might be able to make him new. Make him clean.

Even as he lost himself in a hedonistic rhythm, he knew many wouldn't call this salvation. But he did. Because the shattered glory he felt was the closest thing to pure he'd ever had.

And he reveled in it. Needed it.

She flexed her hips and rode him like an expert, and he was enrapt as he watched her. Watched her take her pleasure, watched her give pleasure to him. Her head thrown back, her breasts arched forward, the burgeoning evidence of her pregnancy echoing with deep, primal satisfaction inside him.

And when she came apart in his arms, her orgasm making her shiver and shake, he couldn't hold back anymore. He gripped her hips, pounding his need into a body that felt created for it. Created for him. Until the rush of release roared through him.

Then she collapsed over him, her hair falling over them like a curtain, her heart pounding fast against his.

"Creed," she whispered. "I love you."

She could feel it, the tightening of his muscles, the resistance in his body. What she'd said was the last thing he wanted to hear.

He wasn't happy to hear her say the words at all.

It was what she had been afraid of, except worse.

Because she had hoped… She had hoped that even if he wasn't going to say them back right away, he wouldn't resist them, or reject them.

That he would at least accept what she was offering freely, that he would let the words reach him, let the emotion touch him.

But the way those muscles went taut, it was like he had built a brick wall between the two of them.

A shouted rejection could not have been any louder.

With a firm grip, he set her away from him, putting her naked on his couch, the chill in the air feeling pronounced after she had been cradled so close to the warmth of his body only a moment before.

"It was a nice evening," he said. "Please don't spoil it."

"Oh," she said, feeling mutinous and angry. "Me being in love with you spoils the entire evening? Because I have news for you. I've been in love with you for longer than just tonight. It's only that tonight I realized just how deeply I felt about you."

"Wren, it's not the time."

"Why not? Why isn't it the time? We're married. We're having a baby."

"And I have a suspicion that you're trying to make a fairy tale out of all of this. And I get the appeal. Because you've been Rapunzel, locked away in a tower, and you seem to think I might be able to save you, or that I *did* save you. But that's not true. We're just two people who had unprotected sex. We have chemistry, or we wouldn't have done what we did in the first place. The first time I did it, I had the excuse of youth. But this time? You and I have something explosive. We both know that. We're not kids. We're not inexperienced. But because of our age, you should know that chemistry isn't love."

"Why would I know that?" she asked. "Why would I know that chemistry isn't love? I've been in a lot of relationships, and there was nothing like what we have. Shouldn't you want this? With the person you're going to spend the rest of your life with? Shouldn't chemistry be part of it? Maybe it's not love all on its own, but I think it definitely indicates we are the kind of people who could fall in love with each other. And I did. I don't need you to say you love me, I really don't. But I'd like it if you could take my words and at least…at least accept them. Let them sit inside you. See what they could heal. Creed, loving you has fixed so many things inside me. It's amazing. It's more than I ever expected. If you let it, love could heal you, too."

But she already knew he wasn't going to allow it to happen. Not here. Not now. She already knew he was going to say no, because refusal was written in every line of his body. And she knew him.

Knew him like she'd never known another person, and to an extent she had to wonder if she knew him so well because now she knew herself. Because of all that honesty.

She was really beginning to dislike honesty.

She was really beginning to resent this journey she'd gone on to peel back the layers of herself and expose everything she was. Not just to the world, but to herself.

Because one thing she hadn't appreciated about the life she'd had before all this was the protection she'd had. Because she had been able to hide in plain sight, and tell herself she was doing everything she needed to do, when in reality, following that prescribed path presented little to no risk at all.

And now, here she was, on the path she was blazing for herself, standing in front of a man and exposing the very deepest parts of herself.

It hurt.

It was hard.

And this was why Wren understood—without knowing any of the details—that her mother had chosen a safer life. The one with borders and boundaries and limits.

Because these feelings didn't have limits. And there was no guide for how to proceed.

Because Wren felt simultaneously the most and least like herself in this moment that she ever had.

This was bravery.

And she was leaning into it while he was running scared.

"I love you," she repeated. "Isn't that a good thing?"

"I don't want to hurt you," he said, his voice low. "God knows you've been through enough. But that's not what I was in this for. It's not."

"Me either. I didn't kiss you that day down in the wine cellar so I could fall in love with you. So I could marry you and have your baby. But here we are. This has been the strangest journey, and it was the one I needed. Because it *was* a journey to me, a journey to us. Because it was somehow absolutely everything we were ever going to be. It's all right here. You're the only person who has ever looked at me and asked what I wanted to be. And said that no matter what that turned out to be, you would support me…"

"That's not love," he said. "It's convenience. I want

access to my child, and I want the marriage to be mutually beneficial so you don't leave it."

"Well, your generosity created love in me. Love for myself and my life, and for you. I didn't know that I could love you. I *hated* you. And I realize now the reason I hated you so much was that you called to something in me I wasn't ready to reveal. I didn't want my life to change. And something in me knew that you could change it. Just by existing, you could change everything that I was. Everything that I am. That you would drag me out of my comfort zone. Out of my safety. I wasn't ready. So I fought you. I pushed back against you. Until I couldn't anymore. My life was at a crossroads that day. I felt like an alien in my hometown, an alien in my skin, and it wasn't until I gave in to you that things started to feel right."

"That's good," he said. "And that has to be enough."

"That's the problem," she said softly. "It's not. Because I realized something tonight when we were at the party. When everybody was at their stations with their husbands, and I had to make a choice. What family was I going to join? I realized that my place was beside you. But it's not because of a piece of paper, and it's not simply because I'm carrying your baby. It's because of love. And it's… I've been chasing that my whole life, Creed. I tried to be the best that I could be, but I was looking for love and acceptance from a man who could never give it. I made myself acceptable for my father, and I lost myself. And I can't hide what I am anymore. Who I am. What I feel. Least of all with you. Please don't ask me to go back to hiding."

"Wren," he said. "I can't love you."

"Can't? Or won't?"

"Something broke in me a long time ago," he said. "I failed. I failed at the most important thing a man can fail at. I'm not a father to my son. And I created an enemy to take the blame. I wanted to blame Louisa. But now I realize… I can't."

"Why not? Why can't you blame her, but you can blame yourself?"

"She must have known. She must've known that I wasn't going to do the job that Cal did. And she did what she had to do to protect her life, her child. But it was my responsibility to be better, to do more, and I couldn't. I didn't."

"Because of that you can't love me now?"

"I…"

"Will you love our baby? Or is what you feel for him or her all tied up in the boy you can't have? Because it seems to me that's awfully convenient. To have put all your emotions into something that you lost eighteen years ago. Of course you love your son. I understand that. It makes sense to me, even though you don't know him. I get it. I do. But at a certain point, you're just self-fulfilling a prophecy. You've decided that you'll fail the people who love you, and you've gone ahead and made sure you will by deciding you're not able to give again. You let that first loss decide how the rest of your life is going to go. Not just for you, but for me, for our baby."

"I want to be there," he said. "I want to take care of you both…"

"I grew up in a house that was quiet. That was half-muted with secrets and emotional distance. I have my sisters, and I love them dearly. But our parents… They didn't love each other. My father couldn't love anyone but himself. My mother is just defeated. I won't put our child in that place."

"I'm not your father," he said. "I would never hurt you. I would never hurt our child. I would never hurt another woman…"

"I know you aren't our father. But I still can't face a life without love. A house without love for me and for my baby. That kind of home was my whole existence before. You can't ask me to make it my life again. I finally found myself. All of myself. But I did that through loving you. And this woman I've become isn't going to accept less than I know that we can have. If I didn't think you could love me, then maybe I would take this. But the problem is… If I accept what you're offering now, then I'm going to be robbing us both, robbing our child. Of the life we can have, of the home we can have. Of everything we can build together."

"I gave you a house," he said. "I gave you vows. What more do you want from me?"

"Only everything," she said quietly. "Just everything that you are, everything that you ever will be. Your entire heart. That's all. And I'll give the same back, but you have to be willing to give to me. And if you can't, then… We'll share custody of the baby. I would never take this child from you." She paused, considering. "And you know what, if at this point you can't believe that I will keep my word about custody, then we really shouldn't be together."

"Wren," he growled.

He reached out and grabbed hold of her arm, pulled her to him, pressing her naked body against his. And then he kissed her. Deep and wild and hard.

But with fury.

Not love.

And she so desperately wanted his love.

Because she had come through the clearing, come through the fire, come through the storm. And she was willing to stand through it, whatever the risk.

And because she'd found a way to be brave and honest, she wanted him to do the same.

Because she loved him more than she had ever thought she hated him, and she desperately needed to know that he loved her, too.

She pulled away from him, even though it hurt. Pulled away from him, even though it felt like dying.

It would be easier to stay. Whether he ever said he loved her or not. It would be easier to just stay. But then he would still be in hiding.

And she would be out in the storm alone.

And he would never know…

He would never find this freedom that she'd found. The sharp, painful, beautiful freedom that made her all she was.

Love meant demanding more from him.

Love meant she had to push them both to be the best they could be. She could not allow him to hide, not allow him to remain damaged but protected.

She wanted him to feel whole in the same way that she felt now. Glued back together, those cracks glowing bright because they were pressed together by love.

"I need you to love me," she said. "I need you to find a way. And if it takes years, I'll still be here waiting for you. But I won't live halfway. I won't live in a house with you without love. I won't share your bed without love. I won't take your name without love."

"You're ruining us," he ground out. "Over nothing."

"No, over everything. And as long as you think it's nothing, that difference is not something we can ignore."

Her dreams started to crack in front of her like a sheet of ice. Dreams of a shared life. A shared Christmas. Those Christmases she thought they might have here in this house, starting with this one.

But it was gone now.

Hope.

She whispered that word to herself.

Just keep your hope.

Wren collected her clothes and dressed slowly.

"Your car isn't even here," he said.

"No," she said. "I know. But my sister will come and get me." She stopped. "If you can't fight me now as hard as you did over the winery business, then... I don't know, Creed. I just don't know."

She went outside then. And it wasn't Emerson who ultimately came to get her, but Cricket.

"What happened?" Cricket asked.

"Oh, my heart is only broken," Wren said, pressing her face against the glass in the car.

"Why did you marry a man you hate?"

"Because I never really hated him. I was just afraid of loving him." She sighed heavily. "Because loving him hurts. Really badly."

"That's stupid," Cricket said. "Love isn't supposed to feel like that. It's not supposed to be that close to... this. All these bad feelings."

"The problem is," Wren said slowly, "when someone has been hurt, it's not that simple. And he's been hurt really badly."

"Well, now he's passed it on to you. And I don't think I can forgive him for that."

"I can," Wren said. "If he wants me to."

Cricket scoffed. "Why would you?"

"Because some people are like Dad," Wren said. "They're toxic. They don't love people because they are too busy loving themselves. But some people are wounded. Creed is wounded. What he has to decide is if he wants to stay that way. Or if he's going to let himself be whole."

"It all sounds overrated to me."

Wren thought back to the last few months, the journey that she'd been on, the one that had ultimately led here, which was so very painful. And she realized she would do it all again. Every time. Exactly the same.

Because however it came out in the end, it had led her to this place, where she had decided to be brave and honest. Where she had decided to heal regardless of what he chose to do.

"Someday you'll understand."

"No. I'm not interested in that kind of thing. And when I am, I'm going to choose a nice man who has nothing to do with any of this."

"With any of what?"

"I want to leave the vineyard," Cricket said. "I realize this isn't the best timing. But I want to tell you… I want my own life. One that's totally different from this. I never wanted to be here. Mom and Dad never cared about what I did and…"

"I think Mom does care," Wren said softly. "But I think, like Creed, she's wounded. And sometimes she doesn't know how to show it."

"I'm not wounded," Cricket said, defiant. "I'm going to find a place with people who aren't. Present company excluded. It has nothing to do with you and Emerson. I might want a ranch. I want you to buy out my share."

Disappointment churned in Wren's chest. The idea of Cricket leaving the winery was painful. Another loss, but...

Her sister needed her chance. Her chance to find herself, like Wren had found herself.

"It's okay, Cricket. You have to find a place that makes you happy. You have to find your path."

Privately, Wren knew that it wouldn't be as smooth as her sister was imagining. But she also knew Cricket would have to find it for herself. And maybe... Maybe Cricket would find a nice, simple relationship. An easy kind of love. But somehow Wren doubted it. Because Cricket was too tough and spiky to accept anyone soft. To accept anything less than the kind of love that moved mountains inside her.

And that kind of love didn't come easy.

But if Cricket needed to believe she could find a love that *did* come easy, then Wren wasn't going to disabuse her of the notion.

Because just like Wren's own situation, no one could do it for Cricket. She would have to fight her way through on her own.

"And what's your ideal man?"

"One who isn't half as much cowboy drama as yours and Emerson's dudes. I'm going to get a job at Sugar Cup. I've already decided. I'm going to serve coffee while I build my ranching empire. And I'll meet a nice guy."

"I didn't think you were interested in meeting anybody."

"I'm not," Cricket said.

"So there's nobody in particular that you like?"

"We shouldn't be talking about me."

"I prefer it to thinking about myself," Wren said.

"No," Cricket said. And she sounded so resolute that Wren wondered if she was lying. "I think love should make you feel sweet and floaty. I don't think that crushes should make you angry."

"Oh," Wren said. "Sure."

Sweet summer child.

But again, her sister was going to have to figure all this out for herself. Just like Wren had.

And honestly, even though Wren felt like she had figured a lot out in the last few months, she also didn't know how her story was going to end.

But she supposed that was the real gift. She had learned, through this series of changes, that while chapters of one's life would come to a close, there was always a chance to make herself new. To make her life into the best version that she could.

And she would carry that hope with her.

As long as she was here, she would have a chance to change for the better. The hope of better was what made one brave. It was what made everything worth it. And so, she would continue to hope, no matter how dark it seemed.

If that realization and her baby were the only gifts she could ever get from Creed, then she supposed they would have to be enough.

Twelve

"All right," his brother's voice came behind him. Creed braced himself for what would come next. "What the hell is the matter with you?"

He turned toward Jackson and scowled. "What's it to you?"

"Plenty. Because it's beginning to impact on my life, and I don't like that. You've been scowling around here for more than a week. It's a pain in my ass. Does it have something to do with your wife?"

He gritted his teeth. "She left me."

"What the hell did you do?"

"It's complicated."

"Try me."

"She said she loved me."

Jackson made a choking sound. "What a travesty. Your wife is in love with you. However will you survive?"

"That's not what this was supposed to be about."

"Oh, your marriage isn't supposed to be about love? What the hell is it supposed to be about, then?"

"I told you. It's complicated."

"I'm all ears."

"And why exactly do you think you're an authority on any of this? It's not like you've ever been in a real relationship."

"Maybe I'm not an authority on relationships, but I'm an authority on you. And you're miserable. Which means you need to sort it out."

"There's nothing to sort out. Nothing changed on my end. I offered her everything that was always on the table. I bought her the house she wanted, I told her she could do whatever she wanted when it came to work, and we set fire to the sheets. I don't know why the hell she thinks she needs more."

"It's this weird thing where people tend to want to be loved. Weird, I know. Especially since it's never been a major priority for either of us. But I think maybe it's not astonishingly strange."

"I don't understand why she needs it."

"I don't understand why it's a problem for you. Hell, you seem like you're in love with her."

"It's impossible. I can't do that. I already… Look, I wasted all my emotion. I can't love her."

"You can't? Or you won't?"

"She asked me the same question. But it amounts to the same thing."

"What's the real problem here? Because I don't get your resistance to this."

"The problem is that I didn't… I didn't get to love my son the way that I was supposed to. So now I'm just supposed to move on? Just make a new family, make a new life? I thought I could. For a little while, I thought I could. But I can't. It's wrong. I can't just decide to get a do-over. I wanted to, but it's killing me. The guilt of it."

His brother just stared at him. "What do you mean you didn't love your son? It wasn't your choice not to be with him. Not to be around him. Louisa chose that for you."

"I could've fought harder. I've seen him around."

"Yeah. And you loved him enough that you didn't go crashing into his life and make it about you. You loved him enough that you let him have the family that he knows. Loving somebody doesn't just mean being in their lives every day. And I never would've thought of that if it weren't for you. But I've never doubted that you love that kid. Because I saw what it did to you all those years ago. It tore you up. But you had to make a choice not to make his life a war zone, and you made that choice. And every time you've ever seen him at an event, including the one a few months ago, you've made the choice to put his happiness above your own. That is love, Creed."

"It hurts," Creed growled.

"No one ever said love didn't hurt. Hurt makes sense. But not guilt. You've got nothing to feel guilty for."

The problem was, his brother's words rang true.

And if there was no guilt… Then there was nothing standing in his way. It was all a matter of being brave enough to step forward. Brave enough to allow Wren to have all of him.

Even though his emotions had been savaged, his heart torn to pieces.

He didn't know if he was brave enough.

But what's the alternative?

Another life spent with so much distance between himself and the people who held his heart.

No, he'd never gotten a chance to be a father before. Not in the way he wanted to be.

But he had the chance now. And not just to be a father, but to be a husband.

It was all well and good to fantasize about how well he'd do those things, but entirely different to take the steps toward *being* those things.

"It's terrifying," he said. "I've been so certain all these years that I would've been great at this, but… What if I'm not?"

"Well, then you're not. That's just part of life. Sometimes you're bad at something, and then you learn to be better at it. Was Dad perfect?"

"Hell no," Creed said. "He's still not."

"Do you love him?"

"Of course I do."

"Well, there's your answer. Did you need perfect, or did you need a father?"

"I'm going to be there for my kid, it's just…"

"Remember what Dad said? That he loved a woman who chose easy over him? That leaves scars. Are you going to leave Wren with those kinds of scars? Are you gonna leave yourself with them?"

"There's no easy answer, is there? There's no pain-proof way to do this."

"No. Life is tough. Nobody gets out alive."

Creed didn't like that reasoning. At all. He also couldn't argue with it.

Because that was just it. There were no guarantees. He just had to be brave.

And with sudden, stark clarity, he saw Wren as she had been. Standing there open and vulnerable and naked. Beautiful, demanding that he love her. And he realized that he'd failed her. He'd been a coward. An absolute, complete coward.

She had been so brave, after the betrayals she had experienced in her life. And he was... He was hiding behind his own hurt. Using his pain to shield him from more pain.

But it wasn't going to work. And in the end, it wasn't worth it. How could he choose safety at the cost of what could be the greatest joy he would ever experience?

He was hit with a blinding flash of truth.

If you wanted to have everything life could offer, you also had to risk your heart.

Just like Wren had said.

She wanted only everything.

And nothing else would do.

He understood that now.

Everything was the only answer. Everything was the least he could offer.

"I have to go talk to her," he said, his voice rough.

"Yeah," Jackson replied. "You do."

"I'll return the favor when you're in the same position."

"I won't be," Jackson said, chuckling, the sound sharpened by an edge that surprised Creed. "I'm happy for you. It's plain to anyone looking at you that you love her. And that you ought to be with her."

"I hope so."

She'd said she would wait. She'd said he could change his heart.

But he wondered. And he almost wouldn't blame her

if she wasn't waiting. Because she had stripped herself bare, and he had offered her nothing.

He had rejected her.

"I just have to hope that she'll still have me."

Wren was wretched, and no amount of trying to ensure herself that standing in her truth, standing strong in what she needed, was making her feel any better.

Emerson was deeply sympathetic, having been through something similar with Holden. Cricket seemed like she didn't know what to do with her.

And a surprising source of support and sympathy came from her mother.

"I know it's hard to believe," she said, "but I know what it's like to have a broken heart."

"You're going through a divorce," Wren said. "I don't think it's hard to believe."

"Not your father. My heart broke slowly over the choices I made, but he didn't break it. I was in love once. And I'm the one who walked away from it. It makes such a deep scar. I hope Creed realizes it before it's too late. Because you can't protect yourself by turning away from love. You just sign yourself up for a life of…less."

"That's why I left… I wanted him to love me. To find it in himself to admit that he does. Because if he can't find it in himself to admit it, then the alternative would be something terribly sad."

"It is," her mother said. "Believe me. And it's taken me years to get to a place I could have been in a long time ago if I had just done the work on myself back then. But instead I hid. I hid in a marriage that didn't have love. I hid behind money. I hid here in this house, because it was what I chose. Status. Wealth."

"Mom," Wren said slowly. "Were you in love with Law Cooper?"

But she didn't get a chance to hear the answer because Cricket came running into the room. "I told him to go away," she said fiercely.

"What?"

"Your husband," her sister said, her lip curled. "I told him to go away. But he's still here."

"Oh," Wren said, springing out of her chair and bounding toward the door.

"Forget about him," Cricket said. "He's not worth it."

"He is," Wren said. "And when you're in love you'll understand."

And there he was, standing in the entry of their grand home, looking out of place in his blue jeans, T-shirt and cowboy hat, his face bearing the marks of exhaustion, of sadness.

"You look like I feel," Wren said, staring at him.

"I feel like hell," he said. "It's been...the worst week of my life."

"Mine, too."

"Wren," he said. "I'm so sorry. I thought... I was so comfortable punishing myself for what happened with... Lucas. My son's name is Lucas. And I don't know him. And I've used that pain to drive me. I told myself all the things I would have done differently for him. And I made myself feel confident in this hypothetical version of me. And at the same time, I used the guilt to keep me safe. To convince myself that I never had to love again, because I had already loved and lost it. But I was just using that guilt to protect myself. Because it was easier than maybe being hurt again.

"I never loved Louisa," he said. "But what she told

me was that I might not be good enough, and I let that sit inside me. But I want to be good enough. For you. I want to be everything for you."

"Creed," she said. "What you did for me… You brought me on a journey to myself. And it was the thing I needed most, when I needed it most. I spent my life protecting myself, so I understand how compelling that is. I know what it is to live your life feeling like you might not be enough. But we were just trying to be enough for the wrong people. When we're already more than perfect for each other."

"Wren," he said, his voice rough. "I love you."

"I love you, too," she said, flinging herself into his arms and kissing him with everything in her heart. "I love you so much."

"This isn't just a second chance," he said, putting his hand on her stomach. "It's our chance. And I'm so damn grateful."

"Me, too."

Wren Maxfield loved Creed Cooper more than anything. He was a cocky, arrogant pain in the butt, and he was hers. And suddenly, even with all the twists and turns in the road to get here, Wren knew she was living her life, the best life.

She knew who she was.

She was Creed's and he was hers.

And nothing could ever be better than that.

Epilogue

Creed was the proudest father around. Matched only by how proud of a husband he was.

He loved watching his son grow, and he loved watching Wren learn, as she went through the process of getting her degree so she could become an architectural engineer.

The people he was blessed to love astounded him in every way.

He astounded himself, because he never really imagined he would enjoy a one-year-old's birthday party. But he did. It had been the best day, down to watching his son's pudgy little fingers smash the cake they'd had made especially for that purpose.

His fascination a few months earlier with their Christmas tree—fake because Wren wanted a very particular spectacle, and Mac would eat fallen pine needles—had been just as cute. Though they'd had to anchor it to a wall so he didn't pull it down on himself.

But it was the knock on the door after the birthday party that led to the most unexpected thing of all.

Wren was the one who answered it. And she came running to him, where he was sitting on the floor with Mac, only a few moments later.

"Creed. You need to come here." Wren swooped down and picked up Mac, and then stepped back as Creed made his way to the door.

Standing there, outside, was his oldest son.

"You don't know me," the kid said. "But… My mom told me the whole story. Everything, a few months ago. And she said what I did with it was up to me, but… I thought it was time I came to meet you."

Creed's heart slowed as Lucas looked past him. The color drained from the kid's face. "Oh, I hope I didn't cause any problems."

"No," Creed said. "You didn't. I just… I never wanted to go crashing into your life and cause any problems for you. But there's always been a place for you in my life. And there always will be."

"I guess my dad always knew," Lucas said. "You know. My…"

"He's your dad," Creed said. "He's the one who raised you. But I'd like the chance to be something to you."

Because that's what love did. It grew, it expanded, it changed. And it left no room for resentment.

And Creed was damned thankful that he had a woman who understood that. Because Wren accepted Lucas into their lives with as much ease as he could have asked from her.

And sometime down the road he realized it wasn't love that caused hurt. It was fear.

And his family made a rule not to operate from fear. But just to grow from love.

And that was what they did. From then, until forever. They just loved.

And they were happy.

* * * * *

IN BED WITH
HIS RIVAL

KATHERINE GARBERA

Shout-out to Texas ladies!
Penni Askew, who welcomed me to Texas
when I moved there so long ago.
Kim Gammill and Kathy Ranney,
who were my mom buddies and friends
when I needed one. Eve Gaddy,
who is my soul sister.

One

Piper Holloway loved a wedding. Who didn't? They were joyous events.

Her niece Harley and Grant Everett had waited a long time for their happily ever after. Piper didn't begrudge them their wedded bliss, but a part of her wished she wasn't going stag to all of their festivities.

These happy-couple kind of events always made her reevaluate her life choices, even though she was perfectly content as a single woman. She had her art, which was way more reliable than a man, and a thriving—well *previously* thriving—business. Though she had never had any stake in Wingate Enterprises, many people suspected she might be part of its allegedly shady business dealings, and her clientele was down recently.

But none of that mattered. She was here to celebrate

her niece's wedding day and support her sister, Ava, who'd recently gone through a really tough decision to move out of Keith's house and set up her own residence. Standing on her own after the death of her husband had been a struggle for Ava and she'd leaned on her good friend Keith until she'd realized he wanted a romantic relationship with her. Now, they all needed a fun day.

It was a gorgeous November Saturday in Royal, Texas. As much as Piper loved living in Dallas, there were times when she truly missed Royal, though she had been home a lot recently as her sister and family navigated their way through their business scandal. Of course, she didn't miss the gossips who'd been making her family's life a living hell since the drug-trafficking scandal had broken.

All of the Wingate assets had been frozen and their home seized. Harley wasn't able to be married on the Wingate estate, which Piper knew had been a dream of hers. But Grant's family's ranch was perfect for the small wedding celebration. It was mainly family and friends—those who had stuck by the Wingates and Holloways through thick and thin.

The Everett ranch was large and sprawling, and the grounds were decked out for the wedding, which had been beautiful. Harley was big into the environment and her choice of venue reflected that. Therefore, it seemed apt that she and Grant had decided to be married in the old barn, which had been decorated under the supervision of her older sister, Beth. The chairs were lined up, and despite the fact that the Wingates were no longer the favored family in Royal, there was a nice intimate group of attendees.

Everyone was happy that "Uncle" Keith wasn't in attendance today, mainly because of how that would have affected Ava. Piper's sister was still dealing with the heartbreak of losing her beloved husband a little over a two years ago and no one had approved of Keith's interest in her. Piper had kept her mouth shut because she didn't like to fight with Ava, especially over men, but it had seemed to her that Keith had been a little too overprotective of Ava. Her spunky sister had become a shell of the woman she had once been.

Right now Ava looked gorgeous in her mother-of-the-bride dress, but she seemed tired and thinly drawn. Moving out of Keith's house had only been the first step to Ava taking back her own life. Piper thought that Ava was finally getting past the crippling grief. Though Piper would never say it to her, the events of the last few months had certainly taken a toll on the Wingate matriarch. Ava was nineteen years older, and Piper had always craved her sister's attention and approval.

"What's that you're wearing?" Ava asked, coming up behind her. "Even though the wedding is small, you could have made more of an effort."

Piper turned to face her sister, biting her tongue as she always did. Ava was in a mood and Piper was giving her a little leeway, given that she'd lost her home, her husband and was on the verge of losing her company, as well.

"It's a designer Grecian gown," Piper said, air kissing her sister's cheeks. "I thought it would be perfect for this occasion and when I texted Harley, she said it was fine. Have you heard any news on the investigation?"

"No. I believe Miles is getting closer but there is still nothing but rumors," Ava replied.

"Do they have any suspects?" Piper asked. She wasn't too close to the business side of things, but she knew that Ava was trying to get back into running the company so she would have something to do. But now, with the precarious state of affairs, those plans were up in the air.

"Yes, but I can't really share that with you," Ava told her in a terse tone. "I know you've never been married, but this really isn't the kind of conversation anyone wants to overhear on their wedding day."

"Of course, Ava. I see Zeke and Reagan waving me over. I'll catch up with you later. I'm sure you need to circulate as the mother of the bride, especially since Trent is not here."

Trent Wingate's death had left a hole in all of their lives, and Piper knew that Harley missed her beloved father terribly. She'd escaped to Thailand to start her own business, which was thriving now.

Piper knew her words hadn't been nice, but her sister had a way of making her react like a…bitch. She turned, thinking she should apologize, but Ava had already moved away. There were times when she wondered if anyone could melt the ice around her sister's heart. Piper didn't want to impose on her nephew and his new wife, so she drifted toward the bar.

"Buy you a drink?" a man asked. His voice was dark, sexy and straight out of dreams that she channeled into her art.

She turned to see Brian Cooper standing behind her. He was tall, over six feet, and had thick, close-cut black hair that made his face seem all strong, masculine angles. He had an easy smile and his eyes beamed with intelligence. He'd asked her to coffee more than once and she'd always said no.

He ticked a lot of her boxes. Whip smart with oodles of charisma…and the innate ability to make her forget things that she shouldn't. She really believed in the adage *older and wiser*. Which was why she had decided to stay away from him.

But it wasn't just the age difference—she was nearly eleven years older—but also the fact that he was Keith Cooper's nephew. Keith had gone from being a family friend to Ava's overprotective friend, and that complicated things. Piper preferred to keep things simple. It just was easier.

"It's an open bar," she pointed out.

He waggled his eyebrows at her. "I know. Figured this way you wouldn't say no."

He was effortlessly charming with the kind of square jaw and impish grin that made her pulse beat a little bit faster. She'd tried to be subtle when she turned him down, but as she'd already observed, Brian was a very smart man. "I'd love tequila straight. But Ava would have a fit if I had one, so sauvignon blanc please."

"Do you always do what Ava wants?" he asked. "She has so much power over everyone in her circle."

"Even your uncle," she pointed out. Keith had been rumored to be taking Ava's decision to distance herself from him without grace.

"Yeah, I guess. I don't really see that much of him normally. I have been busy opening my own law firm in Dallas," he said, then he groaned. "Did I really just say that out loud?"

She had to laugh at the way he said it. "Yes, you did."

"I wasn't bragging. I was just trying—"

"It's okay. What do you want to drink?" she asked as they moved forward and were next in line at the bar.

"Grey Goose on the rocks," he said.

"Damn. Now I'm beginning to rethink my promise to be classy and have white wine," she lamented.

"Why not just be yourself and have what you want?" he asked. "But then again, I'm not related to Ava Wingate…"

Piper appreciated Brian's acknowledgement of that, and yet at the same time, he reminded her that it had been far too long since she'd just let go and been herself. That thought was at the top of her mind as she stepped forward and ordered their drinks, getting the tequila for herself.

She turned to Brian and handed him his glass as they walked away from the bar toward the side of the dance floor. The band was playing and couples moved to the music, but they stood far enough away that they could still hear each other.

"I think I am a bad influence," Brian remarked. "But I don't regret it. Cheers."

"Cheers," Piper said, clinking her glass to his. Although she didn't comment on his admission, she had to admit the tequila tasted *way* better than a glass of wine would have. And truth be told? She felt like herself instead of the perfect sister she tried to be every time she arrived back in Royal. Piper hated that she was forty and still trying to get Ava's approval.

"You just reminded me it's okay to have fun," she said. "I am a little disappointed that I needed that, but I'm glad you did."

Brian enjoyed the vodka but sipped it slowly. It seemed like forever, but in reality, it had only been a few months since he'd first noticed Piper Holloway. She had a cool, funky aura and of course she was so damned hot. He wanted her. She plagued his dreams and left him waking up with a hard-on, and if he was being honest, he'd thought he was way past those days.

He'd asked other women out and taken them home, but no one could satisfy that Piper-sized ache in his gut. He was pretty sure it was just lust and the more she turned him down, the more determined he was to have her.

Possibly he was wrong and the sizzle between them would fade out after they had a drink. His intuition said that would never happen and it rarely steered him wrong. But Piper had been pretty hard to reel in, no matter what he tried.

Was it pride?

He hoped it was something more than that, but as he stood next to her sipping vodka and finally having the conversation he wanted, he didn't care.

They really didn't have much in common—after all, she was a free-spirited artist and he was a high-powered family law attorney—but there was something to be said about opposites attracting...

His eyes slowly drifted over her again.

Piper had a creative vibe, from the way she wore her hair—this month colored dark brown—in an angled bob that was longer in the front than the back, to her Grecian-styled gown in a vibrant sapphire color with a plunging neckline that revealed the inner curves of her luscious breasts.

She was tall, at least five-seven, but she wore heels, giving herself another couple of inches and making it so they came eye to eye. He watched as she savored the tequila, closing her eyes when she took a sip. There was something wildly erotic about the way she drank it, and he knew he needed to play it cool, but he couldn't help but think of throwing back shots with her alone in his place.

God, he could picture her standing next to him in nothing. Hell…just the thought made him rock hard. Earthy and sensual, a bona fide modern goddess, and even though his family and hers had grown apart, he couldn't care less.

"I stopped by your gallery a few weeks ago but you weren't there," Brian said, realizing he needed to up his game around this woman. First, he'd sounded like a braggart talking about his law firm and now this clumsy conversational gambit.

"I was out of town," she replied. "I didn't know you were coming by."

"Of course… I guess I should have called first."

"That's always a good idea," she said.

"But you haven't always been receptive to meeting me," he reminded her. "I did ask you out for coffee at Zeke's."

She flushed and tipped her head to the side. "To be honest, I wasn't sure of you. I don't really like the influence Keith had over my sister after Trent's death. I wasn't sure you weren't the same kind of man."

That was a blow, but not unexpected. She was cautious and he guessed he didn't blame her. While their families weren't the Capulets and the Montagues, they also weren't close as they'd once been, before Trent's death. Brian's friendship with Zeke had made him aware that Ava's family wasn't overly fond of his uncle. And in all honesty, he had thought it a little unseemly how quickly Keith had moved in on Ava after Trent's death. But Ava had seemed to need someone to lean on.

"Fair enough. I'm not my uncle, but I can understand where you are coming from," he said.

"Thanks," she said dryly.

He groaned and realized he either needed more vodka or just to stop talking. The music changed to one of those group dances, the Electric Slide, and Piper looked over at him. "I love this song. Want to dance?"

"I can't dance," he confessed.

"Catch you later then," she said, handing him her empty tequila glass and making her way out onto the dance floor. He stood there, watching her move. There was a smile on her face that lit up the entire room. She moved with lithe, graceful steps, holding the hand of her great-nephew, Daniel, and showing him the moves.

"Dude, why are you standing here instead of dancing with the woman you've been trying to get with for months?" Zeke asked him.

"I can't dance," he repeated to his friend. "It's a disaster and I pretty much haven't been very articulate with Piper tonight, so I don't think I need another strike against me."

His friend just shook his head. "The Electric Slide isn't my thing either, but if your lady wants to be on the dance floor, then that's where you should be."

"She's not my lady," Brian grumbled.

"She never will be if you stand here like a doofus," Zeke pointed out. He left to find Reagan, and a few minutes later Brian saw the two of them dancing along with everyone else.

Brian had never let anything stand in the way of what he wanted and he certainly wasn't about to be defeated by this dance. He finished his vodka in one long swallow, put the empty glasses on the tray of a passing waiter and went for it.

He joined the group on the dance floor next to Daniel. "Hey, can you help me figure this out?"

"Sure can," the four-year-old said. Then Daniel started calling out the steps, and to Brian's surprise, it was actually fun.

Piper looked over at him, laughing when he and Daniel went the wrong way and almost crashed into the line behind them. Finally, the music ended, and Brian stooped down to thank Daniel. The little boy was very happy that he had a starring role in the day's events as his parents had been married. He looked adorable in his tux, cowboy boots and Stetson.

"You really helped me out. I owe you, buddy," Brian said.

"I like jelly beans," Daniel returned with a grin.

"I'll remember that." The music changed to a slower song, and Brian looked over at Piper. "Dance with me?"

"I'd say no, but you really put yourself out there with

the Slide," she said, taking his hand and coming into his arms.

A tingle went through him, and his blood seemed to run heavier in his veins. More than anything, he wanted to take her back to his place here in Royal, but that felt like it might be too fast for this woman who he'd barely been able to get to have a drink with him. Was he coming on too strong? Hell, he didn't know another way to be when he wanted something.

And he definitely wanted Piper in his bed.

But if he'd learned anything from this woman today, it was that she was skittish.

Building trust took time, and Brian had never been long on patience, but for Piper he was willing to be. He wanted to explore his attraction for her and wouldn't let anything stand in his way.

And the attraction that burned between the two of them might be setting him on fire but he wanted to stoke the flames, not just let it go wild and leave nothing but ashes and smoke.

Piper wanted to pretend that she wasn't interested in Brian Cooper, but after spending some time on the dance floor in his arms she knew that was a lie. The large tent that had been erected in the yard of the Everett ranch had sparkling lights draped around the interior and large portable heaters dotted around the area to keep the November chill away. The reception was full of people she'd known her entire life, but after the scandal that her family had been through lately, Piper realized these were the people who mattered. The ones who'd stood by the Wingates and hadn't abandoned them.

Brian was one of those men. He'd helped Zeke and Reagan out—her nephew had told her how much it had meant to them. And, of course, there was this crazy sexual attraction between her and Brian. It had been there since the moment they'd met but she'd done her best to ignore it. That kind of passion she reserved for her art. It was safer that way. She just had never been an all-or-nothing kind of woman when it came to her desires, and with Brian it felt dangerous to let go.

Though with his hand on her back and her breasts brushing his chest as they danced, she was sorely tempted to throw caution to the wind. There was something...*electric*...in the way he touched her, and despite what he'd said about not dancing, he wasn't half bad, swaying to the beat.

She started to feel restless. Usually she didn't feel it in Dallas because she had her routines and her normal life. But here in Royal, when everything was in chaos with her family, it felt like things were changing... Maybe she was too. Starting with when she had ordered that tequila. She'd spent too long trying to be part of the society that Ava always urged her to conform to. Now she was on the edge, ready to do something reckless...

But, as attracted as she was to him, she knew that Brian wasn't the man for her.

He was a family friend. More so than "Uncle" Keith, who Piper's nieces and nephews didn't trust after the way he'd muscled his way into Ava's life after the death of their father. Should she be equally careful of Brian...?

"Another drink?" he asked when the song ended.

"That'd be great," she said.

"Piper, do you have a minute?" Lauren Roberts asked, coming over to her.

"Go on. I'll get our drinks and come find you," Brian said. He turned to walk away, and she watched him go, admiring the cut of his suit.

Down, girl.

"What can I help you with?" Piper asked, pivoting toward Lauren. The brunette beauty was known around Royal for her fabulous food trucks, and her assistant had mentioned Lauren was going to be opening a restaurant soon.

"I was in your gallery while you were out of town and saw a number of pieces I really liked. Your assistant said that it would be better to talk to you so that you'd have a feel for what I really wanted," Lauren said. "I know a wedding reception isn't the ideal place to chat, but I was hoping to catch you so I wouldn't have to go back to Dallas next week. Do you mind?"

Piper shook her head. "No, of course not. I love talking about art, and finding pieces that suit your new restaurant sounds like a fun project. I think someone had mentioned it was going to be a farm-to-table one?"

"Yes. I really want to be as local as I can with the sourcing of the food," the other woman said.

"I think the art should be from the area too," Piper mused, thinking out loud. "I have a few colleagues that I can reach out to in order to find some local artists. Are you looking for paintings or photography?"

"I just want really good stuff on the walls so people will feel like they are in a nice place," Lauren said.

Piper laughed. "So, you're saying you'll know what you want when you see it?"

"Yes. Also Gracie Diaz is investing in my business so she'll be helping me make the choices."

"Okay, let me look around and see what I can find. I'll send some images to the two of you and you can narrow down what you like. Then we can go forward from there. How does that sound?" Piper asked.

"Perfect. Thank you," Lauren said. "I know it's not my business...but are you seeing Brian?"

"No. We're just hanging out together. I guess he didn't bring a date either," Piper said.

"That's good," Lauren said. "I'm sure he's not anything like Keith. I know Sutton thinks he seems like a good guy."

Seemed like a good guy.

"Great," Piper said.

"What's great?" Brian asked, handing her a glass of tequila as Lauren turned to leave.

"The reception," Lauren said, walking away.

"It is nice," Brian told Piper. "I really like that Harley and Grant found each other and that they are going to go back to Thailand. There was a time when everyone would have expected her to give up her life and move back here."

"Not that long ago," Piper said. "Grant's a great guy. I think that even though times have changed, some men still wouldn't follow their woman."

Brian took a sip of his vodka and rubbed the back of his neck. "I'm not sure I'd leave the country, but I who am I to judge someone else?"

"Right. Everyone makes the choices that work for them," Piper concurred.

Watching her niece, she was happy for Harley but another part of her was…leery. Piper had once come close to believing she'd found someone she could share her life with, but she hadn't measured up to his version of perfection and he'd left. And although it had stung for a time, life hadn't ended. She was old enough to know she didn't need a man by her side to complete her. But spending the reception with Brian…exploring the spark of sensuality he'd lit in her…had shown her that she had missed the companionship of having a partner. Not that Brian would be her partner, but maybe it was time for her to start looking again.

She had been put off dating after her bad breakup and watching Ava's marriage to Trent as his health deteriorated. But her nieces and nephews were all finding love and that made her long for something to help fill the void.

That said, she would never try to change for a man again. And she'd never be with a guy she couldn't trust. But laughing and talking with Brian had reminded her of how much she'd shut herself off from relationships. Maybe it was fear or something else that had kept her away, but it was time to stop it.

She turned her attention to the coming week. She was looking forward to getting back to Dallas. Even though he had a law firm in the big D, he wasn't part of her circle. Once she was home, she'd be away from the confusion and desire that Brian was stirring in her.

Two

The Dallas art district was downtown in the city's cultural hub. The strikingly angular Meyerson Symphony Center and the lavish Winspear Opera House gave the area its grounding. Piper's gallery was close to the Nasher Sculpture Center with its exhibits of modern masterpieces in a verdant setting. She had worked hard to be able to have her gallery in the art district instead of on the outskirts of town, but it was important for her clients to know that she was a respectable art dealer. Today she'd started her morning walking through the Crow Collection of Asian Art displays. Sometimes she needed to recharge her inner artist. Especially now.

Wednesdays had traditionally been when she did her accounting and read the reports her accountant sent over. But since the trouble with the Wingate company started and the scandal had broken there had been a steady decline in profits. And if the black-and-white numbers in front of her weren't enough evidence, she also had realized that the gallery crowds were thinner. She could blame the economy, but the truth was no one wanted to be associated with someone—even on the fringes—who'd had assets seized by the DEA.

She'd had one client even go so far as to ask if she could provide proof of her due diligence on the provenance for a painting that they'd purchased almost five years ago. She'd done it, but it had ticked her off because she had never taken a penny of Wingate money and she'd always run her gallery with a strong moral and ethical code. But she couldn't fight whispers, and if she was going to be painted with the same brush as her sister and nieces and nephews, she was going to have to look at a way to expand her business. Find a new revenue stream.

"Hey, boss, here's your chai latte," Coco said, coming in and dropping it on her desk. "Also, Gracie Diaz called a few minutes ago and asked if you had time to see her this afternoon."

"Thanks for the latte," Piper said. "I believe my afternoon is open. I already pulled some slides. Would you mind assembling them in viewing room A?"

"Not at all. And I'll arrange a time with Gracie and put it on your calendar. Also, we've had a few requests for commission work. I know you have the gala piece going up next week. Are you interested?"

"Probably," Piper said. "You know how busy the holiday season can be. We need to also see about renting out the space at night for office parties like we did last year."

Coco sat down in the guest chair and propped her combat-booted feet on the corner of Piper's desk. "I've already started. I have three parties lined up so far and I've got two more who should get back to me next week. One client wondered if we could hang something modern, similar to the party in that *Love Actually* movie. I told them we'd see. We do have those nudes from Maxi that seemed like they might work."

"I like that idea. I'll go over to the warehouse later this week and see what we have. Put on your event planner hat and see if we can do something more with this concept. We need to make a push through the holidays to drive revenue."

"No problem, boss," Coco said.

One of her other assistants—Paul—came to her door. "There's a Brian Cooper here to see you."

"He's been here before," Coco murmured. "Kind of cute, easy smile, nice ass. Want me to talk to him for you?"

"I've got it. Get to work on those paintings for Gracie and get that firmed up. Paul, Coco's going to need your help with a themed office party," Piper said, leaving her assistants and heading out onto the balcony where all of the offices were.

She looked down onto the main gallery floor where Brian was easy to spot. He stood in front of a kinetic wire sculpture she'd collaborated with a local spoken-word poet to create. It was called *The Border* and spoke directly about Xavier's struggle to stay on the right side of the law. The sculpture was one body but two faces looking in different directions. One contemplative, the other angry. In one hand was a notepad and pen, in the other, a gun. She was proud of it but she saw the parts she could still improve. For instance, the angle of the jaw on one side was sharper than the other.

As much as she loved creating, there was also a part of her that hated it. Seeing the image in her head and then witnessing how close she got to it, without ever quite reaching it, was a constant struggle.

She tucked a strand of hair behind her ear and shook off that mood as she approached Brian. He wore a suit that was cut to fit his broad shoulders and tapered to his narrow waist sending a sensual thrill through her.

"Hello, Brian. I wasn't expecting to see you today," she said,

He turned to face her with a good-natured smile, drawing her gaze to his mouth. He had full, chiseled lips that looked like they were made for kissing. She should have kissed him on Saturday at the reception so she'd have that out of the way. Instead she was staring and wondering how his firm mouth would feel pressed against hers.

"I hope you don't mind. I was in the area for a client meeting and thought I'd stop in and see if you had time for lunch?"

"Um," she said, thrown. He had mentioned seeing her and she'd had time to think about it since the wedding. She'd decided to stop running from him. "Let me check my schedule. I told my assistant I was free for an appointment this afternoon. I'm helping Gracie Diaz pick out some art for Lauren's new restaurant."

"Sure. I'll wait while you check," he said. "I can't

believe she won the lottery. I've never known anyone who won before."

"Me either," Piper replied as she scrolled through her calendar. A part of her hoped she had a lunchtime meeting scheduled, but then realized how cowardly that was.

Even though, in her defense, she knew she was just being cautious.

Brian raised all kinds of emotional red flags for her. He was a man who knew what he wanted and wasn't afraid to go after it. That appealed to her on so many levels. Which was beyond dangerous.

Especially now, when he was watching her with an intensity she'd have to be blind to ignore.

She opened the group chat app her staff used so she could let Coco know she was going to go out for lunch with Brian. "Looks like I'm all yours."

"Great!" he said.

"What'd you have in mind?"

"Well, this is your neighborhood. Do you have a place you like to go?" he asked.

Piper had to smile at the way he didn't seem to mind putting the ball in her court. She realized this was a small thing, but she knew his uncle would never have let Ava pick a place.

There was more to Brian than what she'd come to know of the Cooper family. Or was she simply seeing that to justify her attraction to him?

"There is a really great street taco place around the corner. It's casual, pretty much outdoor seating."

"It's a nice day," he said. "I'm game for whatever you suggest."

"That's exactly what I like to hear," she murmured,

dropping her phone into one of the pockets of her duster cardigan. He might be the one pursuing her, but she *wasn't* his prey, and deep down she wanted him too. Maybe enough to take him to her bed? She wasn't sure yet, but she wasn't ruling it out. It had been too long since she'd simply let herself go.

Brian followed Piper, watching the sway of her hips and the way that each step she took seemed to be designed to turn him on. When he'd driven by her shop he'd decided to build on the ground work he'd laid on Saturday at the wedding. He wasn't going to let her shove him back into the acquaintance zone. Brian had had too many long, restless nights of dreaming about her and knew that the time to try to exorcise her from his mind with other women had passed.

He needed Piper. Naked and willing and *his*.

However, he had the feeling that if he pushed too hard, she'd write him off and walk away. So he'd stacked the deck in his favor, making sure he had the right suit on today. One that showed off his success without saying he was trying too hard.

She led the way up the block and stopped shading her eyes against the sun. "Did you just happen by or was this planned?"

"Happened by," he said. Just because he was craving her as much as his next breath didn't mean she had to know. He had seen how badly damaged his uncle was when Ava had moved out of his place without taking his feelings into account. It had seemed…callous. And he wasn't sure that Piper wasn't the same way. Maybe she got off on teasing a man and watching him fall for her.

After all, she was single by choice.

"Oh." She sounded disappointed.

"Also I just opened a big office building and I'm in desperate need for someone with a good eye to help me pick the art for the lobby and the walls. I want to incorporate Texas art but also relevant modern stuff."

She tipped her head to the side. "I haven't done a lot of that type of work, but I do like the sound of it. Since this is a business lunch, I should take you somewhere nicer than—"

"Don't be silly. I'd rather eat at your favorite place while we talk than anywhere else," he said.

The November day was sunny and bright, and as they walked through the art district in downtown Dallas, he couldn't help but notice how Piper fit in with this neighborhood. While at the wedding, she'd stood out. She'd been an exotic flower among the Texas roses that were her nieces and her older sister, but here she made sense.

Brian realized that he, however, didn't fit in. He looked and felt too corporate. Not really a part of this world, but he admitted to himself that that was the appeal of Piper. She knew her own mind and was her own woman. A lot of the gals he'd dated lately had been looking to him to help shape who they were. She wasn't like the other women he encountered. That was part of why he'd initially been drawn to her.

Dancing with her on Saturday, talking to her at the reception, had just honed that desire from lust at first sight into something more tangible. She wasn't just an attractive woman to him, she was *more*. And working with her on his building would be the first step to seeing how much more to him she would be. This spark between them would most likely never develop into anything more than a few nights together, but he was willing to take that chance. He needed to get this lust under control and return to his real life.

"Okay then. Do you want only established artists?" she asked once they'd ordered their food and were sitting at small table set apart from the others to the side of the food truck.

Brian finished chewing the bite he'd taken then wiped his hands. He hadn't given the project much thought beyond his initial conception. "I want the place to give anyone who comes in the feeling that they are going to be successful. If you recommend an artist who you think is a good investment then I trust your judgment."

"I'll need to see the space," she said. "Do you have any artists that you really like?"

"I can send you a list if you want. I have some ideas of what I don't like. We specialize in family law so I don't want anything too abstract. It should convey a sense of stability and unity. Even though legally their world is changing, we want them to feel secure."

She smiled at him. "I've never heard a lawyer talk like that."

He shrugged. "I'm not like other lawyers."

"I'm getting that. When did you come back to Dallas?"

"Sunday morning. You?" he asked.

"Sunday evening. I stayed with Ava and caught up with her," Piper said.

"How is it, having your sister so much older?" he asked.

"I don't know anything else, so it seems normal to me. Of course, my nieces and nephews are all more my contemporaries than Ava is, but it's just how our relationship has always been."

"That makes sense. When I was younger, I used to wish for siblings but I don't know that I would have liked it. I'm pretty competitive with just me. If you add others to the mix…"

"Disaster?"

"Maybe. I don't know," he said wryly. "I can't imagine being any other way."

"Me either," Piper admitted. "It has caused some friction with Ava over the years. She wants me to be more like…everyone else, I guess. She grew up with such a firm vision of the perfect family she wanted to create, and anything that doesn't match that image is a problem for her."

"You were a problem?"

"I tried not to be, but I can't conform to what anyone else wants me to be," she said.

And that was why he was sitting across from her on this Wednesday afternoon getting wildly aroused while they discussed business. But there was a part of him that felt like this was more than just lust. And yet another part of him didn't trust what was happening between them because she was Ava's sister. Was she playing him? Was he playing her? Should he just walk away?

His libido wasn't going to let him. Not until he'd had a chance to explore the sensuality she kept letting him get glimpses of. "I'm glad."

They finished up their lunch and made plans to meet later in the week, and Brian contented himself that he'd see her again soon at his offices. He knew that the best things in life took time.

* * *

Gracie Diaz had the kind of long, straight brown hair that Piper envied. She also had beautiful olive skin and big brown eyes. Piper smiled when she saw the woman she'd known since she was a girl. Gracie's father had done work for the Wingates until his untimely death. She'd recently had a huge lottery win and was now a mega-millionaire. Something that Piper suspected the other woman was still trying to come to terms with.

Gracie had been waitressing to put herself through school and working hard to support her mom and brother over the years. After she graduated, Beth Wingate had offered her a job as her assistant and showed her the ropes of event planning. But now, due to her good fortune, she would never again have to worry about taking care of her family.

"Hi, Gracie," Piper said, giving the other woman a warm hug.

"Hello, Piper. The gallery isn't as busy as the last time I was in here," Gracie murmured.

"It's not. I think some people aren't sure how closely tied my gallery was with the Wingate companies. But that's not a problem. We're doing just fine. I spoke to Lauren and she mentioned that you were going to invest in the restaurant and help her decide on the art for your new restaurant venture."

"I am," Gracie said. "This is so exciting! For the first time in my life if I want to help someone, I can just do it. I love it."

"I bet." Piper smiled brightly. "I've pulled a few different paintings and some prints for you to look at, and we've set them up in the viewing room. Can I get you something to drink while we look at them?"

"I'd love some water," Gracie said.

"You got it," Piper replied. "Head into the room at the end of the hall. I'll be right there."

Piper entered the break room where Coco was eating a chimichanga that smelled strongly of chilis and seasoning. Piper grabbed two refillable water bottles that were monogrammed with the gallery's logo and headed out into the hallway where she noticed Gracie bolting toward the bathroom. Concerned, she closed the break room door and went after her.

From outside the locked bathroom door she could hear the other woman throwing up, then the sound of a flushing toilet. "Gracie, are you okay?"

The door opened and Gracie wiped her pale face with a towel. "Yes. I think I might have a stomach bug. Sorry about that."

"Here, have some water," Piper said, leading her into the viewing room and helping her take a seat. "I don't think we have anything bland to eat. There might be some butter cookies."

"I'm okay. The water is perfect," Gracie reassured her, looking at the paintings on the walls. "I love that longhorn image. Do you have more from that artist?"

"I do. I like it too. His work reminds me a lot of Ansel Adams's black-and-white photos. They are so evocative," Piper said. "I left the book of prints in my office. He's done some limited lithographic runs, so that's an option too."

She left Gracie looking at the other works they'd assembled in the viewing room and went to collect the artist's portfolio. She returned to find the younger woman standing under a picture that was titled *Broken Giants*. It was a photo of the oil derricks that dotted the landscape out toward Royal and Midland. The land was vast and empty except for the derricks with the sun reflecting off the tops.

It was a very different image from the longhorn steers, but she could start to get an idea of the kind of subjects that Gracie liked.

"Do you like that?"

"Yes. It reminds me of how oil has given so many wealth, yet at the same time there is still all that land with nothing," she said.

"So true," Piper said. "Here is the first artist's portfolio. I have another artist who is doing something you also might like, but he's not established, and his art would be more of a risk than an investment. Do you want to see it?" she asked.

"Yes. I think Lauren and I both want the restaurant to have the right feel, and if the art is an investment that's great, but it's secondary to the feel of the images."

"Okay. Look through that while I find his work on my tablet," Piper said. They had a lot of different ways for their patrons to view the art that the gallery sold. As an artist herself, she got that. It was easier to represent herself through her art than to allow people to see the inner emotional part of her in real life. Safer, she thought. She knew that some of that was baggage from her past failed relationship, but it had felt less risky to let herself be free in the studio instead of with…men. Unbidden, a vision of Brian's sensual mouth drifted through her mind.

She shook her head, forcing herself back to the work.

Some of the artists she'd worked with were more old-school and liked to send in slides that the gallery had to reproduce. Others sent in jpg images. She liked the variety because it reflected how the art and those who created it were all so different.

She and Gracie spent the next hour going over everything they had in the gallery that had the feel of the artwork that Gracie had been initially drawn to, and at the end of their meeting, Gracie had agreed to purchase several paintings and then asked for that new artist to come to the restaurant and create a custom piece for her.

Piper felt good as she wrote up the bill of sale and took the deposit from Gracie. Her business wasn't going to get back on track from one customer, but Gracie Diaz was proof that not everyone who was interested in art was from the same faction that had once rubbed elbows with the Wingates.

And, of course, she had the commission from Brian's building. She would make that work. Piper had always known that, as much as she loved making her living working with artists, the art world was a tricky business.

Brian. She had to remember they were working together, and as such, their relationship was strictly professional. Or was it…? She'd been way too giddy to see him in her gallery this afternoon. Brian stirred something inside of her that made her feel edgy and dangerous. But he was too young for her, and besides, he was Keith's nephew. Ava had a complicated history with his uncle, to say the least.

Which meant Brian was the last person she should be thinking of, but there was just something about him that Piper couldn't forget.

Three

Brian had several cases that were taking a lot of his time. The new clerk he'd hired was good but still making mistakes, and his uncle had called several times to talk about Ava Wingate. To say that Brian wasn't having a great day was an understatement. He needed a stiff drink and a night off, but he was holding a charity event for underprivileged children at the Mavs game tonight in his corporate box, so he still had work to do.

While he washed up in his private bathroom, he heard his assistant moving about his office. He came out with his shirt off since Tony was bringing in the new Dallas Mavericks jersey that he'd ordered to wear to tonight's game. His phone pinged and he glanced at the screen as he stepped into his office—it was a message from his uncle asking him to call. *Again*. He heard a sharp intake of breath and then a wolf whistle and looked straight into Piper's dark green eyes.

Her gaze drifted to his chest, making him start to harden. He flexed his muscles before he realized what he was doing, causing her to draw in her breath as she looked farther down his body.

Piper took a step closer to him and lifted her hand as if to touch him, but then she dropped her arm, shook her head and turned away.

He forced himself to go back into the washroom even though he wanted to move closer to her. See what she'd do next. However, he suppressed that urge because he was aware they were in the office and he had to act like a gentleman. He grabbed his dress shirt and pulled it on. "Sorry about that. I thought you were Tony."

"He wasn't at his desk and I knocked but came in. I should be the one apologizing, although I have to say, Cooper, that was a nice surprise."

He smiled at her and lifted one eyebrow. "Glad you liked it. Um, did we have an appointment tonight?"

"No," she said. "I was downtown at a meeting and thought I'd drop by and check out your offices."

"I'm happy to see you. I've got about thirty-forty minutes before I have to be at the American Airlines Center for the Mavs game. I can show you around. Let me find Tony and then we can go. Do you want a drink?" he asked. "Help yourself to anything in the mini fridge."

Brian went back to his desk and pulled up the chat group for his executive staff. There was a message from his assistant saying he'd had to go down and sign for the jersey. He'd be back in ten.

Brian messaged him that he was showing Piper around and to leave the jersey in his office. Then he stood up as his phone pinged again. He looked down at the screen. Keith again. He was tempted to block him.

"Not a message you wanted?" she asked.

"No. Not really. It's from my uncle. He's at his wit's end now that your sister has moved out of his place," Brian admitted. "But I don't really want to discuss him."

"Me either," Piper said. "His actions aren't exactly the best lately. I'm not sure he didn't take advantage of Ava's grief."

Brian didn't know about that. His uncle had fallen hard for Piper's sister. From where Brian stood it seemed like his uncle's feelings had gone from friendship to something deeper and that Ava had encouraged that. Leading him to believe that there could be something real between them without any intention of ever following through. "I mean, he really loves your sister. I'm not sure how that is taking advantage of her. That would be—"

"I think it's probably best if we don't discuss this. You're going to naturally defend your uncle and I get that, but I don't want that to come between us. I like you, Brian."

He wished he could just walk away from Piper. For both their sakes. But he wanted her, and as he got to know her, he was starting to like her too. He felt as if he was in a better position than his uncle was with Ava because Brian hadn't always been secretly in love with Piper. Just in lust, he thought. Pursuing her wasn't the smartest course of action, but it was also something he had to do right now.

He wasn't sleeping because of his torrid dreams about this eclectic beauty, but he knew himself well enough to know that once he'd had her, his fixation on her would start to wane. She might be different from the other woman he'd dated, but *he* wasn't different. He was still more dedicated to his career and building his legacy than he was to starting a serious relationship.

"I like you too, Piper," he said, dropping the subject as she asked although he knew that Keith was always going to be between them because of his past with Ava. "As you can see, the atrium is huge and I was hoping to find something to fill it up. I was thinking either a sculpture or maybe a mural?"

She looked over the railing into the open space outside of his office which was a big great space that was open all the way down to the lobby. There was a brass railing on one side that offered a view of the atrium and then on the other side had two couches and a bank of windows that looked out over downtown Dallas. "I like that idea. I think we'd have to commission a mural—I don't have that many artists I work with who do murals—but I do have a piece that might fit that space so you can look at that first." Pulling her notebook from her shoulder bag, she jotted down a few notes before stowing it back in her bag.

"Sounds good. I'm really in your hands. I just want the place to look good. To reflect our clientele and all the hard work I've done to start my own practice."

"I can definitely do that," she said.

Brian wasn't surprised. Piper was a woman who made things happen. He took her through all the other spaces and showed her the different spots he thought needed art.

"I have to leave when we get back to my office, but I want to get the paperwork rolling on this. Do you mind if I pass you off to my assistant?" he asked.

"Not at all," she said. "You're a big Mavs fan?"

"Yes, even when they aren't winning, but tonight I'm hosting an event," he replied, looking down into her eyes and realizing he didn't want their time together to end. Should he invite her to come along? It seemed like the quickest way to see if they were going to hook up. But he also admitted that the more time he spent with her, the more this wasn't just about lust and ending his sexual torment about Piper.

"What kind of event?"

"I sponsor a program with the local elementary schools. If someone gets all As for the grading period, their name goes into a draw and I bring the winners to the game," he said.

"That's a great incentive," she murmured. "I wouldn't have expected this from you."

"Thanks. What did you expect?"

"Someone more driven to ensure his company's success at all costs," she admitted. "Taking care of kids like this is really the kind of gesture that helps to build their futures."

"I thought so. Also, some of these kids would never get to go to a game otherwise," he said as they reentered his office.

Tony stood there with a sheaf of papers in his hands and the look that meant that Brian had more things to do before he left.

"You have about ten minutes until you need to leave. I've got a car waiting downstairs for you, so you don't have to worry about parking. The charity has confirmed that ten kids and a parent and/or guardian will be there. They have one boy whose older brother would like to come I told them yes," Tony said. "Also, I need your signature on these."

"Thanks, Tony. Would you get Ms. Holloway's details and write up a contract for her to do the art for the building?"

"Yes, sir. Ms. Holloway, please have a seat," his assistant said.

"Of course," she replied. "See you later, Brian."

He hesitated. He was seconds away from inviting her, but he needed to get himself in hand before he did that. He was in lust with Piper. He wasn't about to start getting emotionally entangled with her. That was a complication that neither of them needed.

"Later," he said.

Piper curled up in her pajamas later that night watching the Mavs game and thinking about Brian and Keith. Were they the same type of guy?

She had spent a lot of time over the last five years decorating her house in Frisco, one of the northern suburbs of Dallas. She'd haunted estate sales and online auction houses to get everything right. Her goal was to purchase pieces that were solid and could keep up with her eclectic and changing tastes. Piper looked at the tribal art she'd purchased recently and smiled to herself. She'd been slowly updating her collection and the new goddess mask suited the new phase of her life.

A tinge of sadness flowed through Piper as she thought about Ava exiled from her own home and struggling to get her company back from the brink. Piper wondered if there was some way she could help the Wingates. She had overheard some snippets of conversation at the wedding that suggested Keith might know more about the troubles at Wingate than he let on. He'd been helping out and making decisions for Ava while she'd been overwrought with grief for her husband.

If Piper had another reason to see Brian, would she feel safer somehow? Like she could go out with him because she knew she was doing it for her family. Though she wasn't involved with the business or really that close to Ava.

She started a group text with her family, wanting to ask them what kind of information from Keith they were looking for, but every time she tried to word her text it just sounded like she was Nancy Drew trying to solve a mystery on a bicycle. She had no idea how to get information from Brian. He'd brought his uncle up today, so she felt like she could easily ask him about Keith if she needed to, but she was stymied as to what she should ask.

Piper called her sister, but it was after nine and Ava's phone went straight to voice mail. She didn't leave a message. What could she say?

Rubbing the back of her neck, she headed to her studio. She had been spending more and more time in here lately. Her art had always provided an escape from the real world and this trying time was no different.

She was working on a second piece based on a spoken-word poem she'd heard at a café down the street from her gallery. The author of the poem was a nineteen-year-old man who'd spent most of his teen years in and out of juvenile detention, and the last time he'd gotten out they'd warned him he'd likely go to prison if he got in trouble again.

Xavier had challenged himself to find another life, but his poem spoke of the struggle to live within the law and not take it into his own hands. The idea for the sculpture had come to her one night while she'd been sleeping. She'd thought that would be enough for her. But she'd been called to the canvas and had been working on an abstract painting that showed both sides of Xavier. The intelligent young poet and the tough gang member who wouldn't hesitate to kill. She'd seen now they both existed inside the same man, the struggle constant as each side fought to remain in control.

Piper had asked his permission to use his poem and likeness for the sculpture, which she'd be donating to be auctioned off for Habit for Humanity at the end of the month. But she wanted to gift Xavier the canvas. She was almost finished with the piece. The figure had pen and paper in one hand, a gun in the other. His eyes were still haunting her.

She couldn't get the intelligence just right. Unbidden, an image of Brian's eyes as he'd talked to her about his building flashed into her mind. He had that inner core of intelligence and determination…that was what she'd been missing for this piece. She went back to work, furiously working until she stepped back and saw Brian's eyes in Xavier's face.

She was pleased with what she'd accomplished. Glancing down at her watch, she was surprised to see it was after midnight. She wandered out of her studio and noticed her phone was buzzing on the coffee table where she'd left it. Her heart skipped a beat when she saw it was a text from Brian.

Brian: I know you are probably sleeping, but I wanted to apologize for how I had to leave this evening.

Piper: Still working in my studio. You don't have to apologize. I dropped by unannounced. How was the game?

Brian: Dismal. I know we are in a rebuilding season, but tonight was painful.

Piper: I don't follow sports but...hugs?

Brian: [[Laughing emoji]] Thanks. What are you working on so late?

Piper: A portrait. It really needs to be finished but I was struggling to get it done.

Brian: Does that happen a lot? I don't think I ever realized that you were an artist.

Piper: It's not my main thing. It's just an outlet... sort of more hobby than occupation. I do a lot of collaborating.

Brian: I really liked the sculpture I saw at your gallery. I'd love to see some more of your work.

Piper: Maybe you will. [[Wink emoji]]

Brian: Maybe?

Piper: I mainly do commissions. This piece is a gift for a collaborator that I worked with for a charity auction.

Brian: Which one?

Piper: Habitat's Boots & Boas at the end of the month.

Brian: I have a table. Want to join me?

Yes, she thought. But was she being too impulsive? Her mind tried to reiterate all the reasons she'd been listing since she'd first danced with him about why spending time with him was a bad idea, but she pushed them aside. Piper had realized in her mid-thirties that she regretted the things she didn't do more than those she actually did. She had the feeling she'd always regret not going with Brian. Plus maybe she could information from him to help her family.

Piper: Yes. I have to get to bed now. Talk to you later about the art for your building.

Brian: I wish you didn't have to go. Good night, Piper.

Piper: Good night.

She put her phone down and went to shower before she did something impulsive like invite him over. There was still too much standing between the two of them for her to be this interested in him. She knew it, but she pointedly ignored that part. And besides, it wasn't as if this flirtation could develop into anything serious anyway. She was just going to take what she could with him and let that be enough.

He was fun and attractive. And, damn, the man was *ripped*. Piper never would have guessed that underneath his perfectly cut suits he was in such magnificent shape. She'd been trying very hard to forget what he'd looked like with his shirt off, but as she drifted off to sleep that night her dreams were filled with him naked and moving seductively over her.

Piper had been in and out of his offices for the last week, and Brian had caught a few glimpses of her but there hadn't been time to talk. He'd had a case that should have been handled in mediation go to court and it had been a hell of a fight. He was ready for Friday night when he walked into his office and saw Piper hanging a portrait on his wall.

She had on a flowy white blouse with the sleeves pushed up to her elbows and a pair of leather pants that made her legs seem even longer than he had noticed them being before. A few locks of her short dark hair were tucked behind one ear.

"Who's there? Tony?" she asked. "Come help me with this. I should have waited—"

"It's Brian," he said, hurrying to her side and taking the weight of the painting from her. "I got this."

Her cinnamony perfume made him think of Thanksgiving and family. But the brush of her hip against his thigh conjured images of a long night spent burning up the sheets. He felt the portrait tremble in his hands, and he forced himself to get his urges under control. Shifting the portrait, he felt for the hooks on the wall and settled it onto them.

She turned toward him, her green eyes glazed with lust, and he realized that he was reaching the end of his rope. It felt like he'd waited years for her and right now, as she stood so close to him, smelling of cinnamon and looking like the only thing he'd ever wanted, he needed to kiss her. To taste her full mouth and see if the passion he'd felt from the moment they'd met was real or just a figment of his imagination.

The door was open, and he didn't want her to feel pressured so he took a step back and stumbled over the small toolbox he hadn't realized she'd left on the floor.

She reached for him, her hand grabbing his forearm as he steadied himself, drawing her off balance. He caught her easily with one arm around her waist.

She put her hand on his chest and their eyes met. Something unspoken passed between them. Both of them were wary of pushing this and losing the chance of friendship. Or at least that was *his* concern.

"Thanks," he said. "Sorry for being so clumsy."

She didn't step back but stayed where she was with her hand on his chest. "I think we both know that you aren't clumsy."

"I feel like it around you. I seem to lose all my chill with you, Piper."

She shook her head, worrying her bottom lip between her teeth, which made him close his eyes so he wouldn't be so focused on her mouth. He wanted to kiss her. *Needed* to, actually. He literally felt like if he didn't put his mouth on hers, he'd stop breathing, which he knew was ridiculous.

But with his eyes closed, the touch of her hand on his chest and the scent of her was stronger than his rapidly waning self-control. He was surrounded by Piper Holloway. The woman he couldn't stop thinking about. The woman he'd promised himself he'd let set the pace. He had to get away. He let go of her, opened his eyes and moved away from her. She watched him go and then wrapped her arms around her waist, turning to look at the portrait she'd hung.

He did the same. Anything to draw his attention from her lithe body and her sensual mouth. The portrait was a surprise. It was a version of the corporate photograph that he'd had taken earlier in the year. But this oil painting had somehow captured his energy and passion. He looked like a man who would conquer anything.

"Who did this?"

"I did," she said softly. "I hope you don't mind. If you hate it, I'll take it down."

"I love it. You flatter me with your rendition of me. But I wish I was that man," he said.

"You *are* that man, Brian. I was going to just hang the picture you had taken for the law journal but then… I haven't been sleeping and somehow found myself at the canvas. Anyway, this is a gift and not part of the commission to decorate the building."

He moved closer. Was this how she saw him? He hadn't been paying attention to her words but then they sank in. "I'm paying for it. I should have thought to have you do this earlier. But I hadn't seen any of your work."

He'd had the feeling she didn't want him to see her work and now he understood why. There was something very intimate about the way she'd painted him. And she'd revealed a bit of herself in the work as much as she had stripped away his outer layers, showcasing parts of him that he'd shown to her in conversations.

She'd really captured what he hoped to be. But it was an idealized version of him. Could he be that guy? Did he even *want* to be? She'd somehow seen through the outer man to the person he truly was.

Brian wasn't too sure he liked it. He didn't want anyone to see him this way—it made him feel vulnerable and he didn't want to be. But maybe that was because she made him feel that way? And perhaps, deep down, a part of him hungered to live up to what she saw in him.

"It's interesting. I like it," he said, knowing he

couldn't say that she'd seen him in away that made him feel vulnerable.

She turned to face him, and he saw that questions lingered in her beautiful green eyes. She seemed nervous about his reaction. "Good. It's hard to gauge my own work. I always like it until I'm waiting to hear what someone else thinks, and then I just see the flaws."

He moved closer to her because he hated being even a few feet away. "I'm not just being nice. It's really good."

She turned then, and this time as their eyes met, a jolt of awareness sizzled between them. He knew he might regret it but he also knew he couldn't wait another moment to kiss her. To get a little bit closer to this complex, exotic woman who had turned his life upside down.

Four

Piper hadn't intended to be here when he saw the portrait. She'd spent too many nights working on it and pouring her sexual frustration into it. Sure, she wanted Brian, but they were busy people with very different lives, and she was old enough to know that just wanting a man didn't mean he'd ever be hers. So she'd painted him instead.

But now he was holding her in his big, muscular arms, looking like he wanted to kiss her but also hesitating, as if he didn't want to pressure her into anything. She put her hands on the sides of his face, felt that strong jaw and the stubble that wasn't visible as she went up on her tiptoes and brushed her lips over his.

An electric tingle went through her body and everything feminine inside of her screamed *it's about damned time.* The next time her lips grazed his, he took control of the kiss. His lips moving under hers, he angled his head and his tongue swept over her lips. Gently at first, and then demanding entrance so it could probe deep inside.

He tasted minty, and as silly as it might seem, *manly.* Brian held her loosely, never making her feel trapped, as he deepened the kiss. She slipped her hands down the sides of his face to his neck, caressing the tendons there as she slowly moved her touch to his shoulders. Piper knew how ripped and in shape he was. Felt the strength in his shoulders and in his arms as he lifted her slightly and turned so that his back was toward the open door of his office. She tore her mouth free of his and their eyes met. She didn't want this to end. There was something in his eyes that seemed to say the same thing.

Brian rubbed his thumb over her lips and another sensual shiver went through her all the way to her toes. Her lips felt too sensitive, full and hungry, she thought. She was hungry for more of him. More of his kisses and definitely more of him without his dress shirt on.

He sighed and stepped back from her, but not before she felt the brush of his erection against her thigh. "That nearly got out of hand."

"Nearly," she said softly. Knowing that she would have been very happy if it had. She was used to men who…heck, she wasn't used to *any* man. Truth was, she was leery of men, having been ill-used by her fiancé back in her twenties. And, as a consequence, she kept a wall up and kept her distance.

She moved back from Brian. She only had to look at the portrait to see what she felt for him. How much she wanted things from him that she knew weren't in the cards for her. She had no business kissing him, and not for any other reason than she was too old to have her heart broken by a ripped body and a mouth that made her forget her own name. Too old.

Too wise.

Ha.

She was supposed to be entering the wise goddess period of her life, but she felt as untried as she had felt at twenty-one. This wasn't going to work. Hook-ups were one thing, but…whatever this was—just no. She wasn't going to do it.

"Um, I've got to go." She saw her shoulder bag on his guest chair and started walking toward it, her own sense of panic growing. Not because of Brian but because he'd done something she hadn't expected. He'd awakened that feminine part of her that she'd shoved way down and tried to kill. And this was wrong…on so many levels. Because he sparked a desire in her for things that she knew she couldn't have. Things that still made her want to mourn.

"I'm sorry," he rasped. "I didn't want to push you."

She paused in the doorway and looked back at him. Even now it was all she could do to keep from closing the door and ripping off his shirt. Giving into the fiery passion that was coursing through her and making her hands shake.

Wise goddess.

She hoped that reminder would be enough.

"You didn't. I pushed and I shouldn't have. I'm not… I'm just not ready for this," she confessed. "I'm glad you like the painting. I'll be back with more pieces next week."

She turned to leave but he was there, his hand on her elbow, just the brush of his fingers against her arm, slowing her down. "How do you feel about dinner?"

She looked at him over her shoulder.

"To discuss the installation? I don't think we need to consult any more unless you don't like the pieces."

"I like them. I was asking you out…on a date," he said sardonically.

She had just pretty much decided it was more than passion in her mind, but he was making everything real by asking her for a date. "We can't date. I'm too old for you. You should find someone—"

He put his fingers over her lips and stopped her from talking. "There is no one I want like I want you, Piper. If you don't want me, that's one thing. But our ages aren't a big deal. When we are together it's honestly not even something I've ever thought of. Please, come to dinner."

She looked up into his dark brown eyes and felt her will weakening. It had been just one kiss and she could control this attraction. She was a wise goddess not a sex-crazed woman. She had this under control. And, honestly, dinner sounded nice.

Better than nice. She hadn't been on a date in a long time. Partly due to the walls she used to keep men at arm's length, but mostly because she worked all the time.

"Okay. I'd like that. Where should I meet you?"

"How about CRU Food and Wine Bar in The Shops at Legacy?"

"8:00 p.m.?"

"Yes," he said. She turned to leave again and this time he pulled her back into his arms and pivoted them out of the doorway. He tipped her head back, kissing her again, and this time he held nothing back. And long breathless moments later, when he finally lifted his head, she didn't feel wise. She felt empty. Lonely. Unfulfilled. Like she'd had a taste of something she desperately craved and that made her hunger for so much more.

"See you soon."

She walked away, wondering if she'd just taken a reckless leap into the unknown.

CRU was an upscale Texas wine bar. They'd been the first to offer over thirty wines by the glass and had vino from all over the world and at every price point. They also had a relaxed atmosphere with Napa-style foods and delicious, wood-oven pizzas.

Brian had chosen it because it was close to her home and he knew the general manager. Working in the city had given him a great network of connections and he was glad tonight that he'd been able to secure a reservation through that. He didn't mind waiting for a table, but it was his first date with Piper and he didn't want to spend the time with her standing in the waiting area.

Plus, it was a relaxed atmosphere so there would be no pressure on either one of them. He wanted to be cool about this, but he knew himself and how he felt about this woman, and there was nothing chill about that. But tonight, he reminded himself, was about Piper. Her wants. Her needs.

And doing everything he could to make her feel comfortable.

But damn. That kiss…

That portrait she'd done of him had changed the game. He wanted to stay focused on the lust side of it, and boy had he gotten his wish. Because her kiss had made him want to make her come in his arms again and again until she was exhausted and she forgot about that man she'd painted.

But, in a way, that lip-lock had been the sweetest kind of torture too. Because the attraction between them wasn't something he wanted to walk away from and now he knew it with bone-deep certainty. That she'd started to walk away warned him he needed to be careful.

He'd been surprised when she mentioned their age difference. Because, to be honest, it was as he'd told her…he hardly noticed the eleven years between them.

Blowing out a breath, he tossed his keys to the valet and walked into the restaurant. He looked around the lobby for Piper and didn't see her so he gave his name to the maître d. A minute later Hugh—the owner—came over to greet him. They shook hands. "Good to see you, Brian, and not during billable hours."

Brian had to laugh at that. Hugh and his wife went through periods where they both wanted to divorce but they had never gone through with it. "It is nice. Thanks for helping me out tonight with a table."

"Not a problem. I'm guessing this was a last-minute date," Hugh said.

"Yes," Brian replied, not wanting to discuss Piper with the other man.

"Say no more. If you need anything let me know," Hugh said, as one of the waiters came to get his attention.

He walked away as the door opened and Brian turned to see Piper walk in. She wore a halter top under a black leather biker jacket, a pair of boot-cut black trousers and heels, and seemed to stand out from everyone else in the waiting area. Their eyes met and she smiled when she saw him.

He noticed the way everyone's gaze seemed to follow her and realized she didn't see that. Didn't realize how she drew attention just by being the woman she was. He wondered how much of it was down to what she'd said about Ava always wanting her to fit a different mold.

"Hello, Cooper," she said. "I hope you haven't been waiting long. I got stuck at a red light."

"Not long at all." He grinned. "Let me tell the hostess we are ready to be seated."

"You got a table?"

"Yes, the owner is a friend," he said. "This place is more popular than I realized when I first suggested it."

She nodded and followed him to the hostess station, and they were led to their table. The after-work crowd was changing to couples out for the evening. He put his hand on the small of Piper's back as they moved through the tables following the hostess—more to touch her than to guide her.

She didn't seem to mind it and he took comfort in that. He had wondered earlier if he'd pressured her into the date, but she was here and not pushing him away. He knew that they still had a way to go, but this was the first step.

Brian wanted her to get to know him. So that his reassurance that their ages didn't matter wasn't something that would ever bother her again. Plus, he wanted her to realize she wasn't a novelty to him. He wanted Piper because she was *Piper*, not for any other reason.

They were shown to a high table for two in the back and he held her chair as she seated herself. Then he took the bar stool across from her. "Thanks," she said. "I hate these high stools. I always feel like I'm not going to be able to get down."

"I don't think they have a low—" he began.

"Stop. I'm being silly. Ava's told me more than once to stop complaining about bar stools."

Brian quirked a brow. "Do you go out with her often?"

"Not really. When we are in Royal sometimes. I tried to get her to go out when Trent was so sick," Piper said. "It was hard to see Ava go from being such a glamorous, feisty woman to sort of fading away as Trent's sickness lingered and then worsened."

"That did seem to put a strain on her. Uncle Keith said he tried to distract her. It was hard on him, losing his best friend," Brian said.

"I think it changed them both," Piper admitted. "Ava hasn't been the same since."

"To be honest, neither has Uncle Keith. I think he saw Trent's death as a second chance for him to step up and be the man Ava needed." Brian sighed. He hadn't really intended to talk about his uncle tonight, but Keith seemed to be on Piper's mind.

"Maybe. I think he took advantage of her grief," Piper said.

"Ava Wingate?" Brian asked. It was hard to think of Ava letting any man take advantage of her.

"Even a strong woman has vulnerabilities, Brian," she said, pointedly drawing the menu toward her and opening it up.

"Of course. I didn't mean to imply that she didn't. I guess I don't like to think of Uncle Keith manipulating her. I know he loves her."

"Fair enough. And I don't like it when other people point out how bitchy Ava can be," she said. "Besides, we aren't here tonight to talk about them."

"No, we're not," he agreed. "We're here to see if there is more than just a spark from one kiss."

By mutual agreement they kept the conversation off of Ava and Keith, and talked instead about sports—Brian's passion—art, which was hers, and movies. She wasn't sure how, but they managed to cover all of these topics and found they had a lot in common.

"Are you interested in going to a Cowboys game?" he asked. "I've got season tickets and I usually go with my college roommate but he's going out of town. You know they always play Thanksgiving Day."

"I don't want to seem like I was faking most of the earlier conversation, but I didn't know that. Do they play here in Dallas?"

"This year they do," Brian said. "What about it? My folks have a big family gathering at their house in Southlake. I should let you know we are diehard Cowboys fans."

"I wouldn't have guessed after you told me how Tom

Hicks donated the land out here to build an elementary school," she quipped.

He blushed, which was cute and made her want him that much more. He was fun and easy to tease, and she could tell that family meant a lot to him, which made it harder for her to probe for information about Keith even though they'd agreed not to discuss him. She didn't want him to betray his uncle—unless of course Keith had done something suspect.

Which right now no one could seem to prove.

Every one of her nieces and nephews just didn't like Keith and thought there was something off about him. Ava had moved out of his place, and that should have pacified them, but it hadn't. Which was making her think that there might be more to their suspicions than just irritation at Keith for swooping in so soon after Trent had died.

"So I guess I was gushing."

"Yeah, just a bit," she said, "but I like it. I would love to go to that football game with you."

"Good. And we have the gala for Habitat. It seems to me we might be dating," he said.

"Do we have to put a label on it?" she asked, but secretly she liked the sound of that. *Dating.* She'd be part of a couple and not the odd person at the table. Which she had been for the last few months, as it seemed everyone except her had a significant other.

"No, I don't need a label. I just wanted to make sure you knew I was thinking about us in a serious way."

"How serious?" she asked. A part of her was afraid to let him in. She'd seen her own strong sister disappear inside of Ava's complicated relationship with Keith.

Was there something about Cooper men that was overwhelming? Manipulative? Could she be getting in over her head with this hot, sexy man?

"Not too serious. This is only our first date," he said.

His answer was perfect. Again, was he just saying the right things to win her over? What would he want from her? Actually, she couldn't imagine a man who was better for what she needed than Brian. He was young and fun. The kind of guy who wasn't looking for more than a few nights in her bed. And that made her cautious. Brian was good at reading people; she'd read about that in an article that had profiled him the previous year. It was one of the skills that made him so good in the courtroom. Was he reading her now?

She shook her head, took another sip of her sauvignon blanc and refused to let her niggling doubts ruin her evening with him. Even if they were dating, it was casual. They weren't going to ever get serious, or at least not right away. She was a wise goddess, she reminded herself.

"Do you date a lot?" she asked curiously.

"I do my fair share," he said. "But I haven't been serious about anyone since I graduated law school. I have been too busy trying to get my career going."

She could see that. Brian seemed to her the type of man who wanted to give his all to everything he did, be it career or relationship. She took another sip of her wine and realized she was almost done with her second glass. The older she'd gotten, the easier it had become to drink more wine than she intended. She set her glass aside and reached for her water.

"And what about you? Do you date a lot?" he asked.

She shook her head. "Not really. My relationships tend to be more like this one. It happens when the right person comes along. Not because I feel it's time to date again."

He nodded. "I like that idea. I try to do the same thing, but my work requires a fair amount of socializing, and at times it's better to have someone on my arm."

"You need a corporate wife," she said. "Someone who can be your partner."

Even as she had the thought, she realized she'd said it out loud as a warning to herself. She needed to remember that, whatever else this was, she was an independent woman. Piper never wanted be Brian's social plus-one. *I just want to have fun*, she reminded herself. And as he'd said, this was just their first date. There was no reason to overthink this.

"I don't need anything," he said. "And I'm very happy where I am tonight."

"Me too," she admitted. "I think I should be finished with gathering the art for your building soon."

"Tony took me to see the other pieces you've put up and I have to admit I do like what you've done. He said that all of the pieces are on a three-month temporary display." Brian glanced at her with interest. "What is your thought behind that?"

"I want to make sure that the work suits your building. Once you see it daily, you'll be able to determine if you want to keep it or not," she told him.

"Good idea. Is that something you do with all of your customers?" he asked.

"It depends on the client. If they buy it at auction, then it's theirs, but if we work together to find a piece for their home then I do give them some leeway. And it's an exchange policy for the same artist's work. It's not a refund."

"That makes sense. Art is subjective, isn't it? Just like couples," he murmured.

"How do you figure?"

"Not everyone who looks like the perfect couple will be one," he said.

Five

When the meal ended, he didn't want the night to end but he'd asked her to dinner…that was all. He needed to keep his desires in check to avoid scaring her off.

The Texas sky was big and clear that night; the light pollution from Frisco usually made seeing the stars almost impossible. And he wished they were on his ranch in Royal. They could go for a ride and he'd show her the stars.

"Do you ride?" he asked as he helped her into her coat.

"I do. I'm not really good but I enjoy it," she replied. "Why?"

"Just thinking tonight would be perfect for a ride."

"Yes, but we're in Frisco," she said with a slight smile.

"We are," he admitted gruffly. "Want to take a walk before we head home?"

She shook her head. The Shops at Legacy were an outdoor mall area that mixed restaurants with retail outlets and a large city park. But she didn't want to walk in public with him. She'd wanted to be alone with him.

Brian had promised himself he'd be chill, so he forced a smile and comforted himself with the knowledge that they'd had a really nice time at CRU. He could handle that. He'd call in a few days and invite her out again.

"Fair enough. It's been a long week," he said. "Did you valet park?"

"No," she answered.

"I'll walk you to your car, then."

"Why don't you get your car and drop me off?" she suggested. "Then you can follow me to my home, and we can have a drink and I'll show you my studio."

He looked into her dark green eyes, searching for a clue as to what she actually wanted from him, but he didn't find an answer. He just saw interest, and honestly, that was enough for him. "Sounds great."

He got his car from the valet and drove Piper to hers. He followed her to the gated community where her house was and was waved through by the security guard after Piper spoke to him. Her house was a large stone abode similar to the one his parents had. It was too large for one person, he thought, but it was obvious to him as soon as he stepped inside that Piper liked the space and had made it her own.

"House tour or drink first?" she asked. "November always makes me want to curl up by the fire and drink Baileys."

"November makes me think of turkey and football, but I think I might like your idea better," he said.

She smiled at him. "I'll pour the Baileys if you get a fire started. I was thinking we could sit on the back patio by the fire ring," she said, nodding toward the French doors.

"I'm on it. I was an Eagle Scout."

"I'm not surprised," she said. "Be right out."

He let himself out onto her patio and easily found the seating area surrounding the fire ring in the back yard. The lights had automatically come on as he stepped outside, so he immediately saw the cord of stacked firewood near the built-in outdoor kitchen. The patio floor was inlaid tile and the design was very Texan in scope. A big bold vista with a large sun in the center that her fire ring had been built into.

He used some kindling to get the fire started and then slowly added one of the larger pieces of wood to it. Dusting off the chairs, he moved two of the padded seats closer to the fire with an end table between them. He glanced up as the door opened.

Piper had draped a heavy blanket scarf over her shoulders and had a tray with the bottle of Baileys and two glasses with ice in them on it. After he took the tray from her, she went to one of the cabinets and grabbed two plaid throws. He noticed they were monogrammed with her initials when she handed one to him.

"In case you get chilly. This is my favorite time of year," she said. "The nights are longer and it's not too horribly hot most of the time."

He watched her wrap the blanket around her shoulders and almost offered to pull her into his arms. They could share some body heat and he'd keep her warm. Just thinking about it aroused him.

"I don't think I have a favorite time of the year," he admitted. "I do love summer and fishing out on the lake. But that's not a time of year thing...that's just a fishing thing."

"Do you eat what you catch?" she asked.

He shrugged as she offered him a glass with two fingers of Baileys in it. Their fingers brushed and a shiver went through him. "Mostly release them. I like the sport of it."

He wanted to pull her onto his lap and show her what he really was in the mood for tonight. Piper. That's what he wanted and he was trying to be a good guest but the struggle was real.

"I find it sort of soothing to be out on the boat while other people are fishing," she confided. "I usually take one of my portrait books with me and sketch."

"How does that work? Do you have to have some sort of inspiration, or do you just doodle and it turns into something?" He grimaced. "I'm not creative at all."

"I don't believe you aren't creative, but it might not be in the traditional I-make-art kind of way. I bet you come up with unique ways to solve problems in your life all the time...that's being creative," she pointed out.

"You sound very passionate about this," he noted, taking a sip of his drink .

"I am. I hate when people act as if being creative is something only given out to a few of us. Everyone has that inside of them. It might not produce art, but that creativity is there in everyone's daily life."

He wasn't sure he agreed but he could see what she

was saying. "I think that might simply be more our uniqueness."

"Fair enough," she said. "I'm afraid I get a bit zealous when it comes to anyone denying they can be creative. I think it's like anything else in life. If it was important to you, you would do it and then nurture that skill. Then you would be creative."

"I can agree with that," he said. "I see that all the time when everyone says I'm so focused. It's just because I know that if I'm not, I won't be successful. Focus has given me my career and I work at it. It would be easy to grab my phone and check in with work during the day, but if I'm working on a brief then I finish it first."

"I can see that about you." She flashed a smile. "You are a man who doesn't stop until he gets what he wants, aren't you?"

"I am," he said.

"And what do you want right now?" she asked, putting her glass down and shifting in her chair toward him.

"You."

Brian kept surprising her with his intelligence and his boldness. She'd had an idea of the man he was, but he pushed away those cardboard cutout images and replaced them with his broad shoulders, smoldering dark eyes and firm jaw. Inviting him back to her place hadn't been her plan, but the longer she'd spent with him, the more she wanted him.

That kiss in his office had dogged her all afternoon and evening as she'd waited for their date. She'd told herself to be the wise goddess, but right now she didn't want to. In her mind the wise goddess was ancient and had long gray hair that hung to her waist. She watched life instead of participating in it. And Piper freely admitted she wasn't ready to be that woman. She still felt young and vibrant, and Brian accentuated that.

He made her want give in to temptation, even though there were still alarm bells going off that he wasn't the right man for this moment in her life. But she'd never listened to that type of caution. She'd always been more of a leap-and-the-net-will-appear kind of gal. So she'd leaped by inviting him into her home, and now she craved him more than ever.

But was she prepared for what came next?

He set his Baileys glass on the table and shifted in his chair so that he was facing her. Both of his legs were on the ground in front of him and she couldn't help but smile when she realized he was wearing a pair of boots. She had gotten used to the men in Dallas being very urbane, not necessarily Texan gentlemen, but Brian had been born and bred in Royal and there was a big part of him that was a maverick.

"Boots?" she asked. "It's so not what I expected from you. How did I miss them at the restaurant?"

"It's Friday night," he said with a wink. "That's my night to get back to my roots."

"My daddy used to do that too. Get all duded up on Friday night and put on his boots and hat," she murmured. She hadn't thought about that in a long time. Her parents had both passed away when she'd been in her early twenties and Ava had stepped in to pick up the slack but she had her young family. She still missed them terribly. This memory was an unexpected surprise, like a warm breeze.

"Mine too. He was a lawyer during the week, but on the weekend, he's just a good old boy," Brian said. "I guess I like to think I'm a bit like him."

"I bet you are. You're not really anything like your uncle," she mused.

He groaned. "I know. Keith is a Royal man through and through, but my branch of the family tended to like the big D."

"I can tell. You fit in here very well, but there is a part of you that's very Cooper of Royal," she said. "I see your rancher roots at times."

"Ranching is definitely in my blood," he admitted. "Yours too, right?"

"Yes," she said. "But not in *my* blood, per se. I mean, I liked the ranch, the wide-open spaces and finding a quiet place to hide and sketch. But the actual ranching parts…well, aside from riding, I don't think I'd make a very good rancher."

"Luckily you don't have to be." Putting his hands on his thighs, he leaned forward toward her "Do I unnerve you, Piper?"

Did he?

She wanted to say no, but a part of her acknowledged that would be a lie. After all, she'd asked what he was focused on and he'd said her. *Her.* Piper Holloway. The woman who'd walked a solo path for a long time by her own choice.

And she'd liked the idea of his focusing on her.

She tried to frame it in her mind that it was sex. Just the playing out of the kiss that had happened in his office, but she knew it was more. She didn't normally go out and she certainly hadn't invited a man back to her place in a long time.

"I don't know," she admitted. "You said what I was hoping you would, but now I'm not sure…"

Several moments of palpable tension passed between them. "Would you like me to leave?" he asked at last.

She was torn for a minute. There was so much she was unsure of, starting with trusting her own instincts when it came to him. But she knew he wasn't Keith. In fact, the more she got to know him, the less the two of them felt like each other.

"No," she said. "I don't want that at all."

"Then why don't we sit over there on the double lounger and watch the fire," he suggested huskily. "No pressure to do anything but enjoy this fall evening."

She looked over at him. Would that be enough? For another man it might not be, but she could tell from the earnest look on Brian's face that holding her while they fire crackled would be enough if it was what she said she needed.

Piper nodded. She got up and moved over to the big double lounger and maneuvered it closer to the fire. Meanwhile, Brian fiddled around with his phone until she heard some music start playing. It was George Strait. That native Texas son who seemed to always speak straight to Piper's heart.

The song was *"You Look So Good in Love."* An older song that was set to a country waltz. "My daddy used to love George Strait," he told her. "Want to dance instead of sitting?"

She remembered he had said he didn't like dancing. Yet right now he was holding out his hand to her. It was hard to resist the song *or* the man. She had been alone for a while by her own choice and she liked her life just fine like that, but tonight, with Brian, she was starting to realize that Brian had more to offer than she'd expected.

He put one hand on her waist and she put one hand on his shoulder and they joined their free hands. She didn't feel like he was trying to manipulate her. It seemed to her that he was just a guy holding a girl he liked. And she didn't analyze it more than that. She didn't want to worry that she was kidding herself as Brian sang under his breath and waltzed her around in a circle. Smart or not, all of her fears and reservations melted away.

She reminded herself that Brian was here only because she'd asked him. Sighing, she rested her head on his shoulder as he kept singing and dancing her around the patio. When the song ended, she looked up at him. A sizzle of awareness passed between them. Then he caught her jaw in his hand and rubbed his thumb over her lips.

Brian didn't want to rush her, but he could tell that Piper was having second thoughts. All of his life he'd been very sure of his path, but people were harder to manage, so he kept things cool and light because that was safer. He couldn't accomplish his goals if…if he let himself give into the emotions she'd stirred when he'd looked at that man she'd painted. He didn't want to be like his uncle Keith, devastated because of a woman. Brian wasn't that kind of man.

He dropped his hand and stepped back. He should

never have put on George Strait. That man messed with his head and made Brian believe that his heart could be…well, something it wasn't.

"Thank you for the dance," he said gruffly.

"It was my pleasure," she said. "I get the feeling we are both overthinking tonight."

"Oh, yeah," he admitted. "I'm not going to lie, Piper, I didn't just start liking you at Harley and Grant's wedding reception. I've had my eye on you for a while now, which I'm sure you picked up on. And I want to be all cool about this, but I'm not. And something tells me that you aren't either…"

She watched him with that unfathomable gaze, and he wanted her to find whatever it was she was looking for on his face. But the harder he tried to project that, the surer he was that he looked like Ron Stoppable from *Kim Possible*. That TV show he used to love as a kid. His mama always said that a person couldn't be what another person needed; they could only be themselves.

Be yourself.

But he didn't know if that man was what Piper needed…and he wanted her to want him. Not because he was ticking boxes and pretending to be the kind of guy he thought she wanted, but because the man he was would be enough for her.

"Oh, Brian. I can't let you just walk out of here," she whispered. "It might be smart. I hear what you are saying, and I know that those words are driven by my actions tonight, but I'll tell you one thing I've learned over the years…" She hesitated.

"What? Trust me, darling," he said.

She gave him that sad, sweet smile of hers. "I learned

that I never regret being impulsive, but I always regret being cautious."

He pulled her back into his arms, but there was no music playing now. "I like that. I like *you*. I don't know if we will last more than this night, but I don't want to walk away either." He gazed deeply into her eyes. "So you really want this too?"

She nodded, as if words weren't going to be enough, and put her hands on either side of his jaw just like she had earlier in his office. He got instantly hard. Then he felt the warmth of her exhalation a moment before her lips touched his and it felt like his blood was running heavier in his veins.

Brian put his hands on her waist and lifted her off her feet and into his body, her stomach rubbing against his erection. Then she lifted one thigh and wrapped it around his leg. He pushed his tongue deep into her mouth because this kiss made him ravenous for her. Made him hungry for something that he could only get from Piper Holloway. Something that his cold and lonely soul had been hungry for.

He shifted around and moved until he felt the stone pillar of her patio at his back. Canting his hips forward, he let her rest against him. Their breaths mingled as her breasts pillowed against his chest and his hands moved up and down her body.

She tasted like Baileys and moonlight. Like the conversations they'd had and the ones that he wanted to have with her. Like every kiss he'd always wanted but had never had until this moment, and he knew he wasn't going to be able to ever just walk away from her.

This night would stay with him for the rest of his life

and that felt right deep inside. He let his hands roam up and down her back, cupping her butt and drawing her more fully against him, rubbing the tip of his erection against that notch at the top of her thighs. She tore her mouth from his and her head dropped back as she took in a deep breath. He noticed the deep V in the halter top she had on and how her breasts rose and fell with each of her inhalations.

Brian drew one finger down the center of her sternum, tracing the gold circle charm that was nestled right above her cleavage before moving his hand farther down, grazing the side of her breast and feeling her heartbeat race as he did so. Their eyes met and he had no trouble reading the raw desire in hers.

He knew it must match the same in his own gaze. He lowered his mouth again, wanting to kiss her slowly. Wanting to take his time and make this moment last. However, needing her more than he needed his next breath, he knew that going slow was going to be impossible.

He wanted her spread out underneath him completely naked. And he also wanted to take her here against this post. To make her his so he could breathe again and then he could make love to her. Soft and slow and sweet. But first, he needed to claim her, with fierce unbridled passion, so that there would be no doubt as to what he wanted and who he was to her.

Six

Piper took his hand in hers and led him away from the post back to the big double lounger that she'd moved closer to the fire. This night was the kind that she'd missed. Companionship and sexy times were one of the few things she regretted about her choice to live her life on her own. But tonight, that wasn't a concern. Brian was here and doing things to her that she'd missed for such a long time.

She pushed him down and he leaned against the back. Emboldened, she climbed onto his lap, settling herself over his erection and rubbing her center over him. The low groan he let out made her breath catch in her throat. Then he cupped her butt in his hands, rubbing against the boot cut trousers she wore. She put her hands in his thick hair and tipped his head back. Then forced herself to close her eyes because she didn't want to think any more about what she saw on his face.

She just wanted to *feel*.

Life had been more than a little stressful lately and she needed this evening with Brian. He was complicated but so damned hot that she was just going to overlook the other parts. Just enjoy every second she had with this man. She loved the strength in him. He wasn't someone who was trying to pretend he didn't want her. Every movement of his body drew her closer to him. Made her want him even more. If she was so hungry for him, she should take her time, but she needed him.

Inside her.

Now.

His jaw had stubble on it and she liked the way it abraded her fingertips as she rubbed them over his skin. And that mouth of his, so wide and sensual with his full lower lip that just beckoned her closer, was too much to resist. She shifted up on his lap and his hands slid under her halter top, his large palm warm against her back as he splayed it against her skin.

She shuddered and brushed her lips over his and then angled her head to the side as he thrust his tongue into her mouth. Sucking on it, she drew it deeper inside, then felt his fingernail scraping along the base of her spine. She shivered again and lifted her head to look down at him.

"You feel even better than I imagined."

His eyes were heavy lidded—half-closed—and his lips were swollen from their kisses. There was a slight flush under his skin and his breathing was heavy. She pulled the halter top she had on up and over her head, tossing it aside. His eyes went wide open as he looked at her full breasts in the lace-covered bra.

"Fair enough," he said. "You are even sexier than in my dreams and they were pretty hot."

"How hot?"

He cupped her left breast with his free hand, his thumb rubbing over her nipple until it was taut. She shifted her shoulders and he fondled the fullness of her breast as she shifted forward, nudging his lips with her nipple. He licked her through the bra and sucked it into his mouth.

"Like Texas in the middle of August," he said, against her skin. "But hotter."

Piper moaned and spread her thighs so she could sink down on his lap and feel the ridge of his erection between her legs. She rocked her body against him as he continued to lave her nipple. He reached for the fastening of her bootcut pants and undid it, pushing his hand inside the back, under her panties, to cup her butt and drive her harder against him. Throbbing with pleasure, she rode the ridge of his cock. She wanted more. *Needed* more from him.

"You are," she said.

God, it had been so long since she'd felt this good in a man's arms. She reached for the buttons of his shirt and tore them open, pushing the material aside so she could dig her nails into the firm muscles of his pectorals. He flexed them, the hand on her ass squeezing her cheek before he wrapped his arm firmly around her waist and rolled them over. He held himself above her and she felt his hot breath fan against her face. His chest was bare, with a light dusting of hair, and she couldn't help running her fingers over it.

Then, with his eyes burning into hers, he pulled the strap of her bra down her arm until her breast was free from the fabric and did the same with the other side. She lay underneath him, aware that she wanted him more than she wanted her next breath, and reached between their bodies to caress his erection through the fabric of his jeans. He groaned, capturing her wrist and drawing her hand up to his mouth. Then he kissed it and held it loosely next to her head on the cushion.

"What are you doing?" she asked.

"Trying not to come in my pants," he said, his voice coarse and gravelly.

She almost laughed at how good those words made her feel. "I don't want it slow—"

He put his hand over her mouth. "Woman, I'm hanging on to my control by a thread," he admitted.

Piper licked the palm of his hand and watched his pupils dilate as he moved it and brought his mouth back down on hers. She felt his hand stroking down her body, sliding underneath her to undo the clasp of her bra, and then she felt it being shoved down her arms. A moment later, she pulled them free to tangle her hands in his thick hair.

She shifted, parting her legs to try to rub her aching center against his hard-on. He groaned again and she felt his hand between their bodies working at the button fly on his jeans. She brushed his hands away to take over the task.

Brian shifted out of her grasp, though, pulling her pants down her legs and cursing when they got caught on her shoes. He turned to take them off and she sat up, gliding her fingers down his spine. Then she reached around his front to feel his erection. She stroked him, undoing the rest of his buttons before pushing her fingers into the opening of his jeans and taking him in her hand. He was hot and hard.

Brian shifted around, moving delicately to make sure that he could get Piper's hand out of his pants and not harm himself. He hadn't been this horny since he'd been in his early twenties. She got to him faster than he wanted to admit. He shifted around and looked up her body. She lay back against the cushion, her arms up above her head, her thighs slightly parted. Watching him with that direct gaze that almost seemed to dare him to look away. He couldn't.

He wanted her totally naked and she was, except for that tiny pair of red bikini panties. Lifting her with one arm around her waist, he slowly drew the silky material down her legs and tossed it aside. Then he stood up next to the chair and toed off his boots. It took longer than he wanted it to, but he didn't want to stop looking at the goddess in front of him.

He looked down at his shirt. "You've ruined one of my favorite shirts."

"I'll buy you another one," she said with a wink. "It was kind of your fault for being so ripped."

He shook his head. "Fair enough."

He'd never had a woman compliment him so often on his physique, and while he admittedly worked out to relieve stress and to keep his mind focused, from now on he thought he'd always think of Piper when he did.

Brian tossed his shirt aside after undoing the buttons at the wrists and then pushed his pants and underwear down his legs, stepping out of them.

"Are you on the pill?" he asked. His voice was gruff again because she'd reached out to cup his balls as soon as he was naked.

"I am," she said. "I use it to regulate my period."

"Great." He was glad he didn't have to use a condom, unless she wanted him to. "I don't have a condom, but I'm clean."

"That's fine," she said. "I am too."

It was a conversation that he never felt awkward about having. They were in a new relationship, and it was the responsible thing to do.

"Now that we have that out of the way… I'm going to learn every inch of your body," he rasped.

"I like the sound of that," she said. "As long as I can explore too."

He realized he was going to have to keep himself under control because he wanted that, as well. Mutual pleasure had always been his goal when making love to a woman and tonight was no different. He crawled back onto the double lounger next to her after snagging one of the thick fleece-lined blankets, draping it over them so she didn't get cold.

Turning on his side, he drew her into his arms, kissing the side of her neck and slowly moving his way down the curve to her shoulder. Her cinnamon-scented perfume was a bit stronger there and he licked at the spot, tasting her skin. Then he moved lower, realizing that she had a tattoo on the inside of her forearm that he'd never noticed before. He shifted back so he could see it more clearly.

It was roman numerals in a classy font. He struggled to convert them to numbers but soon realized they were for the year 2001. "What is this for?"

As he ran his finger over the tattoo, gooseflesh spread down her arm and her nipple tightened.

"My annus horribilis. Just a reminder to myself that I made it through a year that I thought would kill me."

He turned his head, saw the shadows in her eyes and kissed her. "I'm glad. I bet it made you stronger."

"It did," she admitted. "Every time I see it, I stand a little taller, knowing I can handle anything that this crazy life throws at me."

Brian traced it again—he'd seen the steel in her more than once and knew that she'd have been shaped by her experiences. He wanted to know what had happened, but didn't ask. Instead, he resumed making love to this woman who was consuming him, body and soul.

Turning her on her side, facing away from him, he drew her back against his chest. He kissed her shoulder again, his hands cupping her breasts as he rubbed his erection between her butt cheeks. She shifted her legs, draping one thigh over his and pulling his top hand down her body and between her legs.

Brian cupped her in his hand, tracing over her center until he parted her and felt the tiny nub that was her pleasure center. He tapped it and she moaned a low deep sound and pulled his hand back, but she pushed herself against him.

"I liked that," she breathed.

He did it again, lazily plucking at her other nipple

while dusting kisses along her back and tapping her clit. She writhed in his arms and he shifted his hips, rocking himself against her, causing her to gasp in pleasure. Then she reached up to push her fingers into his hair, and he brought his mouth hungrily down on hers as he drove her toward her climax.

Her nails rubbed against his scalp as her hips gyrated faster against his hand and his hard-on. He wanted to shift and enter her but he also wanted her to orgasm first. Wanted to see her body go tight and as she came.

She started making tiny sounds, quick and fast, and then she tore her mouth from his and screamed his name as her body spasmed in his arms. He held her, stroking her between her legs until she turned in his arms and pushed him onto his back, straddling him.

Brian felt her hand rubbing up and down his cock. He jerked forward and realized his control was more slippery than he'd imagined. Watching her orgasm in his arms had almost sent him over the edge. He was trying to make this good for her, but he wanted her so badly that he only had to think of the moisture between her legs to feel himself careening over the edge.

He had been laboring hard to get his own law firm off the ground. Working cases and overseeing the construction of his building had consumed his time and hadn't really left him with the chance to do more than hook up. But this was way more intense.

Because it was Piper.

Pleasure surged through him as she trailed her hand up and down his length, her fingernails scraping over his skin. Then, scooting backward, she came up on her knees to look at him.

She took his shaft in one hand, stroking him in her fist. Moving it up and down in a slow and sensuous movement that made his balls tighten. She skimmed her finger over the tip of his erection when she reached the top, and his hips jerked forward.

Cupping his sac in one hand, she squeezed very softly as she tightened her grip on his shaft, causing him to start thrusting in her hand. Then she leaned forward and he felt her breath on his erection a moment before her tongue dashed out and traced the tip of him.

Awareness moved through his body, making him hyperaware of her hand on his shaft. He meant to stay still, but tangled his hands in her hair as her mouth engulfed him.

She sucked on him, her hand fondling his balls, and he felt his control shatter, but he wanted to be inside her the first time they made love. He gently lifted her from him, and she kissed his shaft as she straightened up, looking him right in the eyes. "Too much?"

"Yes. I want to come inside of you," he said, his voice sounding rough and gravelly to his own ears. Like all of the sophistication he'd cultivated over the years had been ripped away. "I don't want this to feel like something I imagined later."

"You imagine blow jobs?" she teased.

"Don't. Don't make me laugh right now," he gritted out, but he loved that she was so free and fun to be with. He lifted her onto his lap and lay back as he put his hands on her hips, thrusting upward until he felt her hot, humid core against his tip.

She smiled at him as she shifted around until he was inside of her, then lowered herself slowly, inch by delicious inch. When she was fully seated on him, she wriggled her eyebrows. "Is this what you had in mind?"

"No," he said, as he put one arm in the center of her back and drew her even farther down. Then, while he anchored her hips to his with his other hand, he drove himself up inside of her. Going as deep as he could. "This is."

"Oooh, I like it," she murmured.

Brian took everything she had to give him, pushing himself hard until he felt his orgasm shivering down his spine. His balls tightened and he heard those tiny sounds she'd made before her orgasm earlier as he let out his own roar and came inside of her.

He kept thrusting up into her until he was empty and then he fell back against the cushions, holding her in his arms. She rested her head in the curve of his neck and petted his chest as they both caught their breath. He rubbed his hand up and down her back, remembering that he'd said earlier they were simply dating. That this couldn't be serious since they'd only had one date. But he knew deep inside that was a lie. This was more serious than anything he'd experienced before. He held her lightly because he wanted to wrap himself around her and make it so he never had to let her go.

But he knew he had to. She didn't want anything serious with him. She'd pretty much said that. So he had to tread carefully.

For both their sakes.

"That was amazing," she said, lifting her head. "Want to spend the night?"

Brian looked up at her. He wanted so much more than that, but he could start with one night. "I'd love that. I have my gym bag in the car… I didn't get to work out today. Let me go and grab it so I have some clean clothes for the morning."

She nodded. "I'll clean this all up and meet you inside."

He pulled his jeans on and looked back at her, lying on the lounger with just the blanket pulled up around her body, her shoulders bare, and he knew he had found something that he hadn't been looking for. He didn't let his mind go there because only time would tell if his gut was right. Instead, he walked through her house and got his gym bag from the car.

Then he showered with her and made love to her again before they both fell asleep in her queen-sized bed. He woke often to look down at her. He'd somehow ended up in the one place he'd wanted to be, and it was both better than he'd expected and a hell of a lot scarier. He'd never been a man to run from anything, but the way Piper made him feel…he didn't want to dwell on it.

The next time he woke it was to the smell of coffee and the sound of Piper talking to someone in the other room. He walked out to find her sitting in her favorite armchair and talking on the phone. She looked up, putting her finger over her lips in a shushing motion.

"I'll call you back," she said, hanging up.

Was she embarrassed to have been with him?

Brian looked at her sitting there, the woman he had wanted for a while now. He'd always been the kind of man who was very good at getting what he wanted, and wasn't afraid to go after the things that might seem out of reach to others. He'd never thought of himself as *less than* until she'd motioned for him to be quiet.

He wasn't embarrassed to be here with her. But he realized that, as much as he might not view them as opponents, she did. She was squarely on her sister's side and she might not want Keith Cooper's nephew in her bed. And while that was her decision and he'd respect it, he didn't want her to have used him the way that it seemed Ava had used his uncle.

Seven

"What was that about?" Brian asked.

His hair was tousled from sleep, and seeing him this morning, looking sexy as sin, just reinforced all the feelings she'd had for him last night.

God he was so ripped that she had a hard time tearing her gaze from his chest. She felt that tingle in all the right places and wished she'd stayed in bed with him this morning. But he confused her. They should be casual but she'd awoken and stared down into his face, feeling something more.

Something that was far from casual.

Piper had always kept things light in her relationships because of her own self-preservation. She'd made up her mind after her broken engagement that she'd never be that vulnerable to a man again. Which posed a huge problem. Because she hadn't realized until this very moment that Brian meant more to her than she had thought he would.

"I just didn't want to have to explain to Ava that you had spent the night," she said.

"Explain? Why would you?" he asked, coming closer to her.

She was having a hard time keeping her eyes off his broad, muscular chest. He wore a pair of boxer briefs and nothing else. He had no tattoos on his body, was one-hundred-percent eye candy. Not a bad way to start the day.

Then his words sank in.

"She's was always mothering me. I think it's the age difference."

"Would you have asked any man to be quiet or is it just me?" he asked her.

She was beginning to realize that Brian was upset about this. "Anyone. Why? Do you think it was only you?"

"Yes. I'm younger. I'm Keith's nephew. I don't know if I was just some booty call for you or not," he admitted stiffly. "And shushing me…well, the last time I shushed a lover, I was sixteen and my dad was knocking on the door."

Piper arched one eyebrow at him. She wanted to know more about that story, but this wasn't the time. "Ava has always grilled me about every man I see. And this morning, when I'm here with you and happy, I simply didn't want that. I wanted to enjoy this Saturday morning, Brian, that was all."

He nodded and she got up from where she'd been sitting and walked over to him. Wrapping her arms around him, she gave him a kiss. Then, to her relief, he sighed hugging her back. "I know you're too good for me. I mean, Ava will probably tell you that."

"I don't care what she says. This is between you and me," she said firmly. "Now, do you want some coffee?"

"Yes," he answered. Then his stomach growled, and he blushed.

"Maybe some breakfast?"

"Yes. But you don't have to cook. I'll make us omelets," he said.

"That'd be great if I had eggs but I'm out. I do have toaster waffles and maple syrup. Will that do?"

"Definitely," he murmured.

She led the way into the kitchen and handed him a mug before pointing him to the French press that she used for her morning coffee. It was better for the environment than those capsule machines and she liked the taste of it better. She pulled a box of toaster waffles from the freezer and looked inside. There were three left. He looked like the kind of guy who would need more than one or two.

She put the three she had in the toaster and then started going through her pantry until she found a can of fruit cocktail. "I'm so not prepared for overnight guests."

"I don't think either of us anticipated this," he said. "I don't regret it."

"I don't either," she admitted.

His phone started ringing in the bedroom and he took his coffee with him as he went to retrieve it.

Piper thought about Ava, who had called early wanting to talk. She'd have to call her back; there had been a note in her sister's voice that she hadn't heard since Trent got sick. Like she was edgy and depressed. Never a good combination in Ava.

"That was a client. I'm going to have to go," he said as he came back into the kitchen. "I wish I could stay for breakfast. Do you want to try to have brunch tomorrow? I'm going with my parents."

Parents? Not sure she was ready for that, she shook her head. "I can't. But I'll see you on Wednesday for the Boots and Boas Gala."

"Do you want to plan to stay at my place downtown?" he asked. "It's closer to the gala and you won't have to drive home after."

Piper liked how he'd made it seem logical; he was being chill about them and that made it easier *and* harder for her. She wanted to pretend he was just a hot younger guy she was sleeping with, but her emotions were already going wild. She nodded. "I'd love to."

"Sorry to have run out like this," he said.

"It's okay. It's your job."

He had put his jeans on and a black Under Armour T-shirt that she guessed had been in his gym bag. Piper followed him to the door, and he bent to kiss her before he left. She stood there in the doorway, watching him leave, until she realized she probably looked like a fifties housewife and closed it.

Piper liked Brian but he was bringing things to the surface that she knew couldn't ever be. She didn't feel safe being the sensual woman that he stirred to life. That woman was reckless and ruled by passion instead of logic. She'd been burned so publicly all those years ago and that was why she'd stayed single.

She rubbed the back of her neck as she felt the worry get the best of her. Why did what had transpired between her and Brian the previous night bother her? she wondered. But deep down she knew the reason. It was because the sensual, feminine goddess inside of her had been broken.

Perhaps irrevocably.

Which meant she should be very careful about what else went on between the two of them. As bad as thinking about her inability to let go and indulge in a relationship with a man eleven years her junior was, talking about it with him would be a million times worse.

Sighing, she went back into the kitchen as the waffles popped up. And though she normally limited herself to one, she put butter on all three of them and smothered them in syrup. She enjoyed her breakfast, telling herself she didn't mind eating alone, but in her heart, she knew she wished he was still there with her.

Brian spent the rest of Saturday taking care of one of his clients whose son had gotten arrested on Friday night. That was not his area of expertise and he brought in one of his former employers who did handle criminal law to handle it. By the time he had a chance to text Piper, it was almost six in the evening.

Normally he didn't overthink his relationships, but as he opened their text string, he knew he didn't want to come on too strong. Despite what she'd said about Ava, a part of him wasn't sure that she was okay with him as her lover. And he wanted to be so much from her. She was still hiding something from him.

But what?

And as much as he'd thought that sleeping with Piper would lessen his need for her, that hadn't happened. In fact, it had simply made him crave her even more.

Hell.

He'd never been a man to hesitate when he wanted something, and he wasn't going to now that he had a chance with Piper. He texted her to see how her day had gone.

Then he put his phone down and went to shower and get dressed. He usually went to the Texas Cattleman's Club in Dallas for dinner if he didn't have plans. And tonight wasn't going to be any different.

He put on his watch and then allowed himself to glance at his phone. She'd texted him back.

Piper: I ended up in my studio and started a new project. It's going well. How about you?

He sat down on the leather wingback chair in his bedroom, then responded.

Brian: Busy day for me but we got things sorted. Are you tired after working in your studio all day?

Piper: Yes. But also exhilarated! I know I said no to seeing each other tonight but I need to get out of my house.

Brian: I was going to head to the TCC for dinner. Want to join me?

Piper: Yes. Thank you. See you in about an hour?

Brian: [[thumbs up emoji]]

He smiled to himself, anticipating seeing her when he hadn't expected to. Was he letting himself get in too deep with her? Was she going to push him aside the way Ava had Uncle Keith? But he had never been able to control his emotions. He didn't fall easily for women, but when he did, it seemed it happened quickly.

He finished getting ready and then called an Uber to the club. He figured he'd be drinking tonight and didn't want to risk driving home. When he got there he saw some new members he didn't know and a few people from legacy families, like his own, who'd belonged to the original Texas Cattleman's Club in Royal. He nodded to the people he knew but kept moving toward the bar. There he ordered a Lone Star beer and found a seat that gave him a view of the entrance.

He caught up on emails and sipped his beer, looking up every time the door opened until finally he saw Piper standing there. She smiled and waved when she saw him. Her pixie cut was styled in a punk-rock look tonight, and she wore a brown suede skirt that ended midcalf and a cream-colored sweater that ended at her waist. How did she manage to take his breath away every time she entered a room?

Piper headed over to him and he got up to hold a chair out for her. She took his hand and gave him a quick kiss before she sat.

"What can I get for you? I put my name in for a table but there's a forty-minute wait," he said.

"Skinny margarita," she murmured. "Maybe some nachos."

"Got it."

He walked over to the bar and placed the order, getting another beer for himself. It was too early in the evening for tequila for him. Carrying their drinks back, he set them down on the table and slid into a seat across from her. He wanted to hear all about her day but tried to play it cool.

She took a long drag on her margarita and sighed. "I was consumed with an idea after breakfast this morning. I thought I'd just do some sketches, but it turned into a full-blown concept and the next thing I know, it's nighttime and I'm starving."

"Does that happen a lot?" he asked with interest.

"Not as often as I'd like, but when it does, I just go with it," she said. "Does that happen to you?"

"Not the same way, but I think so. Sometimes I'll start doing research for a brief and the next thing I know it's midnight," he admitted. He'd always been called obsessive about his work but most of the time he just lost himself in it. He liked uncovering the path to justice for his clients. Finding and noting precedents were one of the things he'd always loved.

"That sounds exactly like it. I was starving when I finished, and as you know there is no food in my house," she said ruefully. "I pretty much pick up something to eat every night on my way home from the gallery, but I've been so busy with the extra work I've taken on."

"Hopefully you can slow down soon," he murmured as their nachos arrived.

"I hope so, but I'm not sure what it will take to change people's minds. You know how small-minded they can be sometimes."

"I do," he admitted. There were a lot of people who thought that where there was smoke, there was fire where the Wingates were concerned, but he'd known that family for a long time now and they were upright people. Not lawbreakers. "I hate that you are being affected by it."

"Me too. I worked hard to establish the gallery, but now everyone wants to believe that I took tainted money," she said, shaking her head. "I don't want to talk about that tonight. Tell me about your day."

He distracted her by talking about how he'd had to be more therapist than lawyer for his client while a colleague took over the case. He couldn't go into specifics, due to lawyer/client privilege, so switching gears, he started telling her about a new modern art exhibit that he'd heard was coming to Dallas.

Somehow after dinner she found herself agreeing to play a game of pool with Brian. She hadn't played since college, when she'd hustled guys who used to hit on her and her roommate, Char, when they went out. Her first shot was wide and not very good, so she wasn't too sure that she was up to this hotshot attorney's level.

He hadn't missed a shot until she noticed that if she bent over her shot, he watched her and not the ball. And though it probably wasn't fair of her to do it, she started using it to her advantage. Which was great for getting her a turn, but she still hadn't sunk a ball.

"You know what might help?" he asked as she lined up for her next shot.

"Hmm?"

He came up behind her. His hips fitted to hers and then he leaned over her. Putting one hand on the green felt and the other on her shoulder, he scolded, "If you stopped trying to distract me and actually paid attention to your game."

She turned and wrinkled her nose at him. "Distracting you is the only thing I'm good at tonight."

He laughed and stood up next to her. "How long has it been since you played?"

"At least fifteen years," she replied. "And I did okay back then."

"Did you do a lot of distracting?" he teased.

"Believe it or not, I thought that was crass behavior and never tried it," she said. "Usually guys would go easy on me and Char because they thought we couldn't play. All we had to do was a get a turn and we'd sink them all."

"So, you were pretty good then," he said.

"We were okay. But you, my friend, have real skills."

"My dad has a table and we played at home," he admitted. "I like it. It forces me to get out of my head. My dad always says I can't debate a ball into seeing things my way."

She had to laugh at that. As free-spirited as she was, Brian seemed equally intense. He was a man who spent his days thinking and arguing and winning people around to his way of thinking. She had to remember that. He was very persuasive.

"Since you are killing me at this game, what do you say we stop playing?" she suggested.

"I don't know. I like it when you pretend to drop something just as I line up a shot," he said.

She threw her head back and laughed. "I'm willing to keep doing it at your place."

"You want to come home with me?"

"I do," she said softly. "If you want me to..."

"Hell, yes." He took her hand and drew her into his

arms, looking down into her eyes. She realized how well they fit together. And while she still had her guard up, she decided to stop worrying needlessly over this thing with Brian. She needed someone in her life who got her and let her be herself. Someone who was on her side, and Brian seemed to be that man.

"Do you want to finish your drink?"

"I'm good," she said. Honestly, she just wanted to be with him. All day long she'd been working on a painting that summed up her life right now. It was abstract, but people had started to emerge as she'd worked. Her sister, of course, her daddy, to whom she'd always been close…and then Brian. The more she'd worked on the painting, the clearer it had become that she wasn't going to be able to just label him as a distraction. He was already deeply rooted inside of her.

So, she'd decided to go with this for as long as it lasted.

"Let's go," he said, leading her out of the billiards room and outside. "I took an Uber, did you drive?"

"I did," she said. "It's damn expensive to get an Uber from Frisco."

"Do you mind leaving your car here overnight?" he asked. "I've had too many drinks to drive."

"I don't mind at all," she said. The parking area was monitored, and she didn't want to take a chance on either of them driving after drinking.

He called an Uber and they were in his penthouse apartment before she knew it. The place was modern, yet had a homey feel to it. He led her into the living room and she admired the view of the glittering Dallas skyline as he made them margaritas in the other room. She took off her boots and wondered what she was doing there, but knew there was no other place she wanted to be.

That thought scared her. So much so, she was seconds away from getting her stuff and leaving.

He came back with two margaritas and handed one to her. "What would you like to do?"

Cuddle on the couch and watch TV, she thought. But she didn't dare say that out loud. She had warned herself against this. He was becoming too important to her and she needed to pull back. Sex was okay. This other stuff...*wasn't*.

"Um... I'm not sure. What did you have in mind?"

"There is a game on," he said.

"God, you are such a guy!"

"Yeah, I am," he acknowledged. "I thought you liked that."

She laughed. "I do."

"What do you usually do at night?"

"Listen to some music and sketch," she said, following him around the apartment.

"Let me go get changed and we can figure something out that's not art or sports... Do you want some sweats and T-shirt to wear?"

She nodded and followed him up to his bedroom. Brian had some art on the walls, and she saw a piece that she knew he'd bought from her gallery. "When did you get this?"

"A few months ago. You weren't in the gallery, but I didn't want to take a chance on someone else buying it."

"It's perfect in this space. I have another piece by this artist that I put in your large conference room. It has the same expansive feel as this landscape. But it's Santa Fe instead of Austin," she said.

"I can't wait to see it," he said. "You have a great eye for quality."

"I do," she acknowledged, realizing that she was looking at him. Brian was the kind of guy she wished she'd met in her twenties. But she hadn't. And they were from families that had a plethora of tension between them. And she needed to remember that she was here for his hot body and sexy kisses.

That was all.

Eight

Piper hadn't been sure what to expect as Brian's date to the Habitat for Humanity Boots and Boas charity gala.

The event was held at the Gaylord Texan Resort and Convention Center. Overlooking beautiful Lake Grapevine, the resort seemed to pay tribute to everything Texas. And it was bigger than most other places. The resort featured a water park and nightclubs along with accommodations and five-star amenities.

They had already started decorating for Christmas and Piper took her time walking through the lobby, admiring the festive decor. She was looking forward to the holidays this year, hoping that somehow her family would be cleared of all charges and maybe life would go back to normal.

Though, what *was* normal? She honestly didn't know

anymore. After all, she was at this public event with a man—something she'd vowed to never do once her engagement had been broken—but Brian was changing her. This was the first event she'd attended in a long time where she wasn't stag. Something she refused to dwell too deeply on.

It was the kind of thing that she had enjoyed before everything had happened with the Wingate family, and she'd been painted with the same suspicions as her sister and nieces and nephews. But being on Brian's arm made her hardly even notice the stares and comments whispered behind hands.

Brian had bought them matching boots from Paul Bond, an American custom boot maker. She loved them. He'd gifted them to her the night before and she'd settled on a cocktail dress with a short skirt that ended above her knees to show off the boots. Brian hadn't been able to keep his hand off her thigh under the dinner table before the auction started, and that was nice too.

She'd always dreaded this gala because when she'd been twenty-four her fiancé had dumped her the night before this very event. It had been her first time donating a piece of art to auction off, and it had made that year's event sheer torture, but Ava had come with her and been her regal above-it-all self. She'd saved Piper that year and that was something Piper hadn't forgotten.

There had been times when it was easy to focus on what a bitch her sister could be, but there was a very soft heart underneath the tough exterior. No one had even thought about saying anything to Piper, despite the rumors that were swirling that Ron had run off with another woman after dumping her.

They weren't really rumors, since that had been exactly what happened. But Ava had saved her. Now Brian was doing the same thing. Only this time he was protecting her from Ava and the scandal that surrounded the Wingate family. Many of the attendees were gossiping about alleged seizure of their property and their company, as well as investigations by the DEA, were pretty damning things, but Brian was her white knight. Keeping the louder gossips at bay and giving her a really fun evening when she hadn't expected one.

"Your sculpture is up next," Brian told her. "I'll let you know I'm going to go hard to get it for myself."

"You don't have to," she protested. "You being here has been more than enough."

"I'm not doing it to be nice. It will look perfect in the lobby of the building. I didn't like the piece you sent over and we have been discussing a mural which I think will make a nice backdrop to this," he said. "You said we needed something bold that speaks to our clients, and that sculpture definitely does. I mean, you captured the heart of what many of my younger clients are actually dealing with. I'm awed by your talent, Piper."

A flush of pride went through her and she smiled at him. "It's not really—"

"Don't do that," he said gruffly. "Take the compliment."

She nodded, and inwardly she thought about how she'd been raised and how it had once been more accepted to demur at kudos. But she had been in her studio day and night to produce this. It was a true labor of love in every sense of the word. "Thank you. I worked really hard at it. I had a recording of Xavier doing his spoken-word poetry that I played while I worked. His voice and word choices change as he moves between the two worlds. I just hope I captured enough of that."

She'd named the sculpture The Border and tried to show Xavier's struggle to stay on the right side of the law. The sculpture was one body but two faces looking in different directions. One contemplative, the other angry. In one hand was a notepad and pen, in the other, a gun.

"I'd say you did," Brian said, then glanced beyond her to where a couple of women were standing and watching them. "I think those ladies might agree."

She looked over her shoulder and noticed that the women were from a local PTA that she worked with to encourage arts. She waved them over. "Hi, Kim and Kathy. This is Brian Cooper. He's a family lawyer here in Dallas. Brian, these ladies are from the Thomas Hicks PTA. I work with them to bring an after-school art experience to the kids."

Everyone shook hands and Brian offered to brave the crowd at the bar and bring them back drinks. Everyone ordered a prosecco and he left.

"I love this piece," Kathy said. "I'm going to go back to our parents and see if we can get something like this for our school. Of course, a piece geared toward younger kids, but I think they all struggle with duality."

"I'd love to do a commission for you," Piper said. "Just let me know."

"We will. I have to warn you there have been some rumors about your family that a few concerned parents have raised with us," Kim informed her. "We know you,

Piper, and have squelched them. But it might be hard to get this approved this school year."

Piper bit her lower lip to keep from saying something and then just smiled at the ladies. What could she say anyway? She couldn't change the opinions of the parents in the school district. Heck, she wasn't exactly sure what had happened at Wingate Enterprises, only knew that her family hadn't acted illegally. No one really seemed sure about who was responsible, though her nieces and nephews had a few leads that they were pursuing.

"There is no hurry for art," Piper said. "Will you two excuse me? I see someone I need to speak to."

"Of course," they said.

She walked away, trying not to dwell on the far-reaching aspects of the criminal activities of a company that she'd never had anything to do with. But that was easier said than done. Instead, she moved closer to the bar, where Brian stood, waiting his turn in line. He looked over at her, quirking one eyebrow.

Piper just forced a smile and indicated she'd be waiting in the corner. She was a social person by nature. But tonight, being in this room, she wanted to shrink into herself. To just blend in with the background until all the hurt that was buried under her skin disappeared.

"You okay?" Brian asked, coming over to her a few minutes later and handing her a champagne flute. She'd noticed he'd had a waiter deliver to the rest of their table.

"Yes. Just overwhelmed for a few moments," she admitted. "I want so much for everyone to see my sculpture for what it is and not filtered through the lens of the criminal activities that have engulfed Wingate Enterprises."

"I'm sure they will," he said.

But she knew that even Brian, who was a very forceful presence, couldn't change anyone's conceptions about herself and her family.

Brian went to a lot of these types of events and normally found them a bit dry and boring, but sitting next to Piper was eye-opening. She'd chilled out after the first prosecco, and since she'd been attending this event for close to fifteen years, she knew some random fact about nearly everyone in the room.

Her little asides had him in stiches as the gala progressed. She hadn't said anything, but it wasn't hard for him to guess that the Wingate scandal was having a profound effect on her life. He knew that her gallery wasn't seeing as much business due to that, and he wished there were some way he could help.

But investigations by the FBI and the DEA, and embezzling and drug dealing weren't necessarily in his wheelhouse. For tonight, though, he hoped he was providing enough of a distraction for Piper to enjoy herself and forget about all of that.

And for himself to forget, as well.

It was hard to be from two families who were at odds and just allow themselves to date. He knew that their rivalry over who to trust wasn't as bad here in Dallas, but when they were in Royal all of it would matter.

He still wasn't sure what her play was here. There were times when she let herself go and was the sensual woman he knew she could be. But other times he saw her barriers come up and she forced a wedge between them.

He knew that Ava had done that to his uncle Keith. Keith had been vocal when he'd spoken to Brian's dad about how he'd been blindsided by her refusing his calls after moving out of his house and into her own place in Royal.

Caution seemed to be more prudent where Piper was concerned but when she was naked in his bed was when he felt he saw the real woman. And playing it safe around her wasn't an option. Because every time he slept with her, he felt something change inside of him.

Fear was a funny thing. Brian used it sometimes to convince his clients to take action, and it motivated them to make the big decisions, but it could be crippling, as well. Right now, he was watching her laugh, her head thrown back in pure and utter delight. She turned to him and he felt a jolt of desire but also a punch right in the heart.

Could he trust her?

She tipped her head to the side. "Why are you watching me instead of the stage?"

"There isn't anything I want up there," he admitted.

She put her hand on him, her fingers caressing his inner thigh as she leaned forward. "But you want me?"

Her whispered words right in his ear made him hard in an instant. She brushed her fingertip over his erection and then wriggled her eyebrows at him. "As soon as my piece goes under the hammer, what do you say we head home?"

"Yes," he said, perhaps a little too forcefully as several heads turned toward them. He just smiled at them and leaned over to whisper in Piper's ear all the filthy things he wanted to do to her.

The emcee announced her sculpture, *The Border*, and once it was brought onto the stage, they started the bidding. She pulled her hand from his leg and knotted hers together in her lap. Brian realized that she was nervous about this part and he couldn't blame her. He would be too. But he wanted her sculpture for his building and raised the bid. Someone on the other side of the room was keen to have it, as well, and kept bidding against him. Finally, Brian just made a huge increase and the room went silent.

"Any other bids?"

To his relief, he won the sculpture and there was a round of applause in the room. He looked over at Piper, who watched him with a look in her eyes that he couldn't read.

"Congratulations to you both," Mrs. Standard said from across the table. "That's a lovely piece and well worth every penny."

"Thank you," Piper said. "Will you excuse me?"

She grabbed her handbag and fled from the table.

"Thanks," Brian echoed. "I am going to go check on my lady."

He got up and followed Piper through the crowded ballroom. She was moving quickly and he had to lengthen his strides to keep up with her as she hurried down a long corridor and out onto one of the patios that were heated with lamps at this time of the year.

"Are you okay?" he asked.

She turned and her face was white, which amplified his concern for her.

"Piper?"

"Yes, I'm fine. I was…you bid a lot of money on my art," she said. "Why did you do that?"

"Because it's a really good piece and you created it. I want to see it every time I walk into my building. It might be based on the spoken-word poet, but I see you in it, Piper. The struggle you feel between being what society and Ava have wanted you to be and the goddess within."

The goddess within.

He saw things in her that no other man had seen before and that made her realize that things were getting too real. She wasn't ready for him. Or for anything like Brian in her life. They were truly all wrong for each other. She'd let this go on for too long because she was wildly attracted to him and had wanted to believe he wasn't the kind of guy to get serious with her.

But the emotions he stirred in her were strong and she wanted to believe—hell, she could see on his face that the feelings went both ways.

"I'm not a goddess," she said. "I'm just a woman who is doing my best to get along. That's really all any of us can ask, right?"

He pulled her into his arms, the expression on his face so intense that she shivered. "Yes, it is. But there is more to you than that. You know it and I think you don't want me to know it. Why is that?"

She pulled away from him, shivering at the cold and yet at the same time hardening her emotions to what she had to do. She had to end this. On this night when she felt so many things. The highs and the lows of her life were centered now on this one man who'd come to mean more to her than she'd ever believed possible.

Which meant she had to cut him out of her life before he left her. There were a lot of barriers between them and they hadn't mattered as much earlier.

She had to do it now before…before he did it and it hurt so much more deeply. And, as selfish as it might be, *she* wanted to be the one to walk away so she could at least feel like she'd saved a bit of her soul.

"What you are seeing is age and maturity. I seem different than the other women you have dated because I have seen so much more of life," she said, channeling her inner Carrie Fisher and being that strong woman she knew she could be. "The truth is, when you are forty, I'll seem like everyone else."

He crossed his arms over his chest and tipped his head to the side as if he couldn't really comprehend what she was saying. "You want me to believe that everything that makes Piper Holloway so special is just age?"

When he put it like that, she admitted to herself, it sounded like an excuse. "You're being a little overdramatic, but yes."

"Overdramatic?" he asked. "I'm pretty much known for being the coolest head in the room. I think you're trying to break up with me and I'm not even sure I know why. We aren't even serious per your design."

Piper sighed. This wasn't going well—she knew better than to start a conversation like this when she was so emotional. She liked Brian. Hell, she might even be starting to fall in love with him, but there was a part of her that knew she wasn't ready to be her true self with him. To expose the parts of herself that she ignored and hated. To give in to the passion that had always been her downfall.

It was as if part of her femininity was at stake and she didn't want to have to admit that to Brian, who was, in her eyes, the perfect male. He was everything she craved and nothing she would allow herself.

"I am breaking up with you," she said at last. "It's been fun but that is all it was meant to be."

"And I'm getting too real for you?" he asked roughly.

"Yes. I think about you a lot more than I should, Brian. And we both know there is no future in this…"

He cussed a blue streak and turned away from her, his head bowed and his hands on his hips. The litany of curses eventually died down, but he stayed that way, with his back to her. And she knew she'd hurt him, which was the *last* thing she wanted, but now she could leave with her head held high and her heart battered but not totally broken.

He turned back around and the pain on his face brought tears to her eyes. She blinked quickly to keep them from falling.

"Why not? Is it because of the complicated history between my uncle and your sister?"

She swallowed hard. "Don't."

The one word was all she could muster. Her throat was tight as she tried to keep from crying while he was baring his soul to her. She struggled to keep hers hidden.

"Why not? I need the truth from you," he rasped. "Or is that something that you won't give me?"

"I'm not the woman you think I am," she said, thinking of how dangerous her unleashed passion could be. And she wasn't ready for this. Being here with him, having him buy a piece she'd made for such a large sum. He was focusing every eye on them and she didn't like who she was in the public spotlight.

"There is literally nothing you can say to convince me of that. I am not falling for an image of who I think Piper Holloway is. I'm falling for the artist who loses herself in her studio for days on end. Who painted a portrait of me that wasn't for show but showed the real man."

He came closer, held out his hand. "Won't you give us a chance?"

She bit her lip as tears did start falling, for she couldn't keep them back any longer. "I can't do this. This is a huge mistake. Goodbye, Brian."

She turned and forced herself to walk back into the hotel and out of his life.

Nine

The hour drive from Dallas to Royal gave her way too much time to think. A million times she'd thought of the other way things could have gone with Brian. But she didn't have time for regrets.

She'd made her choice and she had to live with it.

Besides, better to walk away now before she made a huge mistake. She liked to think that she had life sorted and could roll with the punches. Even if this one was harder to recover from.

Running back to Royal wasn't her style. She'd always prided herself on standing on her own, being able to find her place outside of her sister's shadow. But when Ava called, sounding positively dreadful, Piper knew she couldn't turn her back on her.

The trip was long and uneventful. By rote she drove

to the Wingate estate, which, of course, had been seized and was no longer Ava's home. Piper sat there in front of the mansion and the anger she felt toward Keith Cooper grew.

She knew that, at best, he'd taken advantage of her sister, but he'd been her sister and Trent's friend. He'd been a strong shoulder for Ava, though maybe he should have worked harder to help the family sort out the suspicious activities at Wingate. That would have really helped Ava.

It didn't help matters that she wanted to be angry at men with the surname of Cooper. She hated that Brian had pushed so hard and forced her hand. Made her have to admit that it was time to go back to her typical kind of guy. The kind who was divorced and already had a family or was still single because he hadn't even wanted one.

She put the car in gear and drove to the house that her sister had rented. Ava had been staying with Keith until her children's dislike of the way he tried to control her had finally gotten through to her. Piper took her weekender bag and went up the front steps.

Ava answered the door looking well put together and making Piper rethink the moto-style leggings and AC/DC T-shirt she wore under her leather biker jacket. Especially when her sister raised one eyebrow at her.

"It's not a mystery why you are still single," Ava said by way of greeting.

"They all have heard I'm your sister and are afraid to come too close," Piper said, deadpan.

Ava gave her a slight smile and hugged her. "Thank you for coming."

"You're welcome," Piper said. "I needed a break from Dallas anyway."

Ava led the way into the house and told Piper she could drop her bag in the study off to the left. She went to the eat-in kitchen and offered Piper something hot to drink. She shook her head. "I'm good. After that long drive, I could use a walk. Want to go for a stroll around the neighborhood?"

"Not really," Ava said. "But I will. Let me get changed."

Piper waited while her sister went and put on her Lululemons, donned a baseball cap and a pair of dark glasses, and declared herself ready. Piper wanted to poke fun at Ava for dressing as if the paparazzi were lurking behind her well-trimmed hedges, but she knew her sister had taken a beating over the last few months and kept her mouth shut.

The neighborhood was gated and Ava's privacy from the outside world was ensured, but the neighbors still talked about her. And while Piper knew her sister relished attention, she certainly did not want the kind she'd been subjected to lately.

"I hate this," Ava admitted. "I don't like not having a job to go to or being at odds with the kids. Nothing has been the same since Trent died."

Piper squeezed her sister's shoulder. This was exactly what she needed, someone else's problems to focus on to put her breakup with Brian into perspective. "It hasn't been. How could it be? You two were together so much that his death left a gaping hole in your life."

Ava nodded. "It did. I can only guess that's why I leaned so hard on Keith. I mean, as much as I want to say that he wasn't acting honorably, I have to admit he did comfort me."

"*Comfort* you? In what way?" Piper asked.

"Just as a companion. The trip to Europe did take my mind off my problems, and I let him handle things for me so I could just wallow in my grief and start to heal. He and Trent had been such good friends, especially when we were younger. It was nice to relive those memories and not have to worry about upsetting the kids by talking about their dad with them," Ava said. "But that was it."

Piper put her hand up. "That must have been nice. I don't know what I would have done in your situation."

"Count yourself lucky that you've never been in love and lost," Ava said.

Piper stopped walking. Ava knew about her broken engagement and the fact that she couldn't have kids. How could she say that Piper had never been in love? Sometimes Piper thought the fact that she'd been so in love had been the reason it had taken her so long to fall for a man again. To fall for Brian, who wasn't the right guy for her either, because he had dreams that she wouldn't deny him.

"What's wrong?"

Taken aback, she swallowed past the lump in her throat. "You know that I was in love," she said.

"Sorry, Piper, I thought we were talking about me. Could this just be about me for a few minutes?" Ava asked plaintively.

"When *isn't* it about you?" Piper retorted. She had driven all this way to keep her sister company and Ava was being…well, very Ava about it.

"Sorry. You're right," Ava said. "I just don't know what to do. I feel like I'm losing everyone important to me. The kids are distant and mistrust me because of Keith. And I'm snapping at you, which I know isn't fair."

Piper put her arm around her sister's waist and hugged her, and was gratified when Ava returned the embrace.

"I'll deny this if you repeat it, but I'm so lost."

"I am too," Piper admitted thickly.

They stood there for another moment, and for the first time Piper thought she really understood her sister. That they were both in the same spot and both connecting on a level she'd never expected.

"See? I can be supportive of someone else," Ava said wryly.

"I've always known that," Piper admitted. "You might not like the world to see it, but you care very deeply about your friends and family."

"That's right. I think that's what got me into the mess with Keith. I was just so lonely when Trent died," Ava confessed.

"It happens to everyone. But you're on the right path now," Piper said warmly.

She wished she could say more. Talk to Ava about Brian and everything that was going on right now, but this bond felt so new and Piper suspected it might be fragile if she mentioned a Cooper. The rivalry between their families was real even though when she'd been with Brian she'd never dwelled on it.

Brian was in court and needed to be on his A game, but instead he kept rerunning the night of the charity gala to figure out what he'd done or said to set Piper off. He knew that her emotions had been running high due to people talking about her and the Wingates, and he completely empathized with her for feeling that way. He would probably have gotten drunk and started a fight…except that wasn't his way.

He wished sometimes that he *was* that kind of guy. The kind who just felt things for a moment, expressed them and then moved on, but he never had been. He knew he was ruled by intellect and not passion—normally. Piper hadn't been wrong in any of the things she'd said the other night except when she'd been talking about him.

She didn't know him at all if she thought he'd be influenced by age. That he couldn't see the woman she was. What was he missing? Something he had said must have convinced her he didn't want her long-term.

"All rise," the bailiff said, and Brian stood, making sure his client did, as well. He knew he had to push his thoughts of Piper to the back of his mind until they were done in court.

He charged a respectable rate and his client deserved his full attention. So he did his job, ensuring his client was awarded as much monetarily from the breakdown of her marriage as she was entitled to. He also helped her get the custody agreement she wanted and tried to negotiate her desired move out of her neighborhood, but her husband wasn't about to budge on that front. The judge suggested that they either accept each other's terms or go to mediation, which they'd done three times already. Finally, thinking of Piper and the fact that she'd summarily ended their relationship, he turned to his client during the recess.

"Do you think you'll want to move?"

"No. My kids love that house and it's their home. I just hate that he won't let me," she said.

"We can go back to mediation or we can let him think he's won this and ask for more money," he told her. "I think I can get more for you if you have to stay in that house. At least the HOA fees."

"Sure. I don't want him to think he's won," Karen said. "God, I sound so petty, don't I?"

"You sound like someone who is dealing with a complex breakup. Everyone is petty when that happens."

"Thanks," she murmured. "But surely that's not the case with you."

"Me more than most," he admitted. But the truth was, he didn't want to hurt Piper; he wanted her back. But first, he needed to figure out what he'd missed.

"I doubt that, Brian. You've been so fair the entire time. That's the thing about this. I didn't want a divorce. I liked our life. He's the one who cheated and made it clear he won't stop. I think I want to hurt him because he didn't like our life."

"There's nothing wrong with that. But I don't have to tell you that the law doesn't work like that," he said gently.

"No, you don't. I just wish it did." She sighed. "Okay, see if you can get more money and I want a stipulation that if he moves out of the county, I can move wherever I want."

"I will see what I can do," he said, gathering his notes to go and talk to the other lawyer.

Forty minutes later they had more money and the proviso that Karen had asked for, and he looked at the couple as they both stood in the courtroom. The animosity was gone. There was nothing left to argue about and they both seemed to know it. Brian decided right then that he definitely preferred what had happened between himself and Piper to this. He vowed that if he got married, he'd never end up here. But, of course, Karen hadn't expected to end up in divorce court either.

So was that why Piper was reluctant to take things to the next level? He hadn't been talking about marriage or anything like that. He'd simply wanted to date. Yet, at the same time, it felt like there was more between them than just sex. But maybe he'd been wrong. Did it stem from watching Ava allow his uncle Keith to protect her and help her out? And what had really gone on between those two?

He reached out to Keith via text and asked if he had time to talk, then headed back to his office. The statue Brian had won at Boots and Boas had been delivered and his assistant had overseen its placement in the center of the lobby. Brian stopped and looked at it. Saw the pain and the yearning and truth in the expression on the figure in the sculpture and knew he had to do whatever he could to get Piper back into his life.

He called her number instead of texting to see if she'd answer. The call went to voice mail, but he got a text a moment later from her.

Piper: I am not ready to talk.

He thought of a million different responses but none of them felt right, so he took a picture of the sculpture and sent it to her.

Brian: You're brilliant.

He pocketed his phone and walked away from the statue, pretending that seeing it didn't cause a cascade of feelings that he didn't want to have, but did anyway. Because the woman who had crafted it, the woman who'd seen so deeply into the fact that Xavier was two different men, hadn't trusted him enough to show him hers.

Spending time with her nieces always made Piper feel better. She'd been keeping Ava company when Harley and Beth had called to see if she wanted to join them for pedicures. It didn't escape her attention, however, that they had waited until Ava was at a meeting with her lawyer before extending the invite. She understood it, yet at the same time wished there was some way she could fix this for them all.

"What color are you thinking?" Harley asked. The youngest of her sister's two daughters had medium-brown hair that she wore long and straight. She had green eyes and an easy smile. She was a very natural and earthy girl.

"I was thinking something midnight blue," Piper replied. Brian's eyes were dark and black, but there were times when she caught the slightest hint of blue in them.

"I like it. I was thinking something in either red or maybe a festive autumn color," Harley said.

"Like orange?" Beth teased her. Her eldest niece had dark blond hair and always had highlights in it. She was tall and sophisticated.

"All I can see now is something pumpkin colored," Harley said.

Piper smiled at her niece. "You should have brought Daniel…he has a good eye for color."

"I would have, but he and Grant are having a little daddy-son time," Harley informed her. "As well as packing up. The move to Thailand is taking a lot of hard work. We have to decide what to keep and what to store. We have a shipping container and movers coming to get it all arranged, but I honestly feel like I'm never going to get it all finished."

"I'm glad you took the time to come today. You definitely can use a break," Beth said.

"Me too. Seeing you and Grant married makes me so happy. You are perfect for each other," Piper chimed in. "I mean, you've been through a lot together and clearly are on the same page."

"Are you not on the same page with someone?" Harley asked as they all took their bottles of nail polish and were led to the pedicure chairs.

"Not exactly. It's just that it's hard to be on the same page when you are so wildly different from each other." Piper sighed pensively. "But I have tried…"

"Who are we talking about?" Beth demanded. "I didn't realize you were dating anyone. Although I did see you with Brian Cooper at Harley's wedding."

"I was dating him," Piper admitted. "We called it quits before I came back to Royal."

"Why? Is he like Keith? If so, it's good that you kicked him to the curb." Beth's tone sharpened. "Keith had so much influence over Mom, he was changing her. And not for the better."

"Was he? It's hard to think of our mother letting anyone have that much influence over her," Harley mused.

"He did," Piper said. "It was hard to talk to her about it because she was so defensive."

"Definitely," Beth agreed. "But what's the deal with Brian?"

"He's not like Keith," Piper said. In fact, he was nothing like any other man she'd met. He seemed to get her and to understand that she wasn't marching to the same drum as everyone else.

"So what's the problem then?" Harley interjected.

"He's eleven years younger than me."

"So? I know you don't care about that," Beth retorted. "What's this *really* about?"

Piper looked at her nieces and fought to find the strength to tell them. She'd always felt so much an outsider in her own family but right now she could use someone to talk to. Someone who would understand where she was coming from. Beth was nine years younger than she was and Harley was 17 years younger so she hadn't shared much of her broken engagement with them. They'd been so young at the time. "You're right, it's not the age difference. It's a lot more to do with my baggage. I've had a really bad breakup once before, and I promised myself I wouldn't go through that again."

"But why end things with Brian?" Harley asked, confused.

"He's Keith's nephew, for one. Your mom isn't going to be a huge fan of me dating him."

"Like you care what Mom says," Beth quipped.

"I do. I mean, she can be overbearing at times, but I don't want to ever hurt her," Piper admitted.

"If you like him, Mom will understand," Beth said.

Did she like him? Of course she did. That's why she broke things off with him. And another reason why she'd come home to Royal.

She remembered the way he'd hired her to decorate his building and then left her alone to curate the pieces that she'd use. He was a man who hired experts and then stepped back and let them run with it.

Maybe that was why it had been so hard to leave Dallas the night of the gala. She hadn't wanted to leave him. Truth was, she liked *so many* things about him. But he was young and eventually he was going to bring up kids and she couldn't have them. Didn't want to have to admit that to him. So she'd left before she had to.

"He sounds great, Piper," Harley murmured. "But you haven't answered my earlier question. What's really going on?"

"I don't know how to put it into words," she said at last. "It's just not going to work out."

"Well, I'm sorry to hear that." Beth sighed. "Sounds like he was making your happy for a little while."

"I'm sorry too," Harley said. "But there is more to relationships than just making someone happy."

Her nieces were very smart, and she felt so lucky to have them in her life. Piper changed the subject to Thanksgiving and how nice it was to have Harley back this year. She let the conversation drift around her and when she left her nieces to head back to Ava's she realized she needed to do this more. Talking to them had made her realize that there were other complications in life than just her own fears.

Was it her fear that was holding her back? Or was she justified to feel that Brian might cause her to forget all the safety measures she'd put in place? Her life worked because she kept that wild, passionate side of hers hidden away. Letting it out wasn't something she was sure she could do.

It gave her something to think about as she drove home past the Texas Cattleman's Club where all of the Wingates had been members for as long as Piper could remember—well, the women hadn't been admitted until the early 2000s—but she knew that her family no longer felt welcome at the club since their assets had been seized and their home put into foreclosure.

As hard as it was to face gossip in Dallas, at least she'd been removed from this sort of day-to-day thing. She wasn't sure how she could handle that. Stopping at an intersection, she had an epiphany of sorts while waiting for the light to turn green. She realized she was trying to distract herself from the fact that she still missed Brian.

Piper sighed. It would be nice if parting ways with a man meant that she stopped thinking and caring about him. She knew that her actions were going to be for the best in the long run, but right now she ached. For, despite everything, she couldn't stop yearning for him... which made her feel like a soppy young woman instead of the wise goddess she was trying so hard to be.

But she just shook her head and felt the weight of her gold orb earrings brushing against her neck. She knew that no matter what she wanted to project, inside she was still that twenty-four-year-old with a broken engagement when she thought about forever with any man. Her relationships after Ron and before Brian had all ended by her own hand.

Maybe it was time to stop trying to keep from being hurt again by ending things with Brian until he found the broken thing inside of her that had made Ron leave? But if she did that she'd have to put her heart on the line and she wasn't sure she had the strength to do that. Being a goddess and standing on her own above everyone else was one thing but trusting Brian not to hurt her…that was something bigger. At Harley's reception she'd wanted to have a partner, but she realized now she'd gotten more than she'd bargained for with Brian.

Ten

Piper had typed a text to Brian just to chat and deleted it about eighty-five times. She missed him, but she knew that she should just leave it be. So why couldn't she? Added to the fact that he was Keith's nephew, she knew that it should be enough to convince her to stop thinking about him, but she hadn't.

She'd even woken up in the middle of the night, her body craving his. Only to be filled with dismay to find the empty space next to her. Given that they'd only slept together a handful of times, her intense longing for him wasn't rational. But then, she knew that matters of the heart rarely were.

She was going to have find her way through this. However she did it, whatever that meant, she had to stay strong and be that wise goddess she wished she were.

She didn't feel wise at all today as she watched her sister slowly lose her sparkle as more pieces of Trent's legacy were taken away from her and her children. Her confidence had taken a hit when Trent died, but losing the house and having the company seized was like a knife to Ava. And Piper saw her put on her old attitude when the kids were around or she thought she needed to keep up the pretense, but honestly there were moments when her sister seemed truly lost.

Piper poured them both a glass of wine and went to find Ava sitting in front of the fireplace. There was a nice blaze going and it heated the room. She looked up at the space above the mantel where Ava had always had a portrait of herself and Trent and the kids in her home. It must kill her sister to sit here in a rented house on rented furniture in a place that wasn't home, unsure that she'd ever get back into her own home.

"It's wine o'clock," Piper said to announce herself.

"Thank goodness," Ava said.

Piper handed her sister one of the glasses. "To sisters."

"Sisters," Ava murmured, clinking her glass against Piper's. "Oh, Pip, what am I going to do?"

Piper curled her legs underneath her as she sat down next to her sister on the sofa. "You're going to remember you are Ava Wingate. You raised some great kids and helped build Wingate Enterprises into the success it was. Your family has taken a hit but you're not out of the game."

Ava tipped her head to the side as she took a sip of the wine. "I am that woman, but I'm also the one who was so scared to be alone that I fell into Keith's arms and let him make decisions for me. I just... I just went along with it. That's not me."

"I know," Piper said.

"The kids don't. Harley didn't really even want me at the wedding. I think they blame me for everything," Ava said. "I'm so mad at Trent for dying and leaving me. I know it's not his fault and that makes no sense, but I miss him, and I needed him. He promised me seventy-five years of marriage."

Piper blinked to keep from letting her tears fall. "You know if there was any way in hell that he could have delivered on that promise, he would have. He thought you hung the moon."

Ava let her head drop to the back of the sofa and Piper heard the ragged sound of her breathing. "Sometimes I feel like the real me died the same day he did. And some imposter has been trying to act like me."

Piper scooted closer to Ava, putting her wineglass on the coffee table and pulling her sister into her arms. Ava had never been one to show any cracks in her life and this had to be hard for her. The woman who always used her iron will to make things happen and ensure that her family was safe, was now helpless to keep it from crumbling.

"You did the best you could. I know this will shock you, but you're not superwoman, Ava."

Her sister started laughing and pulled back to punch her playfully in the shoulder. "I know that."

"I think you forget it sometimes. Cut yourself some slack. Keith came to you as a friend and you took him at face value. It's not your fault that you couldn't re-ciprocate his feelings. After Ron reneged on our engagement, I thought I was cool, but after my next few relationships ended, I realized that I couldn't trust a man. *Any man.* Ron had taken that from me. I still struggle with that."

"I know you do. Are you seeing anyone?" Ava asked, wiping her eyes with a tissue.

"I have been. But I broke it off," Piper said.

"Why?"

"He makes me feel reckless…not like the woman I need to be. He's also younger than me."

Ava turned to face her. "Why does that matter?"

"It doesn't. I mean, I know it doesn't, but it is just one more thing."

"So far those obstacles aren't insurmountable," Ava said. "One of us should be in a healthy relationship."

Talking to Ava had made Piper realize that maybe she should give Brian another chance. That long-ago hurt was keeping her from happiness. She wanted to think she was beyond it, but she knew she wasn't. And maybe it was time she made up her mind to let it go. To trust another man.

"Actually, you know him."

"I do?" she asked. "Who is he?"

"Brian Cooper."

Her sister's jaw dropped open. "Keith's *nephew*?"

"Yes," she said.

"I wouldn't have thought of him and you together," Ava said.

"But you just—" Why did she think that her sister had changed?

"You're right. You're smart, Pip. You are never going to let a man walk all over you like I did with Keith."

* * *

Piper had spent the afternoon at the high school in Royal, talking to the art students. She remembered her own time in these halls, which had changed a lot since she'd graduated. Yet there was something so familiar about it. Especially the art room with the smell of acrylic paints and clay. For the first time since she'd left Dallas, she felt like she could breathe. She took a deep inhalation and closed her eyes.

Cheri, the art teacher, was a friend of Piper's, but she'd been surprised when Cheri had invited her to come in and view her students' work and talk to them about career options in the art world. Some of the students were really talented and Piper had made the offer to showcase some of them in her student exhibit in the summer. The teacher had smiled at the idea.

"I'm going to frame it as a gallery in Dallas. Right now, this town is pretty much anti-Wingate," Cheri said, "and although I know you don't have anything to do with the business, some of the parents might not see it that way. This offer isn't something the students should miss because of that."

"Thanks, Cheri," Piper said. She left but felt edgy and ticked off. She hated small-mindedness, and of course she didn't want anyone to think she condoned breaking the law, but her family was innocent.

She had her head down as she walked up Main Street, not really paying attention to where she was going, and bumped into someone. Glancing up to apologize, she stopped in her tracks.

It was Brian.

"You okay?"

She shook her head. "Yeah, thanks. Sorry for bumping into you."

"Don't worry about that. But you look pissed as hell."

"I am," she admitted. "I just came from the high school where I was told in a very nice way that some parents might not want their kids' art to hang in my gallery. I mean, give me a freaking break!"

"That's not fair to the kids or you," he said. "You're not part of Wingate Enterprises."

"No, I'm not. But I am part of the family." She sighed. "I've been dealing with this to a lesser extent in Dallas. Anyway, that doesn't matter. What are you doing here?"

He tipped his head to the side, studying her. "I was hoping to see you. Want to have dinner so we can talk about things?"

Did she? Yes. But the things she'd have to talk about…she didn't want to. She had made a break and she knew if she took a step back toward him it would be harder to leave again. "I can't."

Brian clenched his jaw but then relaxed it into a smile and she realized that he wasn't happy about their breakup, but he was being a gentleman. Wasn't that everything she adored about him? He was *always* a decent guy. The kind of man who deserved everything that life had to offer. A successful career, a sophisticated woman by his side…and kids.

A house full of them if he so chose.

"Fine. But hiding with your family isn't going to last forever," he reminded her.

"I'm not hiding. I'm here to help support Ava. It's a

rough time for her," she said. "She's still trying to get over Keith."

"How do you figure? Ava's not a shrinking violet," he said. "And she broke up with him."

"Why was she not herself when she was living with Keith?" Piper asked, realizing she was letting this devolve into a fight. She wanted to fight. Wanted to yell at him because it would make her feel better about the fact that they weren't together.

But she wasn't going to do that. "I'm sorry. It was nice seeing you."

She walked away and didn't look back. Just got to her car and drove out of town, hoping that it would be as easy to get over Brian as it had been to drive away.

Piper wasn't prepared to see Brian when he showed up at Ava's door later that evening. She and her sister had made tacos for dinner and spent the evening laughing and talking about men. It had been nice to talk to Ava and feel her sister had her back.

For so many years she'd felt like she was on the outside of the family looking in, trying to be someone she wasn't. Brian had offered her a chance to be herself. But dare she trust herself enough to give in to her passionate side and live her life? Or was she always going to be afraid of it?

But here he was on her sister's doorstep, stubble on his jaw, and he looked tired. Like he hadn't been sleeping well. He clearly wasn't about to let her close him out as he stood there. "Sorry to show up like this, but I just didn't want to do this by text."

"That's okay. Um, let me grab my coat and we can go for a walk. This is Ava's home and I don't know—"

"Who is it?" Ava called as she came down the hallway.

"Brian," Piper told her.

"Hello, Ava," Brian said. "I'm sorry to show up unannounced but I need a word with Piper."

Ava gave him a hard look and then shook her head and forced a smile. "You can use the study."

Ava turned and walked away from them both. Piper stepped back to allow Brian to enter the foyer. She gestured to the left where the study was. As soon as he entered, she followed him, closing the door behind them. He moved farther into the room and took a seat on the leather settee while she stood there with her back against the hardwood door, trying to get herself under control.

Now that he was here, she discovered she'd missed him so much more than she'd even realized. And yeah, he looked exhausted, but also so good to her eyes. She was drinking him in as if it had been years since she had seen him instead of days. His voice was a low rumble as he talked, and she realized how much she'd missed the cadence of it. He leaned back, spread his arms along the back of the settee and just stared at her.

"What did you say?"

"I asked if you were going to sit down so we could talk," he said. "Are you feeling okay?"

No.

She was a big hot mess, and spending time with her sister who was in the same boat hadn't really helped her at all. Piper only hoped that he couldn't see it. She forced a smile. "Of course."

She sat down in one of the armchairs, perching on

the edge before realizing what she was doing and sitting back, hopefully to give the illusion that she was chill with this. "What brings you here?"

"Are you serious?" he asked. There was an intensity in him that she hadn't noticed before. She had the feeling she was seeing his courtroom persona, and honestly, he was rather intimidating.

"Yes. I thought we said everything we needed to the other day." Piper crossed her legs and wrapped her arms around herself.

"No, we didn't. I had hoped that once we had some time apart, you'd realize that," he bit out.

"Realize what?"

"That what we have is too good to give up on," he said. "If you don't want to move to the next level that's fine with me. I'm willing to keep things fun and light."

She shook her head. "One of the things I have admired about you is that you don't lie. Please don't start now."

"Fine. I don't want to be casual. Do you think I like feeling like this?" he asked.

"No," she admitted. This was hard and not anything she was prepared to deal with. "How about if we just leave things until after Thanksgiving, and then when we are both back in Dallas we can—"

"No, Piper, I don't want to leave this. I want to fix this. I'm still not sure what your objection to the two of us is," he said. "The age thing is a nonissue, so please don't bring it up again."

"It's more than that. You have a young man's dreams and I don't—"

"Stop." He cut her off as he got to his feet. "You are being closed-minded."

"Better than being ignorant," Piper retorted, standing, as well.

"We both know I'm not," he said. "If you're going to insult me, you'll have to work a bit harder."

"I don't have to do anything. I'm a grown-ass woman and if I decide to end things with you, that's it."

"God dammit, Piper Holloway, you are ticking me off!" he said.

"Good. Maybe you'll understand that I'm saying we are over."

"Is this what you do with all your relationships? End them before they begin?" he demanded.

His words hit a little too close to home and she hated that he'd pegged her so easily. "I don't think that's any of your business."

He tipped his head to the side and strode closer to her, leaving a few inches between them, but she knew it was his own self-control that kept him there and not in her face. God, she wanted to throw herself into his arms and kiss the hell out of him. There was no one quite like this man, she realized. But she also knew she wasn't thinking clearly. Her emotions were out of control, roiling through her like a tornado, and while she was sorely tempted to give in to them, she didn't want to destroy herself and Brian in the process.

"It *is* my business, Piper. I wanted everything with you and you are too stuck in the past to see it."

"I'm not. We just aren't as compatible as you want us to be," she said to reinforce her point.

"Fine. Fuck it. I'm leaving," he snapped, brushing past her and stalking to the door, but when he got there, he stopped.

He was leaving.

That was when it hit her—she loved him. She felt it all the way to her bones. It hurt so much to watch him turning his back on her and walking out. But that was okay. It was better this way.

But it didn't feel better. It felt so bittersweet.

"You know what I think?" he demanded, turning to face her.

She really didn't want to know. Because she was teetering on the edge, on the verge of losing it completely. So, out of sheer desperation, she gathered all the steely emotional armor she'd built over the years around her.

"Please enlighten me," she said, trying not to wrap her arms around herself again.

"You can't let yourself love any man. I don't know if it's a control thing or what, but I'm beginning to realize why you are still all alone."

"You don't know jack shit," she said, losing her temper. "I'm not alone. I have my family and my art."

"Your family is a mess. I'd think you'd want one of your own."

"Don't you dare say anything about my family when your uncle is the cause of what has made my sister ignore the business for so long. I won't take the risk of losing myself in a man. That's when mistakes happen, big mistakes. And I can't have a family of my own. I'm barren. See yourself out," she said, brushing past him and heading up the stairs to her room.

She hated that he'd driven her to lose her temper, but it was better for him to hear it all so he'd realize there was no hope of reconciliation for them.

* * *

He wanted to go after her but when a woman walked away in the home where she was staying, he knew better than to follow. He glanced to the end of the hallway, saw Ava standing there. She didn't say a word, but he felt her censure.

"She doesn't know me at all if she thinks that I give a damn about her reproductive abilities," he said, then he turned and walked out of the house, getting into his car and driving faster than the speed limit down the road toward the front of the gated community.

He slammed on the brakes when he noticed people walking on the sidewalk with fishing poles. Damn. She was making him stupid and reckless.

Hell, she hadn't made him anything. Love had. In his mind, the rant he wanted to have at her ran on an endless loop. When had he said that he wanted only biological children? When had he said that he wanted her to choose him over her family?

What kind of man did she think he was? Had she even tried to get to know him? He knew the answer had to be no. If she had, she wouldn't have made such blind and wrong assumptions about him and what was important to him.

He pushed those thoughts aside and drove to the house he kept in Royal. His uncle had been texting him to get together since it was close to Thanksgiving, but given that Brian had been dating Piper, he had thought it best to stay away.

But now...hell, did it really matter if he had dinner with Uncle Keith? It didn't matter that the Wingates all suspected Keith of somehow being responsible for their trouble. They had no proof, and as he'd just witnessed in Piper's irrational diatribe against him, they weren't above jumping to completely false conclusions.

In no mood to go home and be alone, he stopped at the Texas Cattleman's Club. He knew he needed to get drunk. But getting sloshed alone was never a good idea. If he did, he'd probably give in to the temptation to drive back over to Ava's rented house, lie to the guard again and stand outside in the yard doing something asinine like yelling her name or playing the song that had been playing the first time he held her in his arms.

He wasn't going to let that happen.

He had pride.

Sober, at least, he had pride. The drunk version of him had always leaned more into his emotions than his rational side. And he knew better than to go back to Piper. She had made herself clear twice now. How many times did he need to hear a woman tell him she didn't want him before it sank in?

He saw some friends who were about his age that he'd known while growing up and joined them. They were drinking whiskey and talking about the Cowboys, and it was just what Brian thought he needed until he remembered that Piper had agreed to come with him to Thanksgiving at his folks' house and then the Dallas Cowboys game.

"Dude, you okay?"

"Yeah, why?" Brian asked.

"You're staring at that whiskey like you are planning to throw it against the wall," Leon said.

"Just had a bad breakup," Brian admitted.

"Well, hell, boy, why didn't you say? We should have ordered tequila," Leon said.

"No one wants to admit he got kicked to the curb by a woman," Brian grumbled, downing his whiskey in one long swallow and signaling the waiter for another one. "And tequila on a weeknight is never a good idea."

"I know that. But my old lady is in College Station with her sorority sisters and I've got nothing to go home to," Leon said.

"Me either. That's what I've been trying to fix. How'd you and Viv get together?" Brian asked. "I always thought I had some kind of game, but recently it seems as if I have nothing."

Leon played with the whiskey glass, rolling it between his palms before taking a sip. "We got together after graduation. I came back to take over the ranch and she took one look at me in the diner one day and said, 'You want to ask me out.'"

Brian laughed. That sounded like Vivian. She'd always been ballsy and unafraid to go after what she wanted. "And you were smart enough to do it."

"Damn straight. A woman like Viv doesn't come along twice in a lifetime," Leon said. "Tell me about your gal. I'm guessing you want her back?"

"I do," Brian said, taking another swallow of the whiskey. He did want her back. No matter how many times she pushed him away, he still couldn't stay away from her. But a man had his pride. He couldn't keep going back, could he? "She's, um, Piper Holloway. You know her?"

"I know of her. Dang boy, she's pretty sophisticated and out of your league."

"I'm a high-paid, highly respected lawyer, Leon. I've got some polish," Brian reminded his friend.

"I know, but Piper has something else. She just seems more metropolitan. But as you pointed out, so are you. So it's not that. What is it that's keeping you two apart?"

It was on the tip of his tongue to tell him what she'd said but he knew better than to share that with another living soul. She'd claimed she was afraid to lose herself in him. But why? Had he been too forceful, too domineering? And how could she lose herself in him when she'd been hiding her true self from the world?

"She says we are too different, that we want different things from life," he said at last.

"And all you want is one with her," Leon murmured.

"Exactly. I'm fucked," Brian said.

Eleven

Ava was gone when Piper woke up in the morning and she contemplated going back to Dallas. Her sister was going to be okay and Piper had realized overnight that she would be too, eventually. What had always worked in the past when she'd ended a relationship was to pour herself back into her art.

She had a commission for a client in New York who missed Texas and wanted something that reminded her of her home state. Piper pulled out her sketchbook, but her mind was empty. No matter how she tried to come at the work, she couldn't think of anything. So she just started sketching because sometimes moving her pencil over the paper sparked ideas. She liked the sound of the scratching and started simply, with just a face. Then, over time, she made the jaw a little bit stronger before drawing crossed lines to place the eyes and the nose.

The eyes she drew were wide-set and the nose a sharp blade that reminded her very much of Brian's. She pushed that thought aside, let go of her conscious thoughts and just sketched. It wasn't long until the image took shape, and more than the nose looked like Brian. It *was* Brian.

She'd drawn him as he'd looked when she told him she couldn't have kids. And it would be easy to tell herself that the look on his face had been disgust, but it had been a shock and, of course, being Brian, empathetic, as well. He'd been ticked at her, but more because she'd misjudged him.

Tossing the sketchbook aside, she stood up to pace to the window that looked over the backyard. She saw that her sister hadn't left the property but was sitting on a bench in the backyard. By herself.

This was it, she thought. This was what the Holloway women had come to. Two lonely women who had lost on love. Ava when Trent died and when she'd trusted the wrong man, and Piper…well, she'd lost because after Ron she'd never been able to trust *any* man. She'd never let herself love again because she was afraid to be hurt again.

This time, though, she was pretty damn sure she'd hurt Brian. Badly. She could justify it ten ways to Sunday and tell herself that he'd get over it—get over *her*— and find someone closer to his own age. But would she?

Could she move on from pushing away the only man she'd fallen in love with? She knew better than to believe that it would be easy. But Brian was gone. There was no way he'd come back after what she'd said to him, and really, how could she rebuild his broken trust when hers was still tattered and in pieces?

She'd have to let down her guard, really just start being herself and be comfortable in her own skin. Was that even possible? She wasn't too sure.

Piper could only feel safe thinking about trusting him because he had left and that had been final. She sank to the floor and drew her knees up to her chest, resting her forehead on them. *This*. This was why she wasn't the wise goddess she projected at the gallery. She was still broken from something that had happened in her twenties, and like someone who hadn't had their wound properly attended to, she had learned to live with that fractured part of herself.

And while she had pretended that being broken didn't really matter, and that she was fine, deep down she wasn't. She hadn't been since her engagement had ended…until Brian danced with her at Harley and Grant's reception. He'd swept her off her feet, starting a cascade of change inside of her, but she'd just kept putting rocks back in the dam to keep it in place. And she'd succeeded in driving him away.

This time for good.

She was safe. No one could hurt her. Alone. *Again*. By her own design.

"Ugh!" she yelled, getting up from the floor.

She was making herself angry with all the whining she was doing mentally. If she wanted Brian back in her life then, by God, she'd get him. If that meant convincing him that she'd made a mistake—admittedly that was going to be the hardest part, but she could do it.

He was worth it.

Wasn't he?

Ava had pointed out that Brian wasn't Keith any

more than Ava and Piper were the same. He was a good man who'd worked hard all of his life and he was kind and funny. Sexy as hell.

She'd never find another man like him again, she thought.

Never.

That had to be enough to get her out the door. Piper turned and saw her reflection in the mirror. She looked as if she hadn't had a shower in days, and the fine lines she'd been trying to hide with retinol were visible this morning. She looked like a woman who'd given up.

A woman who'd forgotten who she was. She *was* that wise goddess. Piper knew it. She'd worked hard to get where she was in life and to surround herself with good friends and family she loved very much.

There was no reason Brian couldn't be a part of that. She had to deal with any lingering doubts that Ava and the rest of the family had, but then she was going to find a way to try again with Brian.

She winked at herself in the mirror. Feeling loads better now that she'd decided on action. Action was better than wallowing any day.

She showered and put on makeup and her favorite outfit of skinny jeans and a funky sweater before going to find Ava. Her sister was on the phone and that was fine with Piper. She had already made her peace with her choice and she had the insight that only people who were unsure had to rush.

Once you were solid in the knowledge of what you wanted, time didn't matter. She would take as long as she had to in order to win Brian back.

* * *

Uncle Keith was in an odd mood when Brian arrived for dinner. But he was glad to see him. The big house was empty except for this housekeeper who'd served dinner, but then she left too. Keith poured them both a Jack and Coke pretty hard throughout the meal.

"I didn't think you'd be back in Royal until December," Uncle Keith said after they'd retired to his study to watch ESPN.

It seemed to Brian that they'd made the move so that his uncle could be closer to the whiskey, and he wondered if losing Ava was still an open wound for Keith the way losing Piper as for Brian.

He poured them both another Jack and Coke, and took a seat across from his uncle. The room was dark and masculine, smelling of cigars and pine. There were stacks of paper on the desk and the large-screen TV dominated one wall while floor-to-ceiling bookcases occupied the other.

"I followed Piper, hoping…" Brian trailed off. Truthfully, he didn't really want to get into it again. He was turning into a sad sack, first with Leon and now with his uncle.

"Piper Holloway?"

"Yes, sir," Brian said, leaning back and propping his ankle on his knee. "We had been dating, but she ended things abruptly."

"She dumped you?" Uncle Keith asked incredulously.

"Yeah," Brian admitted. "She's so unsure of me. She's afraid she'll lose herself if she's with me."

"Really? She never really struck me as the forceful kind," Keith said.

"Oh, there is a lot more to Piper than most people see," Brian said. That was probably why he'd been so convinced that what they had was special. She'd let him in, and had looked past his barriers and seen the real him, as well.

"Same with Ava. Everyone sees her as a force to be reckoned with, and she is, but after Trent got so sick, she just couldn't hold it together any longer," Keith said.

"That had to be hard for you to see. Losing your best friend and then seeing his widow at the breaking point—I would have been wanted to step in and fix things too," Brian said.

"Damn, boy, we have more in common than I would have guessed. I did the best I could. I love her," Keith said gruffly. "I just wanted to take care of her."

"If she's anything like Piper, she probably wanted to do it on her own."

"Yeah. Just like college," Keith said, getting up to pour himself another drink.

"I thought y'all were just friends in college. Was it more?"

"I wanted it to be, but Trent cut me out. He had more money back then and didn't hesitate to splash it around. Ava soon started spending more time with him," Keith told him, his voice heavy with emotion.

"That must have been hard, but you were young and moved on," Brian reminded him. "I know you had some good times with the women you married."

Keith turned around, his eyes bloodshot and his steps a little unsteady as he made his way back to his armchair, bringing the bottle of Jack Daniels with him. "That I did, but none of those women were Ava."

Had his uncle been pining for Ava Holloway Wingate all those years? That didn't seem like the kind of man that Keith Cooper was. But emotions were something that most men in their family didn't like to talk about.

"Then Trent got sick and she needed me," he said, almost to himself.

"That was a tragedy. I know you were there for them both through the illness," Brian added.

"Least I could do."

"I would do the same for Piper," he said. Would he? He wasn't sure he'd be able to be friends with Piper if she married another man. He'd eventually drift out of her life. But Keith hadn't been able to get that distance.

"I know you would, son."

"So what really happened between you and Ava?" Brian asked. "I thought you two were getting really close."

"We were," he said. "But once we were back from Europe…no one can compete with Saint Trent and the holy Wingate/Holloway kids. They didn't like me and urged her to move out once the business started having trouble," Keith said. "I've reached out to her, but she's made it clear she doesn't need me anymore."

"She might need you, Uncle. They think it was an inside job."

"Do they?" Keith asked. "That would make sense. Only someone with access to the login information of someone at the top of the corporate structure would have been able to set that up."

Brian leaned back, taking another sip of his drink. "Do you have any idea who that could be?"

"I have an idea," Keith said. "You wouldn't believe me if I told you."

"Who do you suspect?" Brian asked, leaning forward, but his uncle had turned his attention to the basketball game playing on the big screen. Keith mumbled something under his breath and Brian leaned in close to catch it.

He shook his head, unsure he'd heard the muttered comments correctly. But it had sounded like something that Brian hoped like hell wasn't true.

"Did you say *you* did it?" Brian asked, horrified.

"What, boy?" Keith murmured.

Brian stood up and walked over to his uncle. "Who do you think is responsible?"

"Given how Ava recently treated me, I suspect it was someone who was close to the family and got cut out because of small-minded assholes," Keith said.

Brian stared at his uncle. Was Keith saying he'd done it? The only person who was outside the family and had the kind of control that Keith mentioned was... *Keith*.

His uncle finished his drink and Brian made his excuses and left, getting into his car and sitting there for a long time. He'd probably heard that all wrong. Maybe he'd wanted to hear Keith say something so that Brian would have a reason to go back to Piper, seem like he was the hero.

Yeah, that was it.

He drove home, but the next morning he couldn't keep from remembering what his uncle had said. After all, Keith had been on the inside for a while. It could have been anyone close to the family.

Suddenly Piper's reservations about his uncle made more sense. Had she picked up on something from Keith that the rest of them had missed?

Brian made up his mind to go to the investigator and mention that Keith thought it could be someone who'd been close to the family. Zeke had mentioned they were working with the FBI to track down leads.

Should he go to them? Could he trust the ravings of a drunk?

At best, his uncle would be investigated and cleared...

Brian's conscience wouldn't allow him not to report this. He knew what he needed to do. Piper had said her family was the most important thing to her, and loving her as he did, he wanted to help them in any way he could. Even if that meant turning in his own uncle.

Ava went to meet with her children about the investigation into Wingate Enterprises, and while she was gone Piper started baking pies for Thanksgiving. She wasn't a traditional person by nature but there was something about this time of year that always made her want to have pie. Her mother had started baking them on the first of November when Piper had been a girl.

Piper started with pecan—her favorite—and there was something soothing and homey about the scents that filled the kitchen in Ava's rented house. She baked pumpkin pie and apple and mincemeat. Then she moved on to breads—banana and pumpkin—doing everything she could to keep her mind off Brian. It had only been a few days since she'd ended things for good, but it felt like a lifetime since she'd seen him. And the more time that passed the harder it was to say to herself that they would ever make it work.

She was seeing all the obstacles again. They had always been there, but when she had been with Brian—

really been with him, not in Royal where she fell back into childhood patterns and attitudes—those hurdles hadn't seemed as big or insurmountable. It was only when she was lying alone in her big bed, missing him, that she reminded herself she'd kicked him out.

She'd broken up with him and he'd probably come to his breaking—she quickly shut that thought down. It was pointless to start feeling sorry for herself. Those thoughts and feelings inevitably followed a breakup. She knew her flaws better than anyone and loneliness just made them stand out.

The front door opened, and she heard voices as Ava, followed by her children, entered the house. "Everything smells delicious in here."

"Thanks. I wanted to do something productive," Piper murmured.

"I'm not waiting for Thanksgiving to partake," Zeke said. "Unless…"

"Of course we don't have to wait. I'm ready for a slice of pecan pie," Piper said. "How'd the meeting go?"

"Well, better than I think we expected. Seems Brian was over at Keith's the other night and he said some leading…" Ava broke off and turned away.

"What did he say?"

"Brian said it might have been the alcohol, so we don't want to get too excited that this will lead to anything, but he mentioned that the embezzling and drug trafficking had to be an inside deal and that it had to be someone close to one of us at the top." She sighed. "That pretty much only leaves Keith. When Brian pressed him, he didn't say it out loud but winked and said he couldn't say more."

Brian? Why had Brian done that? Was he trying to prove he wasn't like his uncle? Of course, he couldn't. "That's good, but how are they going to use it?"

"They've asked him to wear a wire and go back and see if Keith says anything else. Right now, it's all hearsay, which Brian was adamant wouldn't stand up in court," Ava said. "So he's going to try to see if he can get Keith to admit it again. Ironically it was breaking up with you that led to the conversation."

"Sorry about that, Piper," Harley said, coming over and giving her a hug.

"If it helps the family then it will be worth it," Piper said. They sat around the dining room table in the rented house drinking coffee and eating the pies she'd baked, and Piper realized something about home. With her sister and her nieces, nephews and their partners this *was* home. It wasn't the big Wingate mansion or her home in Frisco. It was these people and… Brian. She missed him at this gathering. He'd have loved it.

She had said some things to him that were going to be very difficult to retract because she had meant it when she said that family was the most important thing to her, but she had just realized that somewhere along the way Brian had become family to her, as well.

She wanted to text him but had no idea if he was with Keith or if she'd interfere with his sting operation so she kept her hands off her phone. Instead, she played canasta with some of her family, and smiled and pretended that she wasn't worried about Brian. Keith might not be a physical danger to Brian, but he was dangerous.

If he was to blame for everything, then he had a powerful hate for their family, and anyone who helped him would be branded a traitor, especially his nephew. She couldn't keep her mind from wandering to a worrying place, and she tried to force her thoughts to the present, but after everyone had gone home and she and Ava were alone, it was exponentially harder.

"I misjudged Brian," Piper said to her sister as they were sitting alone in the living room. "I'm surprised he's done this for us."

"I'm not," Ava said. "I saw his face when you ran upstairs the other night. He looked like you'd pulled his heart from his chest and stomped on it. We misjudged him. I'm sorry for my part in that."

Piper nodded. But there was a huge lump in her throat, and she couldn't speak. So she just curled up in the chair, her mind swirling with the thought that she might have been too good at letting her fears rule her mind, and as a consequence, had hurt Brian in a way that he would never forgive.

He might be helping out the Wingates just to prove to her she was wrong and then…he'd walk away leaving her with the knowledge that she'd lost the only man she should have trusted.

Piper stared into the fire, wishing she could go back but knowing she would have made the same choices as before. Because the truth was, she hadn't changed until she'd hurt him. She hoped it wasn't too late after everything was over with the sting that Brian was running to frame Keith and save her family.

Twelve

Brian hadn't expected Piper to call. That was under-standable, considering what was currently happening with their families. He was letting her have some space to think, but when the time was right, he was going back for her.

He loved her.

And he wasn't letting her walk out of his life. Not again.

However, right now he had to do something else that he knew was right no matter how much he hated it. He stood in one of the rooms at the Texas Cattleman's Club being wired by the local police. No one thought he should be seen leaving the police station, so they'd come to him instead.

He was going to try to get his uncle to talk and give up the name of the person he thought had committed the crime. That would make Keith an accessory because he hadn't come forward with the information voluntarily, but in the end, Brian had to believe it was the right thing to do.

Except that he wouldn't let his uncle get away with criminal activity. Obviously, it would be nice for Piper to see Brian as a hero, but morally it was wrong. So even if he hadn't been going out with her, he would have done this. Brian still wasn't one hundred percent sure what his uncle would say when he went back to talk to him since Brian couldn't ask leading questions. He had to just let the conversation make its way to Ava. *Let Keith take it there*, the agent who'd briefed him had said.

Brian was almost ready to go over to his uncle's house. His parents were expecting him back in Dallas for Thanksgiving, so if he didn't get the information today, he'd have to try again in a few weeks. The FBI agent and the Wingate family wanted the information sooner rather than later, and Brian didn't blame them at all.

He rubbed the back of his neck and put on his shirt over the wire.

"Okay, when you talk, the recording will start," the agent told him. "It's voice activated so you won't have to do anything. As a reminder, don't bait him. If you do that it will make it harder to use it in court. It might be enough to indict but we want a conviction too."

"Yeah, I got it. The other night he started talking about it when I brought up Ava's sister…" Brian paused. "I think he saw us as both loving the same type of woman."

"Just use your gut. You know him and you know the

law. Don't feel like you have to force it, either," the agent said. "If you do that you won't sound like yourself."

Brian listened to more advice from the agent, and after he tested the device the agent left him alone. Brian sat there in the room at the back of the club going over the evening in his head. The other day, Keith had already been drinking. What if he wasn't today?

Then he took a few deep breaths and put on his lawyer persona. Sure of where he needed to be and what he wanted to have happen. He wasn't going to be more ready than this.

Leon and his friends were in the bar again and waved him over, but he pointed to his watch and made a *maybe next time* gesture before walking out. Dusk was falling and the November evening was crisp and cold. Starting to feel more like the holidays, he thought. He remembered the plans he'd made with Piper that would probably not be happening now.

Brian exhaled roughly. He didn't kid himself into thinking that bringing information to help clear her sister and family was going to make it any easier to win Piper back over. She needed to get to the point where she could trust him to stay. And trust herself enough to admit she loved him.

Piper usually had a pretty clear read on most people. He wondered what it was she'd seen in him that had led her to that conclusion, but then he shook his head and pushed all of that aside.

The only way he was going to get Keith talking about Ava again, regardless of whether he'd been drinking or not, was to convince his uncle that he hated Piper Holloway and the Wingate family as much as Keith must.

He went off book and stopped at the liquor store and bought a couple of bottles of Jack Daniels. He'd never drive drunk so he drove to the park near Keith's house and had a few swallows to give his breath the smell of the liquor and then spilled a little on his sleeve so it would seem like he'd been drinking all day.

To be honest, he might have been doing that if Keith hadn't said what he had the other night. Brian would have gone home and drowned his heartache in whiskey. Somehow doing this was almost cathartic.

He felt like at least Piper would be able to see he was a good, decent man. Maybe it would be enough to make her see that he'd never meant to hurt her the way he had. After driving the short distance to his uncle's house, he parked his car in the drive. He had poured out three quarters of one of the bottles and was holding it loosely in one hand, and he had a full bottle in the other hand.

Brian knocked on the door and waited. The housekeeper showed him to Keith's den where he was drinking, and when his uncle looked up and saw him, he welcomed him in.

"Glad you're back, son. No man should have to deal with a broken heart on his own," Keith said.

"I agree, Uncle," Brian replied. "I brought a bottle for you."

"Come in and we'll get started on it," Keith said with a grin.

Brian took a deep breath and stepped into the den, not knowing what his uncle was going to say. But he needed to get to the bottom of this. And then he'd figure out how to win Piper back.

He'd made a promise to himself that he wasn't going to let her walk out of his life again.

And he'd meant it.

"It has been a crazy year," Brian said.

As an opening gambit he wasn't sure it was a great one, but he needed to lead the conversation naturally to Ava and the sabotage at Wingate Enterprises. And frankly, at this time of year, he always reflected on the past.

"Opening your own law firm is quite an accomplishment. I know your daddy is proud of you, as he should be," Uncle Keith murmured.

"He is," Brian said. "He and Mama are anxious for me to settle down."

"Be careful who you choose, boy," Keith said. "I know you said you were dating Piper. Are you sure that's over?"

"Probably. My parents thought she seemed great, and they were not happy that we broke up. They don't get it like you do…" He knew he was laying it on a bit thick, but he needed to establish a rapport with his uncle. Make them the same. In one way they were. Piper had dumped him because she thought he wanted to change her. Which was beyond ridiculous. But honestly, he wished she'd seen that he wanted her just the way she was.

"Those Holloway women can singe a man to his core," Brian grumbled. "Even Trent didn't always have it smooth with Ava. He used to tell me about her stubbornness."

"God save me from that hardheadedness. Piper is so sure she sees me better than I see her," Brian said, knowing he had to be bitter and angry if he wanted Keith to start spilling. "Like she knows me at all."

"Ave never really saw me either. Just saw what she needed to in me," Keith told him. "I was there when Trent was sick and she started leaning on me to help out at the office. Just lend a hand because she was overwhelmed."

"You did a good thing," Brian said. The way his uncle was talking today, Brian felt more confident that Keith would give up the name of the insider who'd betrayed the family, and he was already determined to represent Keith if any charges were filed against him. Right now, he just sounded like a man who'd lost the woman he loved.

"I did, didn't I?" Keith asked, taking another sip of his drink. "Of course, she didn't see that. As soon as we got back from Europe she started acting different."

"There was the lawsuit after a fire at their jet plant in East Texas," Brian pointed out. "I think that shook her."

"I get that, but I was her rock. I had her back," Keith said. "She should have leaned on me. I think it was Beth who started her thinking of me in a different way."

"How do you figure?"

"I could tell. I don't think the kids were comfortable with her spending so much time with me so soon after Trent's death. I could tell by the way she talked to me. Always a bit standoffish," Keith said.

"It had to be hard. I don't know what I'd do if Dad died and my mom started turning to someone else. Beth was probably just trying to protect her mom."

"Maybe."

"I'm sure that was it," Brian said.

"After that, all the inroads I thought I'd made with Ava when we were abroad seemed for naught. Maybe I'm good enough for her to lean on during grief but that's it," Keith said bitterly.

"Grief is really funny," Brian said.

"Yeah. I thought that Ava was the love of my life," Keith said. "But as it turns out, she just took what she needed and gave nothing in return." Keith was getting angrier with each word.

"Like I was letting her stay at my house while hers was seized just because we were friends. She knew there was more between us."

Brian realized that they were starting into the kind of conversation that he needed Keith to have. He knew that anger was what would make Keith give up the guilty party. As hard as it was, he needed to put himself in Keith's shoes and imagine that he'd never be with Piper again.

"Piper is the same way. I gave her my heart. I told her I wanted her to be my everything and she threw it back in my face. I'm too young for her...girl, you should be so lucky to have man like me in your bed."

"You don't have to tell me, son. She always was a little too good for everyone else. Ava at least is a beauty, so it makes sense. But then, with Ava, she makes sure that everyone in the room knows she's it."

Ava did like the spotlight. Brian took another sip of his drink. He wasn't sure he could keep saying all this stuff about Piper. But so far, other than bitching about Beth, Keith hadn't even mentioned Wingate Enterprises. "She's a tough broad."

"She is. But even she can't control everything. The

company that Trent built is in a freefall and she should have turned to me to help her. But she had to leave my house because of those children and nephews of hers. Zeke never liked me either."

"I wonder why?"

"They think I was controlling her. If I'd had that ability, she would be in love with me," Keith groused.

"She's not?" Brian asked. This was slipping out of his fingers; he could feel it. He needed to talk about wanting to get back at Piper. That was the only way he was going to get Keith to confess to anything, and if he didn't…well then, his uncle was a jerk but not a criminal.

"How much have you had to drink?" Keith asked. "She's definitely not."

"Like Piper," Brian said. "I wish there was some way to get back at her. To make her see that she shouldn't have rejected me."

"I'd go after her business," Keith replied. "Take everything else she has in her life and bring it to ruins. Let her see what it feels like to be ripped to shreds, then she'll have nowhere to turn but you."

"I don't think that would work…" Brian began. Definitely not liking the sound of this. What was Keith saying?

"You're right," his uncle said, taking another long drink. "Trust me. She'd have to lose everything…"

"Ava's lost everything, or at least had it threatened. You mentioned you know who it is. Should you go after them? Then you'd be her hero," Brian told his uncle, realizing as he said it out loud that he was doing just that.

Trying to solve a situation that he wasn't involved in so that Piper would see him as her hero.

"Yeah, kid, it's not going to happen. I started with the fire and embezzling funds, hoping that would drive Ava into my arms, and then I planted the drugs, and everything was seized and she had no place to live. But even being under my roof wasn't enough. She's still lost to me. Because she's still in love with *him*. She'll never be mine."

Brian just stared at his uncle. He hadn't expected the confession he'd just heard. And seeing his uncle's anger, and understanding the heartbreak that had driven him, didn't help at all.

Ava was in a full-on bitchy mood, and then sorry for her bitchiness, but the atmosphere had been tense once the rest of the family had gone home. Ava was dealing with the fact that the man she'd trusted might have been working against her the entire time. Piper understood that her sister would have felt bad even if she were the only one aware of it, but now everyone knew about Keith's betrayal. And that kind of weakness had always been her sister's Achilles heel.

"When are they going to call?" Ava asked for the fifteenth time.

"Whenever they have something. You and I might think it should be over with quickly, but I can't imagine getting Keith to confess something is going to go quickly," Piper said. She was riding a high thinking about Brian doing this for them and she acknowledged, since they still hadn't talked, that she had no clue if he was doing it for her. But deep down she hoped he was.

"What are you smiling about?" Ava asked.

"Just thinking about Brian. I can't believe he is doing this for us," Piper admitted.

"Of course, he is. Everyone likes our family," Ava said. "Did you think he was doing this for you?"

Piper shook her head. She was willing to give her sister some leeway, given that she was on tenterhooks waiting to hear back from the investigator. Knowing that if it was Keith, Ava was going to have to work hard to get her kids to forgive her and to forgive herself for not seeing that her friend was capable of this. She was lashing out, but Ava had always known just how to say the thing that hurt the most. And Piper wasn't going to take it anymore.

Maybe it was that she'd lost Brian because of her fears, and he was standing up doing the decent thing no matter what she'd said to him. Maybe it was her inner wise goddess finding her backbone now that she'd decided to fight for her man. Or maybe she'd just had enough after a lifetime of her older sister bullying her whenever Ava was feeling vulnerable. But something snapped.

"Brian is the kind of man you wish Keith had been. So whatever you are trying to say about him, save it! There isn't anyone to assign the blame to for this, Ava, except yourself." Piper released a quavering breath, trying to get her emotions under control. "Look, you were grieving and I can cut you some slack on that front. You were lost after Trent died and everyone gets that. But you made a mistake…and you're going to have to own it."

"And how do you propose I do that?" Ava huffed.

"Apologize to everyone and try to rebuild your relationships with them. But insulting me and being the queen bee isn't the way unless you want to spend the rest of your life alone." Piper narrowed her eyes at Ava. "There's no excuse for being unkind to me or your kids. This situation is difficult enough without that."

Ava stared at her, visibly taken aback, and Piper nodded at her sister. "And just so you know, if Brian will have me back, I'm going to spend the rest of my life with him. I don't care if you think he's with me for some ulterior motive or if you don't approve. It's my life and I live it on my own terms."

As soon as she heard those words, Piper realized that her past fears had been dictating her behavior since the night of the gala. She'd fallen back into those old patterns as if Brian was her ex-fiancé. As if Brian wasn't the only man she'd fallen in love with after a lifetime of being good on her own. She didn't *need* a man in her life, but she *wanted* Brian. And Ava better get on board with that.

"Oh, and one more piece of advice? Call your kids."

"And what should I say?" Ava asked wearily.

"Tell them you love them and that you screwed up. It won't be an easy conversation, but taking responsibility will go a long way in mending fences. Now I'm going up to my room to sketch," Piper said, turning to leave the living room, but Ava stopped her, touching her arm as she walked by.

Her sister stood up and hugged her tightly. "I'm sorry, Pip. I didn't mean any of that. I just am so scared. I hate to think that everything Trent and I built over a lifetime has been destroyed by a man who we thought of as a friend. And you're right—I am to blame but admitting I screwed up this big...it scares me."

"It scares everyone," Piper said, hugging her sister and then stepping back. "But if everyone knows it was you and you don't acknowledge it, then it will fester and grow. And losing the business is one thing. It can be rebuilt. Losing the family...even the almighty Ava Wingate couldn't handle that."

Her sister wiped away her tears and nodded. "I couldn't. I'd be nothing without my family. I wish I'd been better about protecting them."

Protecting them. Piper had been trying to protect Brian from her own fears and she'd hurt him to do it. But she knew that she couldn't and wouldn't do that anymore. "Everyone is an adult, Ava, they don't need you to protect them that way. They need you to treat them as equals and respect them."

Ava nodded. "How did you get to be so smart?"

"My big sister is a good example," Piper said.

"I love you, Pip," Ava murmured.

"I love you too."

Thirteen

Brian left his uncle's house just after midnight. He was pretty sure they had enough on the tape to indict Keith but he wanted to make sure. He would go back again if he needed to. His uncle had been crazed with anger and bitterness but also that sad love tonight and since Brian hadn't been drunk there had been no denying that Keith was behind all of the criminal activity.

He had to pull over once he was out of his uncle's neighborhood. God, he couldn't believe the lengths Keith had been willing to go to in order to keep Ava in his life. To make her love him.

That kind of manipulation made him sick. Brian hated everything he'd heard tonight. And all the things he'd had to say. He knew that he'd needed to, in order to get the conversation going, but he'd never expected his uncle to confess to everything.

Brian wondered if there was some kind of mental illness in the man. Though he knew from personal experience that losing a woman he loved could cut deep.

He drove to the police station while calling Miles Wingate.

"This is Miles."

His voice was rusty with sleep and Brian realized he might have waited until the morning, but since Miles had been on this from the beginning, he knew the other man would want to know what had happened that evening. He took a deep breath.

"Miles, it's Brian. Sorry to call so late but I've just left my uncle's house and he admitted to everything. He wanted to ruin your mother and your family. He blames y'all for her not loving him, but he really hates her for pushing him aside. I am headed to the police department so the lead investigator can take the wire off, but I wanted to give you a heads-up."

"Thanks, man. I can't believe he admitted it," Miles said. "Do you think it's enough to arrest him?"

"I do," Brian said. "But I'm not a criminal lawyer so it's just what I know from school not from practice. But I'm pretty sure the DA will be able to get a warrant for his arrest soon. With what you've uncovered and his confession they should be able to put together the pieces."

"Damn. I knew it was him in my gut, but I never thought we'd get him like this. Thanks again, Brian. Good night."

"Good night," Brian said.

He hung up, wanting to call Piper but at the same time wanting to finish his part in the investigation. Also, once she heard what he'd said on the tape would she believe anything else he said? And the issue between them was still Piper's belief that he wanted children more than he wanted her. He rubbed the back of his neck as he went into the police station and saw the lead investigator waiting for him.

"I've been listening in. Dude, you were good. I filled in the assistant district attorney, as well, and he's taking the transcript to a judge to get a warrant for Keith's arrest. He should be back soon. Normally we wouldn't do this in the middle of the night, but as slippery as Keith has been everyone wants him in custody. He might realize what he told you and try to leave Royal or even the country."

"He was almost passed-out drunk when I left, but I'd try to get there first thing in the morning before he can remember what he said. I…are you going to share the recording with the Wingate family?" Brian asked.

"Yes. I think they'll want to hear it," the lead investigator said.

"Would you…ask them to think kindly of me? I had to say some of those things to get him talking…"

"I'm sure they will understand," the detective said.

But Brian wasn't so sure. And he knew that Piper would be hurt by the things he'd said. He should text her, but he was done with middle-of-the-night-calls. So he went to his home in Royal after he left the police station and found himself online looking at the digital image of the portrait that Piper had made of him. How could a woman who saw straight to his soul not have known he loved her?

He knew he'd never said the words, that admitting to loving someone like Piper frightened him. She was so self-contained. So sure and confident, he knew she didn't need a man even though he wanted nothing more than to claim her. To find a way to make sure she was his...

Regardless of how the two of them worked out he was happy for his part in helping to catch Keith. He almost texted his dad because he knew his father would want to know what his brother had been up to, but he knew better than to do anything until Keith had been arrested.

He didn't want to taint the arrest or give Keith's attorneys any ammunition to use to get him off the charges. And Keith had good lawyers, so Brian was sure it was going to be an uphill battle in court.

He closed the laptop and tried to go to sleep, but honestly, he couldn't. All he could think about was Piper. Something Keith had said kept running through his mind, about not being able to make her love him. He would never try any of Keith's tactics to get Piper to love him, but he did realize that if she didn't love him maybe she'd said what she had about children to let him down easy. Maybe she hadn't loved him from the beginning, and if that was indeed what was at play here, then it might be time for him to move on.

Or, at the very least, go back to Dallas, away from Royal and Piper and the entire Wingate family.

Piper woke to the news that Keith had been arrested. Her entire family was gathered in the kitchen of Ava's rented house. Her sister was more animated than she'd been since Piper had come back to Royal. She saw relief on her sister's face, now that they had Keith's confession.

Beth and Harley stood close to their mom and Piper couldn't help but think that the worst was probably over now. "What happened? Did Brian get a confession?"

"He did," Harley said. "Piper, he was great. He didn't mention Mom at all…just let Keith bring it around to her."

"I knew he was responsible but hearing the hate in his voice. I had no idea that he'd become so bitter," Beth said.

"You heard the tape?"

"It's a digital recording," Ava told her. "You don't want to listen to it, Pip. Brian had some things to say about you… I don't think he meant them, but it's nothing you want to hear."

Piper wondered what Brian had said. Ava was correct in that she didn't need to hear it. She knew what she wanted from the future and anything that Brian had said in order to get Keith to confess was alright with her.

"Where is he?" she asked. She wanted to go to Brian and thank him for what he'd done for their family. Piper would use it as an olive branch to get a conversation going, then…then she was going to take a big risk and just tell him how she felt. Be the woman he'd awoken with his passion.

"Keith?"

She'd been thinking about Brian, but she did want to know where Keith was, as well. Plus she wanted to talk to Brian about how she felt before she let anyone else know—even her family. "Yes."

"He's being interrogated at the police station. They brought him in for questioning and then arrested him. I think they'll be a bail hearing soon," Beth said. "That's what I heard from the lead investigator. This is such a relief."

"It really is. The boys are heading over and I think we are going to issue some kind of statement," Ava added.

Piper hugged her sister and her nieces before leaving them to talk Wingate business. She pulled her phone out of her pocket just to make sure she hadn't missed a text or call from Brian, but she hadn't.

Piper: Thanks for helping my family. Can we talk?

Brian: I'm at the diner if you want to come and join me for breakfast.

Piper: Give me thirty minutes and I can be there.

Brian: Sounds good.

She had wanted a more private place for their talk but didn't blame him for suggesting the diner. He had been through a lot when he'd come to visit her the last time. She got dressed, fixed her hair and was out of the house in ten minutes. Faster than she'd gotten ready in a long time. But she missed Brian and she was fed up with the distance between them.

Piper knew they had a future. She'd made up her mind when she learned what he'd done for her family. Also she was tired of hiding from life and only pouring her passion into her art. She wanted to live in color with Brian. They brought out the best in each other, and more than anything, she wanted him in her life.

She parked near the diner in Royal and several townspeople stopped her to tell her how glad they were that an arrest had been made, and though some others might have believed the gossip about her family, they never had. Piper had to bite her lip to keep from smiling or saying something sassy as the sentiment was repeated several times. Ava was going to love this reversal of fortune.

Brian was seated in a booth near the back and she made her way over to him. Several people tried to stop her, but she just smiled and waved off their apologies. Royal had been quick to turn on her family, but she knew that was because of the strong sense of justice in the town. They were going to be all over Keith now.

She slid into the booth across from Brian and he smiled when he saw her. He looked tired but was truly a sight for sore eyes.

"Thank you," she said.

"It was nothing."

"It *wasn't* nothing," she insisted. "What you did for my family…especially after how I treated you—"

"It's okay, Piper," he said. "I'm just glad I could help. Turns out your breaking up with me was just the thing to push Uncle Keith into confessing his plot. So maybe I have you to thank."

She shook her head, reaching over to put her hand on top of his. "No. I wish I could have handled things better. You have never been anything other than a gentleman and I shouldn't have gone off like that."

Brian turned his hand in hers and rubbed his thumb over her palm before drawing back. He didn't want to touch her, she thought. *That's not good.*

This wasn't going to end the way she wanted it to, and she had no one to blame but herself.

"No, you shouldn't have," he said. "But I do understand why you did. I think I was moving too fast, afraid to lose you, and then I did anyway. But we hadn't been together long enough to have the conversation you needed to have, and I am sorry for that."

"Me too," she admitted. She noticed the waitress standing a short distance away waiting for her to look up.

The waitress hurried over, poured Piper a cup of coffee and took her order before leaving the two of them alone again.

"Listen, did you hear the recording of Keith's confession?" he asked.

"No. Ava said I didn't need to. She said you had done what you had to in order to get him talking."

Brian swallowed and nodded. "She is right. I had to convince him that I hated you, Piper, and the only way I could do that was by saying some things that could never be true. You are hardheaded but I love that. So strong and independent, and to me that's what makes you who you are. To Uncle Keith, those are the very things he hated about Ava. He wanted her to depend on him, to need him and only him."

"You're not that kind of man. You want to stand next to your woman not make her stay in the shadows."

"I do."

He leaned across the table and kissed her. Piper heard a smattering of applause around the diner, and as their lips parted, she realized that there were some things that were better done in private. This conversation was one of them.

"What do you say we go back to my place and talk details?"

"Naked details?" she asked coyly.

"Anything the lady wants," he said. She scooted out of the booth and he followed her, throwing some bills on the table to cover their food and then leading Piper out of the diner. As soon as they were in the parking lot and out of sight, he pulled her back into his arms.

Fourteen

Piper hadn't thought she could be this happy with anyone after her engagement had been broken but Brian was making her rethink so many things. His house in Royal was a large, sprawling two-story modern ranch. It was quiet as they entered, and he carried her up the stairs to his bedroom.

She knew if they were going to have a future together, she owed it to him to explain her past. She wanted him to understand why she just didn't think she could bring herself to try something as permanent as marriage again.

He put her on her feet on the thickly carpeted floor.

"Um, come and sit down next to me on the bed," she suggested. "It will make it easier to tell you if we're not standing."

He toed off his shoes, climbed into the center of his king-sized bed and beckoned her to come sit next to him. She had to smile at him. Her heart was full of joy and she had to wonder if she was holding to this one old fear for a foolish reason.

But she remembered how it felt to be engaged and then to suddenly be unengaged. She would much rather be Piper and Brian than have any other pressure.

"I was engaged… I think I mentioned it when we were at the gala," she said.

"You did."

"Things were going well and I thought we'd be married soon, but the doctor noticed something abnormal in my yearly pap smear so he called me back in and that's when he told me that it would be very difficult for me to have children," she said, remembering her confusion when he'd said it. "I have a lot of polyps in my uterus. Anyway, none of that matters. I told Ron—my fiancé—what the doctor had said and he asked *how* difficult it would be. I said I hadn't asked but Ron was insistent. So I went back for another appointment and the doctor said that I had a less than four percent chance of conceiving."

She sat down on the bed, staring at Brian's kind eyes and sexy face, and realized how hard this was to talk about. She'd never had to tell anyone the next part. Not even Ava. But she wanted Brian to know. Needed him to understand she hadn't been overreacting when she'd broken up with him. And knowing he cared for her made it easier for her to confide in him.

"Ron was waiting for me when I got home. I told him what the doctor had said and he got very angry and said that was it. We couldn't be married because the entire point was to have a family…" Piper's voice cracked. "I said that was fine. We could just be a couple. He rejected that and told me he wanted more from life than a would-be artist partner and no kids. So I gave him back his ring…well, sort of threw it at him…and told him to kiss my ass."

"You should have done more than that. What a bastard," Brian said. "But his shortsightedness is my gain. You know I don't care about anything but you."

"I do," she whispered. "When everything happened with Ron I promised myself I'd never be that vulnerable again. I channeled all of my passion into my art, and that worked until you came along." She met his eyes. "I hope you know I feel the same about you, but I don't want to be engaged."

"Fine by me. We aren't living it the dark ages," he said with a wink. "As long as I'm yours and you're mine, I'm okay."

"Same here," she said.

Brian leaned forward and pulled her into his arms, drawing her back against his chest. He rested his head on her shoulder and one big hand cupped her breast while the other spanned her waist, the heat of his body warming hers.

They fit perfectly together, something she'd always thought was an urban legend. But there was nothing fake about Brian Cooper. He'd gone above and beyond to prove himself to her and she couldn't believe she'd found a man she could trust with her battered heart and wounded soul.

A partner for the wise goddess she'd become, and she wasn't about to let him go now.

He rolled her over on the bed, coming over her, resting his arms on either side of her body.

"I am so glad you came up to me at the reception," she murmured.

"Me too. I'd been crushing on you for the longest time and I knew I had to make a move, or I'd regret it for the rest of my life."

"You would have," she said, wiggling her eyebrows at him. "You would have missed my kisses."

He brought his lips to hers. "You mean like this?"

His mouth was firm and he took his time kissing her, rubbing his lips back and forth until her mouth parted and she felt the humid warmth of his exhalation in her mouth. He tasted so…delicious, she thought. She wanted more and opened her mouth to invite him closer.

She thrust her tongue into his mouth and rubbed it over his teeth and then his tongue. He closed his teeth carefully over her tongue and sucked on her. She shivered in delight.

His taste was addicting, like the taste of Baileys on a cold fall night. Yes, she thought, she wanted much more of him, not just his kisses.

She put her hands on his shoulders and then higher to that thick black hair and pushed her fingers into it. Brian Cooper was hers now.

His hands moved over her shoulders, his fingers tracing a delicate pattern over the globes of her breasts. He moved them back and forth over the swells until the very tip of his finger dipped beneath the material of her top and reached lower, brushing the edge of her nipple.

Exquisite shivers racked her body as his hands continued to move slowly over her. He pushed her sweater up and over her head, tossing it to the floor next to the bed. She wore a lacy camisole and he leaned back to look down at her chest.

"I would have missed seeing you like this," he said. "I would have had to make do with my imagination."

"You would have," she murmured, arching her back and watching his eyes move down to her breasts. Her nipples were hard and pointed under the lace.

He wrapped his hands around her waist and drew her to him, lifting her. "Wrap your legs around me."

She did and immediately was surrounded by him. His mouth was on her breasts, his hands on her butt, and he suckled her gently. Nibbling at her nipples through the fabric of her camisole as he massaged her backside. When he took her nipple into his mouth she felt everything inside of her tighten and her center grow moist.

His mouth…she couldn't even think. She could only feel the sensations that were washing over her as he continued to focus on her breasts.

One of his powerfully muscled thighs nudged her legs apart and then he was between them. She felt the ridge of his cock rubbing against her pleasure center and she shifted against him to increase the sensation.

She wanted to touch him, had to hold him to her as his mouth moved from her breast down her sternum to her belly button. He looked up at her and for a moment their eyes met. "I can't imagine my life without you, Piper."

He lowered his head again and nibbled at the skin of her midriff, his tongue tracing the indentation of her belly button, and it felt like each time he dipped his tongue into her that her clit tingled. She shifted her hips to rub against him and he answered her with a thrust of his own hips.

His mouth moved lower on her, his hands finding the waistband of her jeans and undoing the button, then slowly lowering the zipper. She felt the warmth of his breath on her lower belly and then the edge of his tongue as he traced the skin revealed by the opening.

The feel of his five o'clock shadow against her was soft and smooth. She thought she'd learned everything she needed to about Brian, but it seemed there was still more for her to experience.

"Lift your hips," he commanded.

She planted her feet on the bed to lift them up, and felt him draw her jeans over her hips and down her thighs. She was left wearing the tiny black thong she'd put on that morning.

He palmed her through the panties, and she squirmed on the bed. She wanted more.

He gave it to her, with his hand on her most intimate flesh and then with his mouth as he drew her underwear down by pulling with his teeth. His hands kept moving over her stomach and thighs until she was completely naked and bare underneath him. Then he leaned back on his knees and just stared down at her.

"You are so gorgeous, Piper," he said.

His voice was low and husky and made her blood flow heavier in her veins. Everything about this man seemed to make her hotter and hornier than she'd ever been before.

"It's you," she said in a raspy voice. "You are the one who is making me feel that way…"

"I'm nothing more than the only man for you," he said.

She shuddered at the impact of his words. He *was* the only man for her, and she knew it. She couldn't be happier to know she'd spend the rest of her life with him. Pleasure rippled through her as he lowered his head again and rubbed his chin over her mound. Just a back and forth motion that made her clit feel engorged. Then he tilted his head down until he could trace the line of hair from the Brazilian wax on her nether lips.

"This is the one thing I should have done when we made love at your place the first time."

"You did," she reminded him.

"I should never have left. Just kept us in bed so we could learn each other's secrets and know each other's heart."

He parted her with the thumb and forefinger of his left hand and she felt the air against her most intimate flesh and then the brush of his tongue. It was so soft and wet, and she squirmed, wanting—no needing—more from him.

He scraped his teeth over her and she almost came right then, but he lifted his head and smiled up her body at her. By this time, she knew her lover well enough to know that he liked to draw out the experience.

She gripped his shoulders as he teased her with his mouth and then tunneled her fingers through his hair, holding him closer to her as she lifted her hips. He moaned against her and the sound tickled her clit and sent chills racing through her body.

His other hand traced the opening of her body. Those large, deft fingers made her squirm against him. Her breasts felt full and her nipples were tight as he pushed just the tip of his finger inside of her.

The first ripples of her orgasm started to pulse through her, but he pulled back, lifting his head and moving down her body. Nibbling at the flesh of her legs. She was aching for him. Needing more of what he had been giving her.

"Brian…"

"Yes?" he asked, lightly stroking her lower belly and then moving both hands to her breasts where he cupped the full globes.

"Take me now," she said. "It feels like a hundred years since I've had you inside me and I need you now."

Piper was shivering with the need to come and wanted more from him. She wanted his big body moving over hers. Wanted his cock inside of her, thrusting hard and deep. She reached between their bodies and stroked him through his pants. Impatiently, she lowered the tab of his zipper, but he caught her wrist and drew her hand up above her head.

"Don't do that or I'll lose it. I thought I'd never have you again," he said.

"Me either. That's why I need you. Now."

"Okay," he said, lowering his body over hers so the soft fabric of his shirt brushed her breasts and stomach before she felt the masculine hardness of his muscles underneath. Then his thigh was between her legs, moving slowly against her engorged flesh, and she wanted to scream as everything in her tightened just a little bit more.

It wasn't enough. She writhed against him, but he just slowed his touch so that the sensations were even more intense than before. He shifted again and she felt the warmth of his breath against her mound. She opened her eyes to look down at him and this time she knew she saw something different. But she couldn't process it because his mouth was on her.

Each sweep of his tongue against her clit drove her higher and higher as everything in her body tightened, waiting for the touch that would push her over the edge. She shifted her legs around his head, felt the brush of his silky-smooth hair against her inner thighs.

Felt his finger at the opening of her body once again and then the delicate biting of his teeth against her pleasure bud as he plunged that finger deep inside her. She screamed his name as his mouth moved over her. The first wave of orgasm rolled through her body.

Her hips jerked forward and her nipples tightened. Piper felt the moisture between her legs and his finger pushing hard against her G-spot. She was shivering and her entire body was convulsing, but he didn't lift his head. He kept suckling on her and driving her harder and harder until she came again, screaming with her orgasm as stars danced behind her eyelids.

She reached down to claw at his shoulders as pleasure engulfed her. It was more than she could process, and she had to close her eyes. She reached for Brian, needing some sort of comfort after that storm of pleasure.

He pulled her into his arms and rocked her back and forth. "I can finally breathe now that you are back in my arms."

"Me too."

Brian couldn't let things rest until he'd addressed what had been said on the recording. The things he'd said, well, he hadn't meant any of them. "In case you ever listen to the recording of myself and Keith, please know that I didn't mean a word—"

"Brian, I know that," she said, reaching up to touch his face as they lay nestled in each other's arms. "You were doing what you had to in order to help my family."

"I was. Honestly, I never expected any of what he confessed. I thought, at best, that he might have known the real person who had mucked things up...not that he was the mastermind behind all of it. But he wanted to burn down everything Ava loved."

Piper shook her head. "I read an article a few years ago about how fine the line between love and hate is, but to be honest I never believed it until now. I am so sorry you had to do that."

"I'm not. When you told me everything, I realized that despite telling you I was mature and feeling in my heart that I was ready to make a life with you, I'd never really given us a chance to talk. I just rushed you to bed and then wanted to make it permanent," he said.

She smiled at him. "Don't take all the credit for rushing me to bed."

He was starting to think that Piper wasn't just here to thank him for helping to catch the criminal responsible for the trouble at Wingate Enterprises. She was talking to him in a careful way. She'd explained how her past affected her feelings about marriage and...did she regret ending things with him?

He took a deep breath, not sure if his heart would survive her rejecting him again. But he had to at least try one more time. He knew his life was going to always seem a little too gray and routine without Piper in it. Stretching one arm along her back, he looked into those beautiful eyes of hers. God, how he'd missed her. It might have only been two days since he'd last seen her but, in his heart, it felt much longer.

A lifetime had passed since he left her at Ava's house. So much had happened and changed, but the one thing that hadn't was how he felt about her. He wanted her as much now as he ever had. If not more so. Having confronted his uncle and heard the way the other man had tried to ruin Ava's life, and by extension, Piper's, had made him want to right the wrongs done to them.

And he had.

There was nothing left but to bare his soul to Piper and see if she'd have him back in her life. If she'd give him the second chance that he so desperately wanted. And if she said no? God, it would hurt like hell, but he'd respect her decision.

"You know I did all that for you," he said. "I mean, I couldn't let him walk away once he'd hinted that he might have had something to do with it, but I did it because you told me how much your family meant to you and I know deep in my heart that one day I want to be a part of your family. I want you to be my family—"

"Brian, I can't—"

He stopped her words with his fingers over her lips.

"Piper, marriage doesn't matter. I want you by my side. I love you," he said. "I know that I probably am moving too fast, but time isn't going to change how I feel about you and I don't want to have to pretend that it will."

He put his hand on her naked hip and waited to see what she would say. She leaned up, meeting his gaze with her own. "I can't have kids. That's not going to change. It might matter to you, Brian, when everyone else is starting a family and you are stuck with—"

"The most gorgeous woman in Texas? The only woman I've ever loved? Unless you don't love me, Piper, there is no reason for us not to be together. There are plenty of kids in the world who need a family, and when we are ready, they will find us."

She smiled at him and he realized he was holding his breath. She hadn't said she loved him or that she wanted him back in her life, but he'd laid it all bare. It was up to her to make the next move, and whatever she decided, he'd abide by it.

Even if it killed him.

"I love you, Brian. If you're sure—"

"Dammit, Piper, I'm a man of my word."

"You are," she admitted, wrapping her arms around his shoulders as she kissed him. It seemed to him that she might never let go; hell, he wasn't going to let go for a long time either.

"I wish I'd taken the time to see what you were hiding from me," he said. "I'm so sorry you were hurt."

"You couldn't have seen it, Brian. I was hiding it even from myself. I thought I had everything I needed until you came along and danced with me at the wedding reception, and suddenly I was thinking how nice it might be to have you in my life."

"Forever."

"Forever."

Epilogue

Hosting Thanksgiving at her house wasn't something Piper had anticipated doing, but she wanted to have her family around Brian and herself. She was little nervous, which was silly because it wasn't as if she needed her family's approval to be with the man she loved, but she still wanted it. And Brian had decided to forgo his traditional attendance at the Cowboys game since he said there was nowhere he'd rather be than by her side.

The turkey was in the oven and Brian was in the big living room, acting as the host. He had the Macy's Thanksgiving Day parade on because that was one of her nonnegotiables. Brian had brought his mom's famous cinnamon pumpkin bread and his parents were coming by later. The arrest of Keith hadn't been easy for the Cooper family, but they weren't that close to his uncle so it wasn't as bad as it could have been.

Beth and Camden arrived first. She sent Camden into the living room with Brian who had a drinks station set up in the corner at a large antique bar she'd purchased a few years ago in an estate sale. Next were Harley, Grant and Daniel, and then Zeke and Reagan, and Luke, who she knew was feeling stressed about finding new ways to revive Wingate's businesses. Finally, Sutton and his fiancée, Lauren, arrived with Ava. Sebastian had texted he would be there in time for football and turkey, and Gracie had gone to Florida to spend the holiday with her family. Piper had everyone together.

She had an open-plan kitchen that spilled into the living room, so everyone moved back and forth between both rooms. Ava pulled her aside and Piper was wary about what her sister would say. Ava had thought Brian was too young for her.

"I was wrong about Brian," Ava said. "Let's get that out of the way first. He's a great man and perfect for you. And I will never be able to forget what he did for us."

She hugged her sister. "Me either. I can't believe how happy I am."

"I'm glad. It's about time you found someone to share your life with," Ava said.

Piper couldn't agree more, and when it was time to sit down to the main meal, she reached under the table to squeeze Brian's hand as she invited everyone to go around and say what they were grateful for.

Much of the sentiment was for new loves, their cleared family name and their plans for relaunching

Wingate Enterprises now that Keith was in jail. Ava was happy to have her family around her. And Piper thought she saw in her sister's eyes that she wouldn't ever take them for granted again.

"I'm glad Keith is in jail, but rebuilding is going to take a lot of time," Sebastian said.

"Y'all are up to the challenge," Piper murmured.

"We are."

"Are y'all making it official?" Zeke asked Brian after they'd had dessert. "Just asking to make sure you're taking proper care of my auntie."

Zeke winked at Piper.

"We are official, though we're not really concerned with things like marriage. But y'all can get used to seeing me with Piper for the rest of our lives."

Zeke toasted them and everyone joined in. Piper realized how blessed and thankful she was for her family.

* * * * *

COMING SOON!

We really hope you enjoyed reading this book.
If you're looking for more romance, be sure to
head to the shops when new books are
available on

Thursday 12th November

LET'S TALK

Romance

For exclusive extracts, competitions
and special offers, find us online:

- facebook.com/millsandboon
- @MillsandBoon
- @MillsandBoonUK

Get in touch on 01413 063232

For all the latest titles coming soon, visit
millsandboon.co.uk/nextmonth

MILLS & BOON

THE HEART OF ROMANCE

A ROMANCE FOR EVERY KIND OF READER

MODERN

Prepare to be swept off your feet by sophisticated, sexy and seductive heroes, in some of the world's most glamourous and romantic locations, where power and passion collide.
8 stories per month.

HISTORICAL

Escape with historical heroes from time gone by. Whether you passion is for wicked Regency Rakes, muscled Vikings or rugg Highlanders, awaken the romance of the past.
6 stories per month.

MEDICAL

Set your pulse racing with dedicated, delectable doctors in th high-pressure world of medicine, where emotions run high a passion, comfort and love are the best medicine.
6 stories per month.

True Love

Celebrate true love with tender stories of heartfelt romance, the rush of falling in love to the joy a new baby can bring, and focus on the emotional heart of a relationship.
8 stories per month.

Desire

Indulge in secrets and scandal, intense drama and plenty of s hot action with powerful and passionate heroes who have it a wealth, status, good looks…everything but the right woman.
6 stories per month.

HEROES

Experience all the excitement of a gripping thriller, with an i romance at its heart. Resourceful, true-to-life women and str fearless men face danger and desire - a killer combination!
8 stories per month.

DARE

Sensual love stories featuring smart, sassy heroines you'd wan best friend, and compelling intense heroes who are worthy o
4 stories per month.

To see which titles are coming soon, please visit

millsandboon.co.uk/nextmonth

MILLS & BOON

MODERN

Power and Passion

Prepare to be swept off your feet by sophisticated, sexy and seductive heroes, in some of the world's most glamourous and romantic locations, where power and passion collide.

Eight Modern stories published every month, find them all a

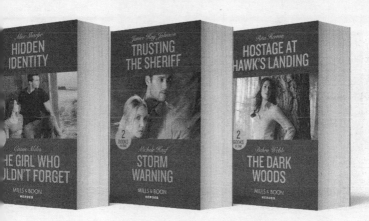